# Pirate Palooza

By Erik Craddock

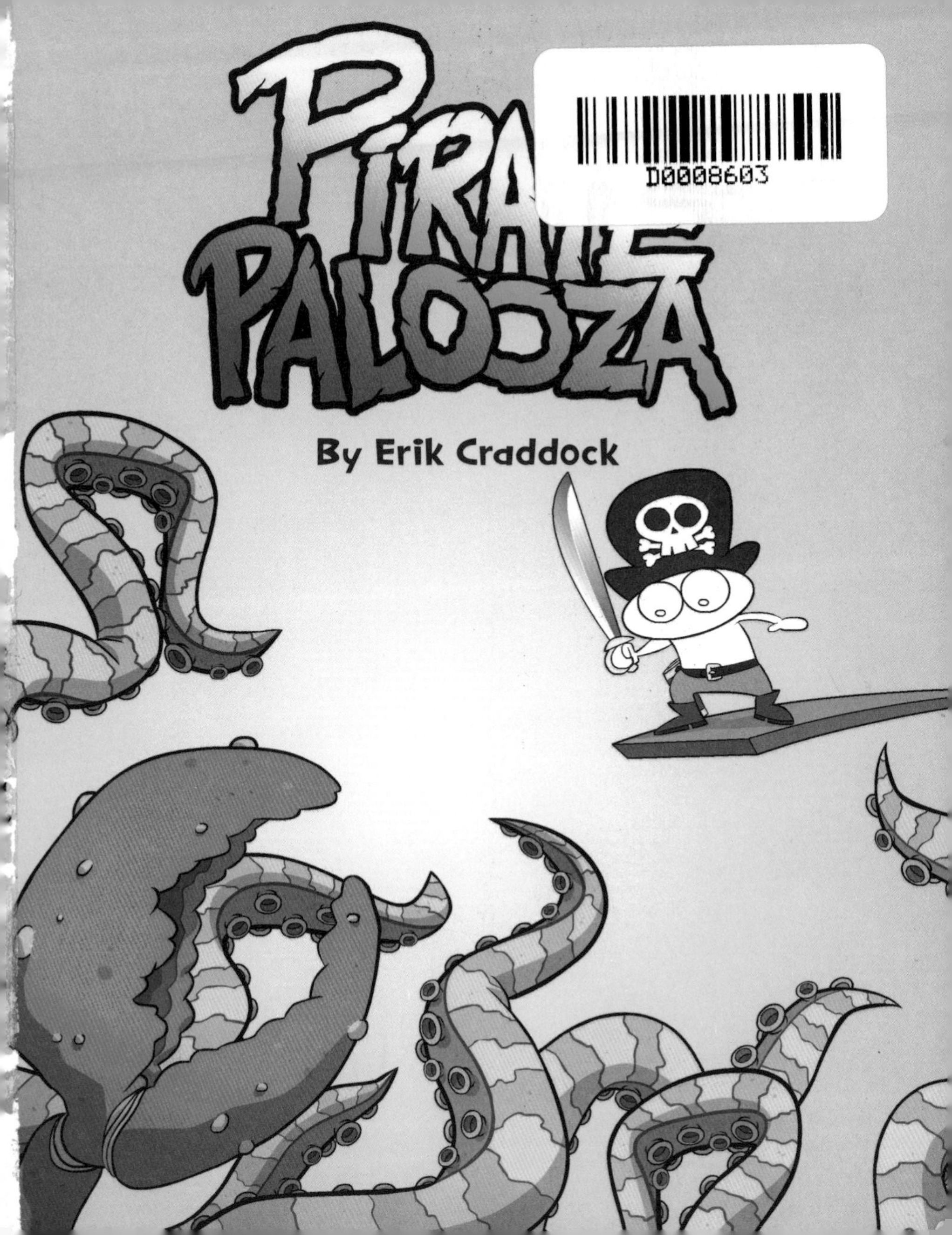

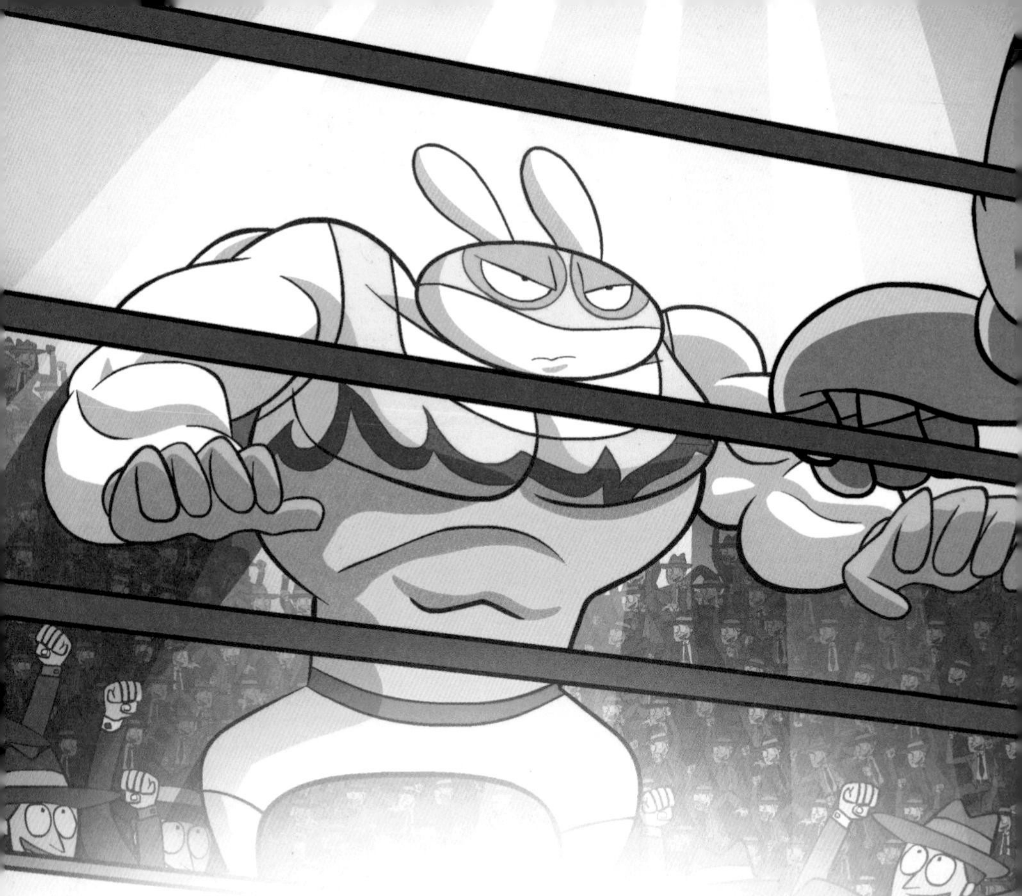



Published in the United States by Random House Children's Books, a division of Random House, Inc., New York.

Random House and colophon are registered trademarks of Random House, Inc.

Visit us on the Web! www.randomhouse.com/kids

Educators and librarians, for a variety of teaching tools, visit us at www.randomhouse.com/teachers

www.stonerabbit.com

Library of Congress Cataloging-in-Publication Data is available upon request.
ISBN 978-0-375-85660-0 (trade)—ISBN 978-0-375-95660-7 (lib. bdg.)

MANUFACTURED IN MALAYSIA

10 9 8 7 6 5 4 3 2 1

First Edition

Random House Children's Books supports the First Amendment and celebrates the right to read.

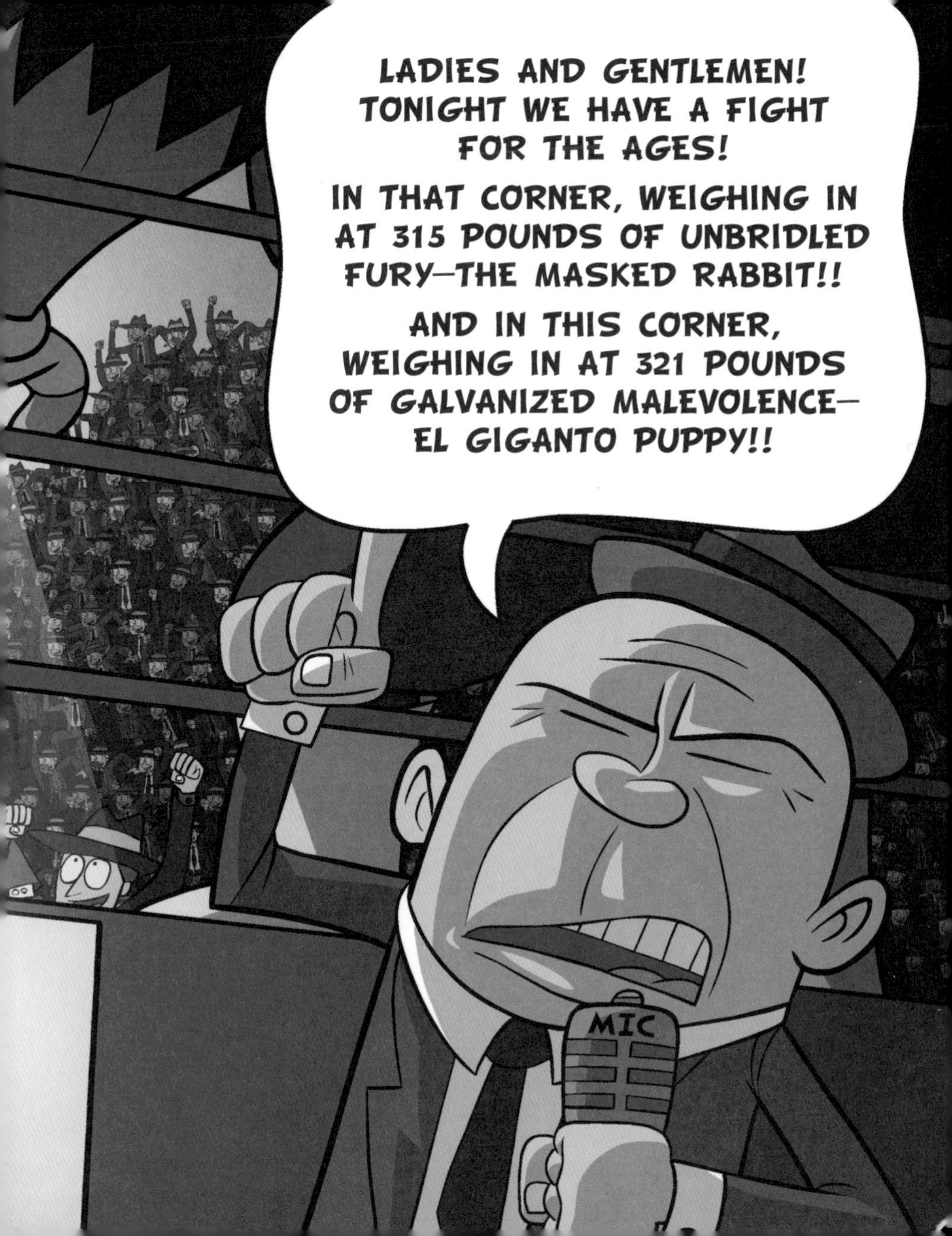
LADIES AND GENTLEMEN! TONIGHT WE HAVE A FIGHT FOR THE AGES!
IN THAT CORNER, WEIGHING IN AT 315 POUNDS OF UNBRIDLED FURY—THE MASKED RABBIT!!
AND IN THIS CORNER, WEIGHING IN AT 321 POUNDS OF GALVANIZED MALEVOLENCE—EL GIGANTO PUPPY!!
MIC

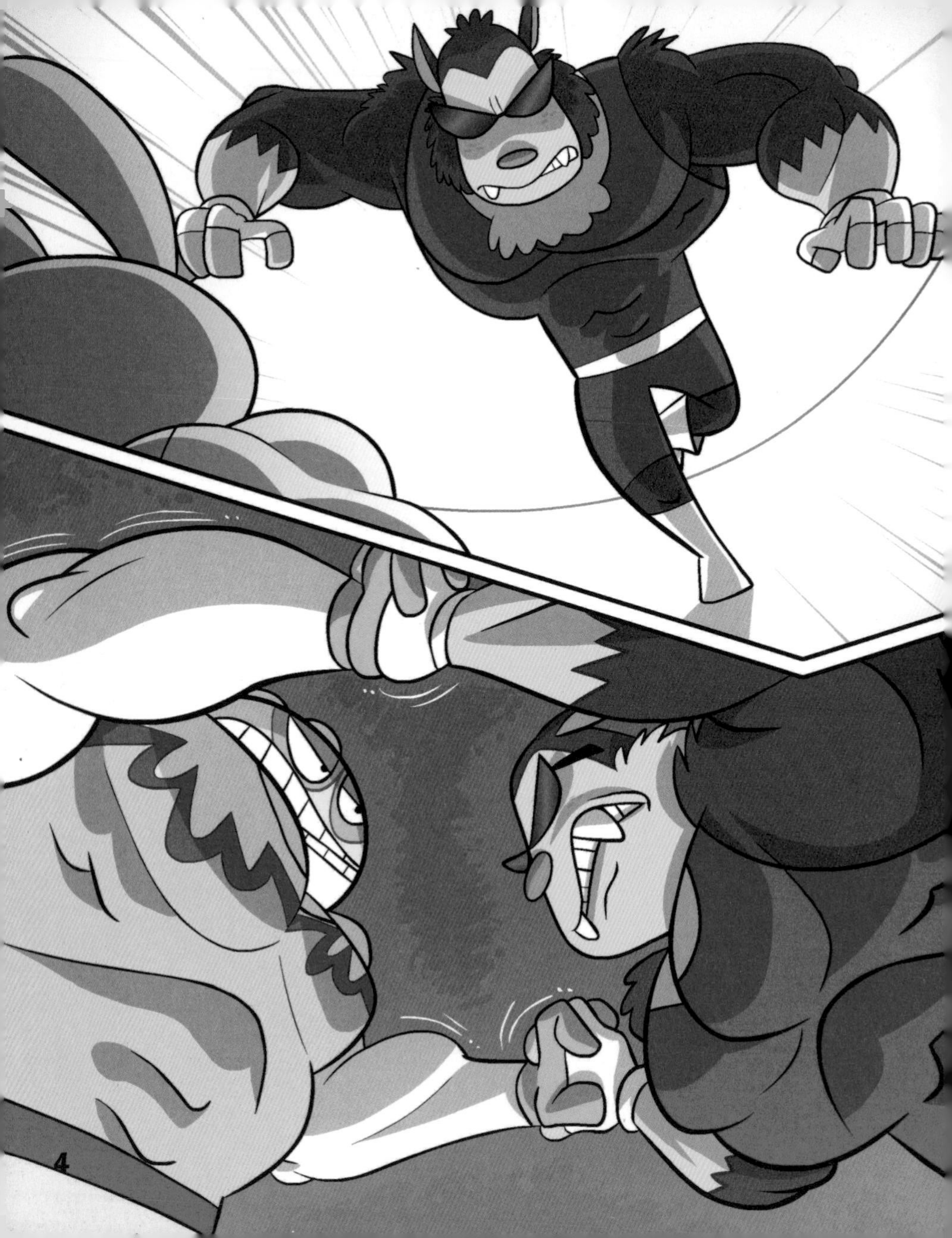

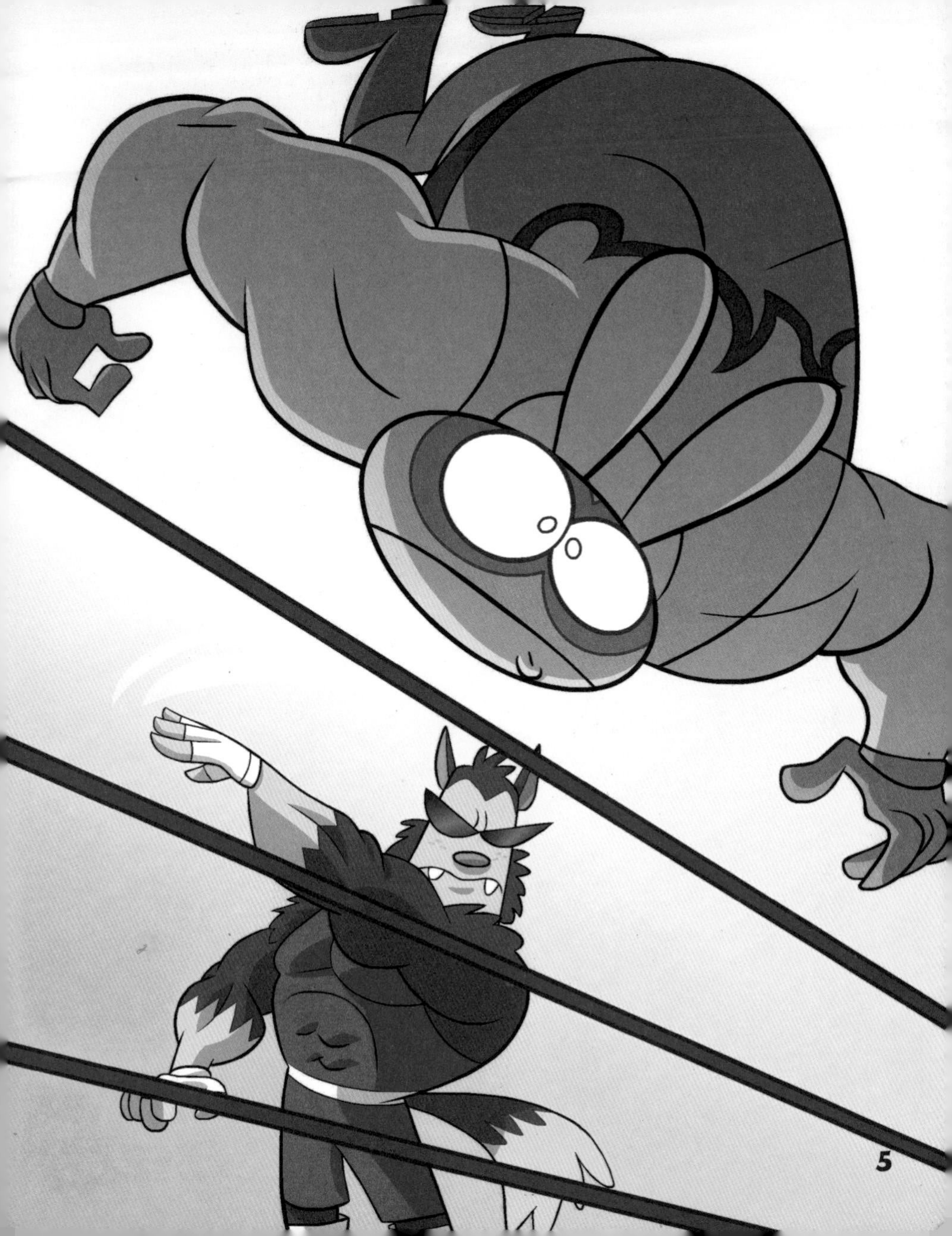

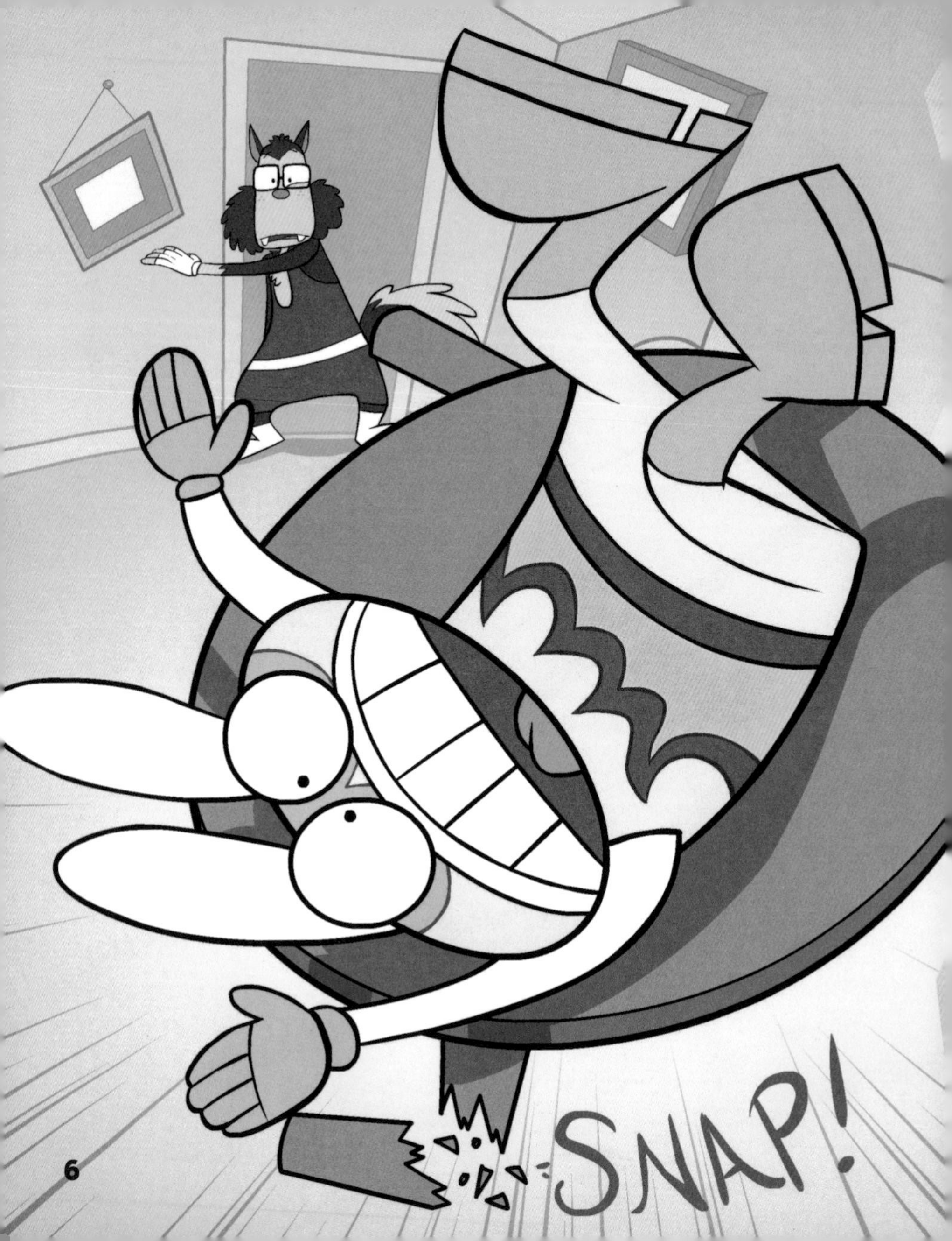
SNAP!

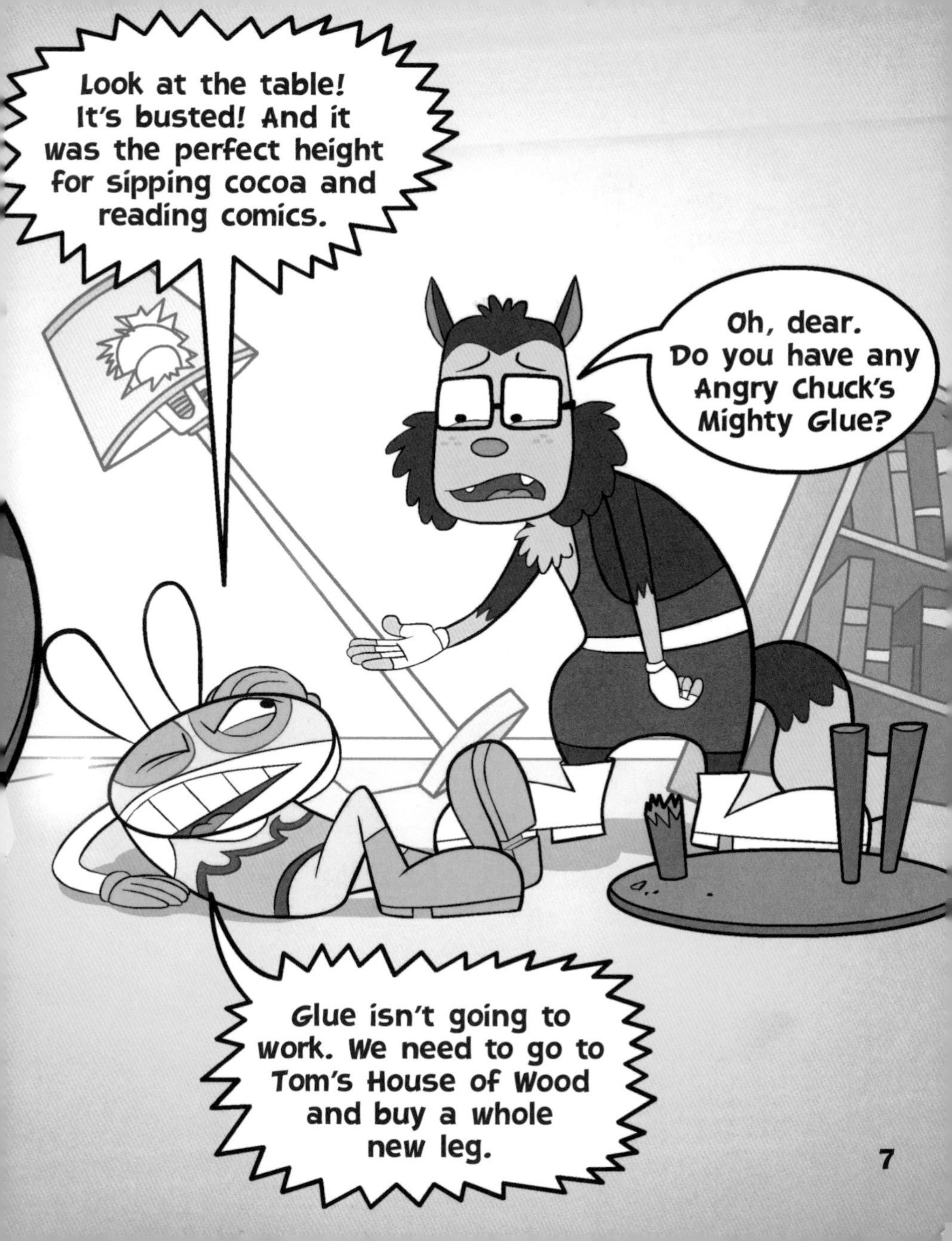
Look at the table! It's busted! And it was the perfect height for sipping cocoa and reading comics.
Oh, dear. Do you have any Angry Chuck's Mighty Glue?
Glue isn't going to work. We need to go to Tom's House of Wood and buy a whole new leg.

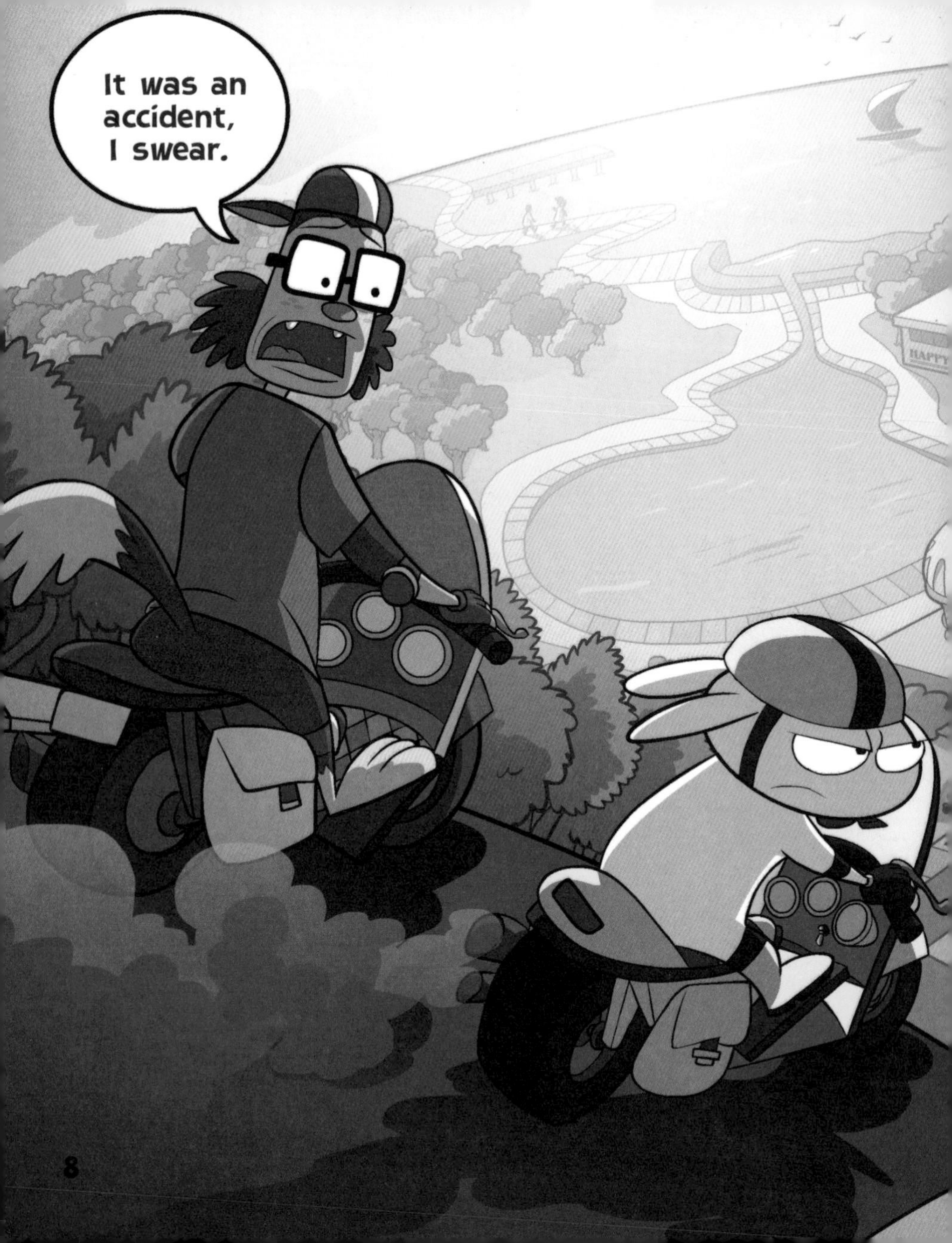
It was an accident, I swear.

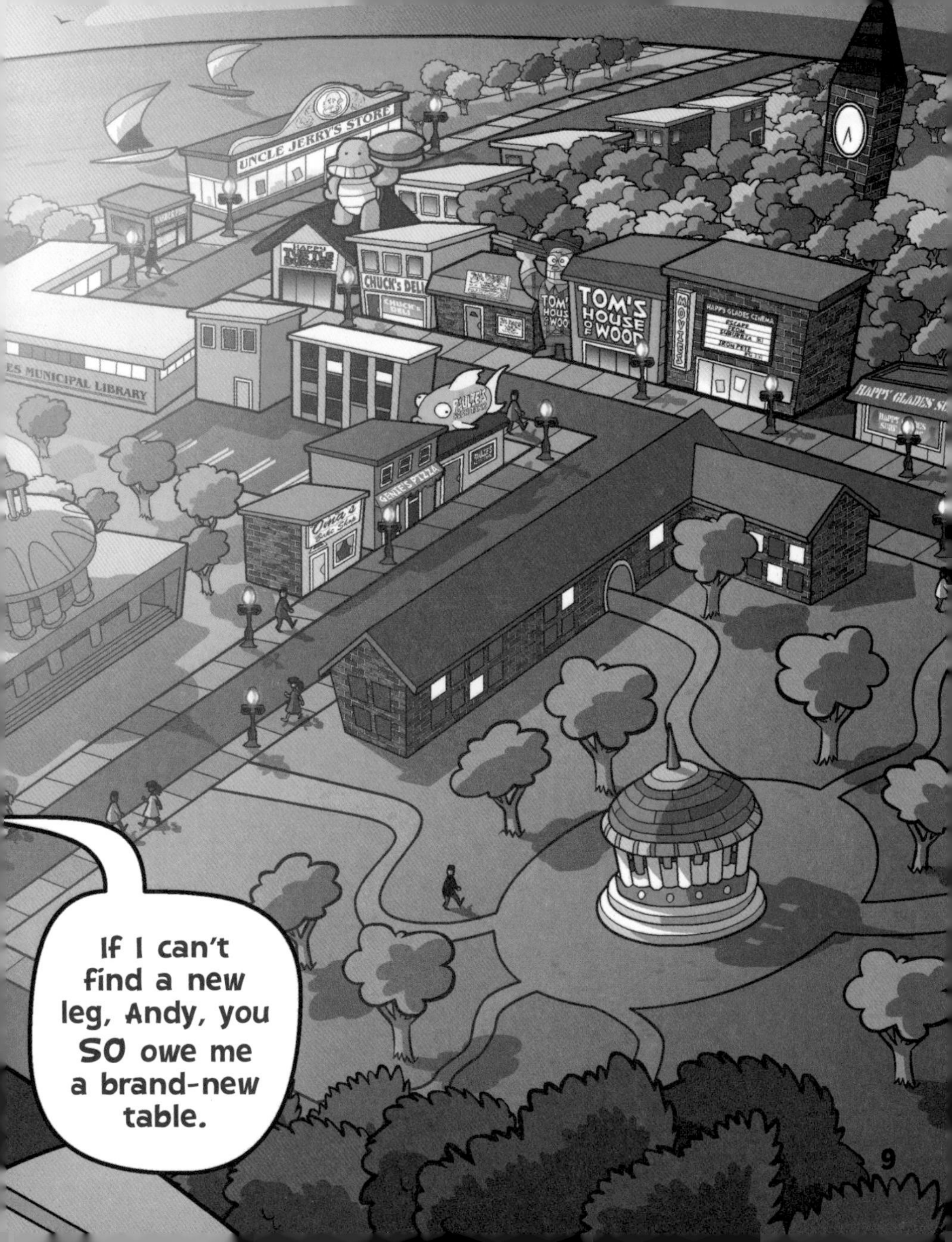
UNCLE JERRY'S STORE
HAPPY TURTLE BURGER
CHUCK's DELI
TOM'S HOUSE OF WOOD
MOVIES
HAPPY GLADES CINEMA
ESCAPE FROM SUBURBIA
IRON PETE
ES MUNICIPAL LIBRARY
GENIE'S PIZZA
HAPPY GLADES S
If I can't find a new leg, Andy, you SO owe me a brand-new table.

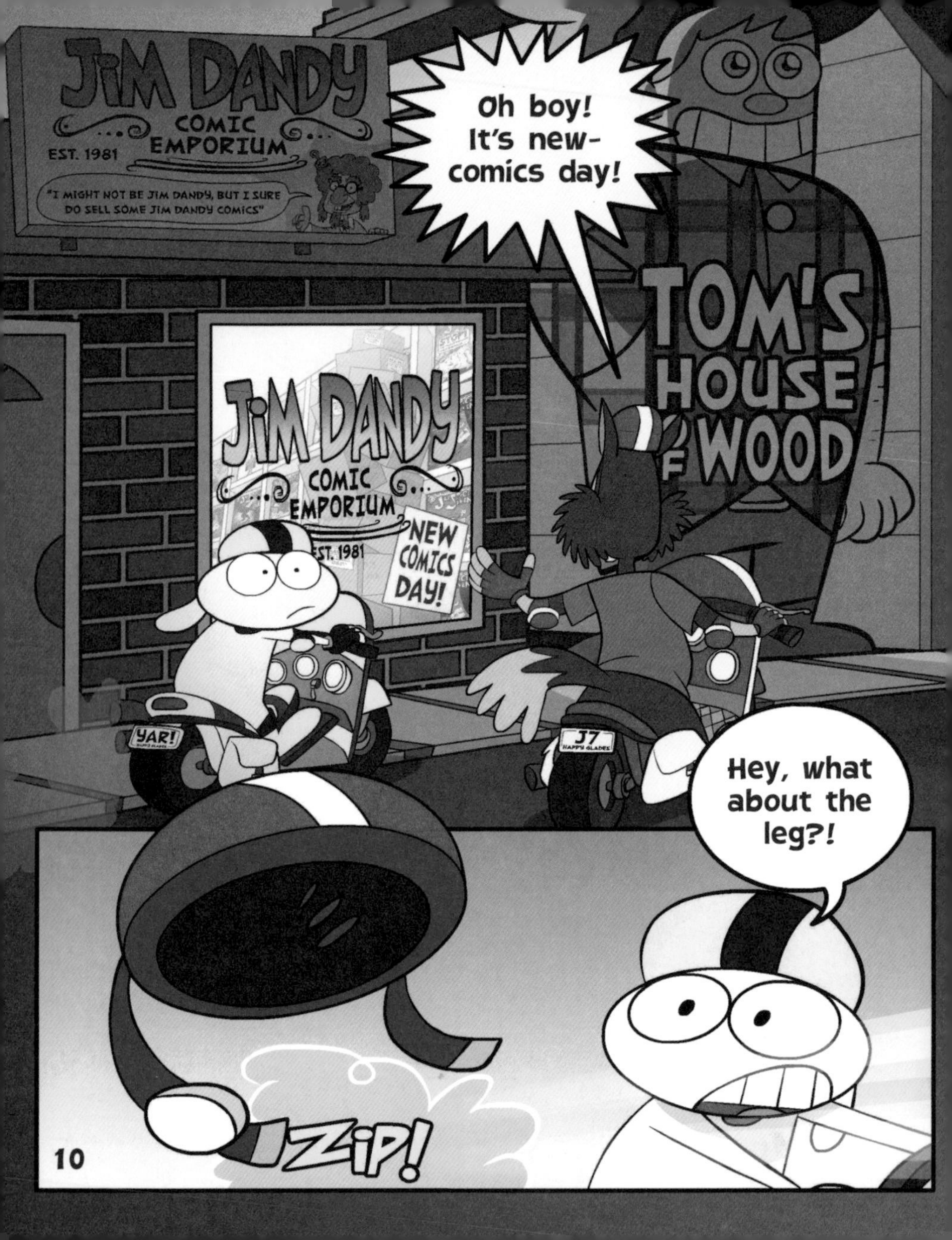
JIM DANDY
COMIC EMPORIUM
EST. 1981
"I MIGHT NOT BE JIM DANDY, BUT I SURE DO SELL SOME JIM DANDY COMICS"
Oh boy! It's new-comics day!
TOM'S HOUSE OF WOOD
JIM DANDY
COMIC EMPORIUM
EST. 1981
NEW COMICS DAY!
YAR!
J7
HAPPY GLADES
Hey, what about the leg?!
ZIP!

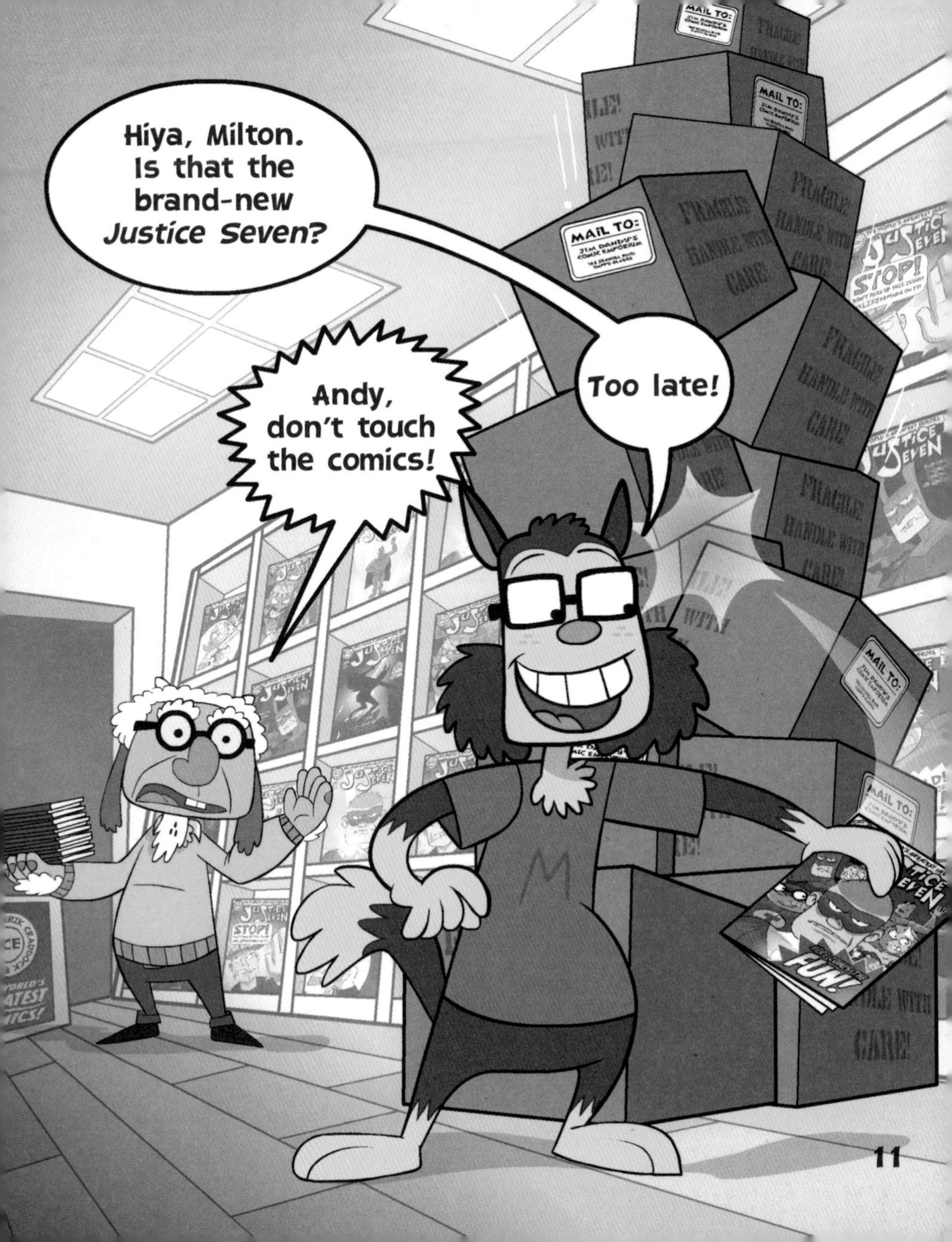
Hiya, Milton. Is that the brand-new *Justice Seven?*
Andy, don't touch the comics!
Too late!

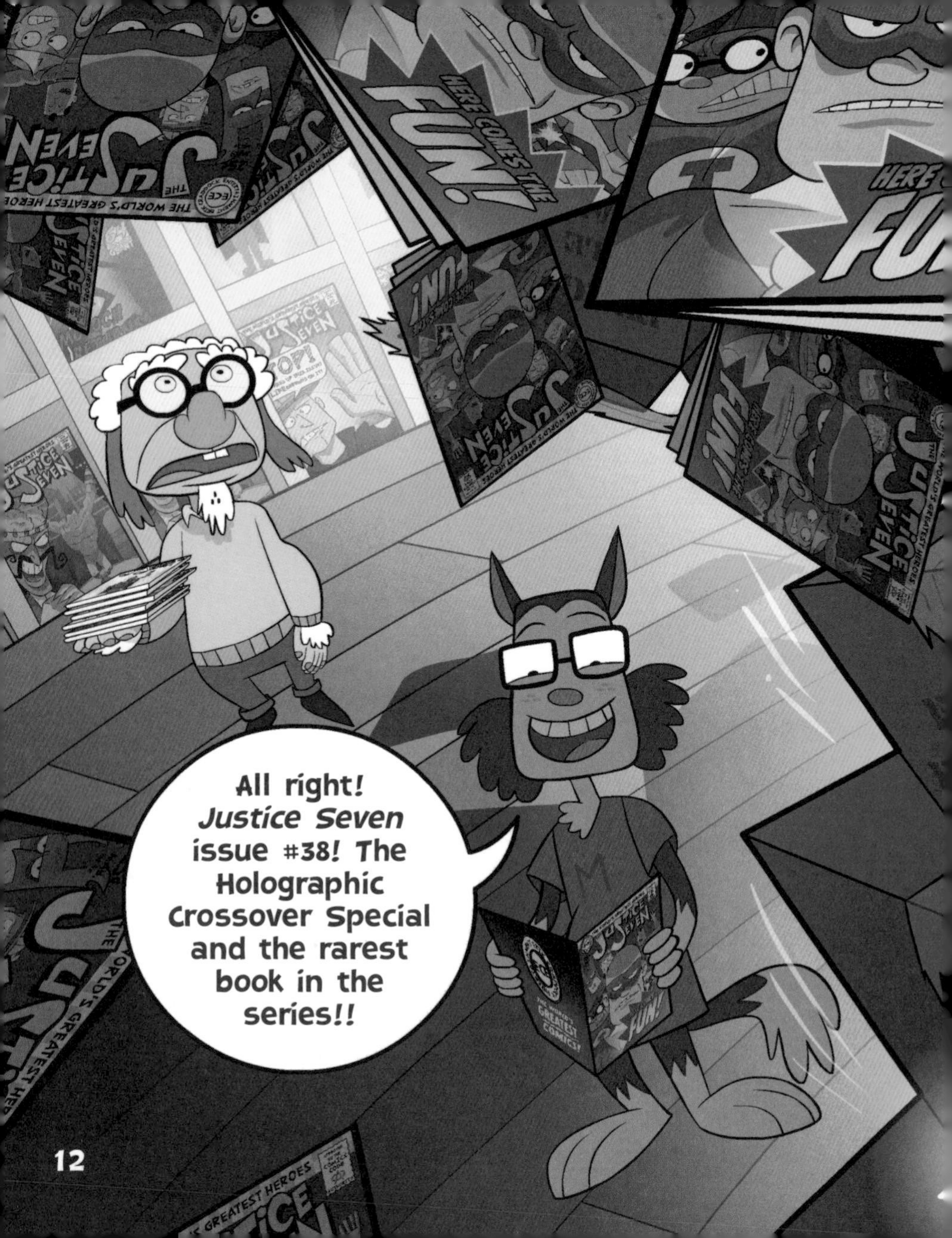
HERE COMES THE FUN!
All right! *Justice Seven* issue #38! The Holographic Crossover Special and the rarest book in the series!!

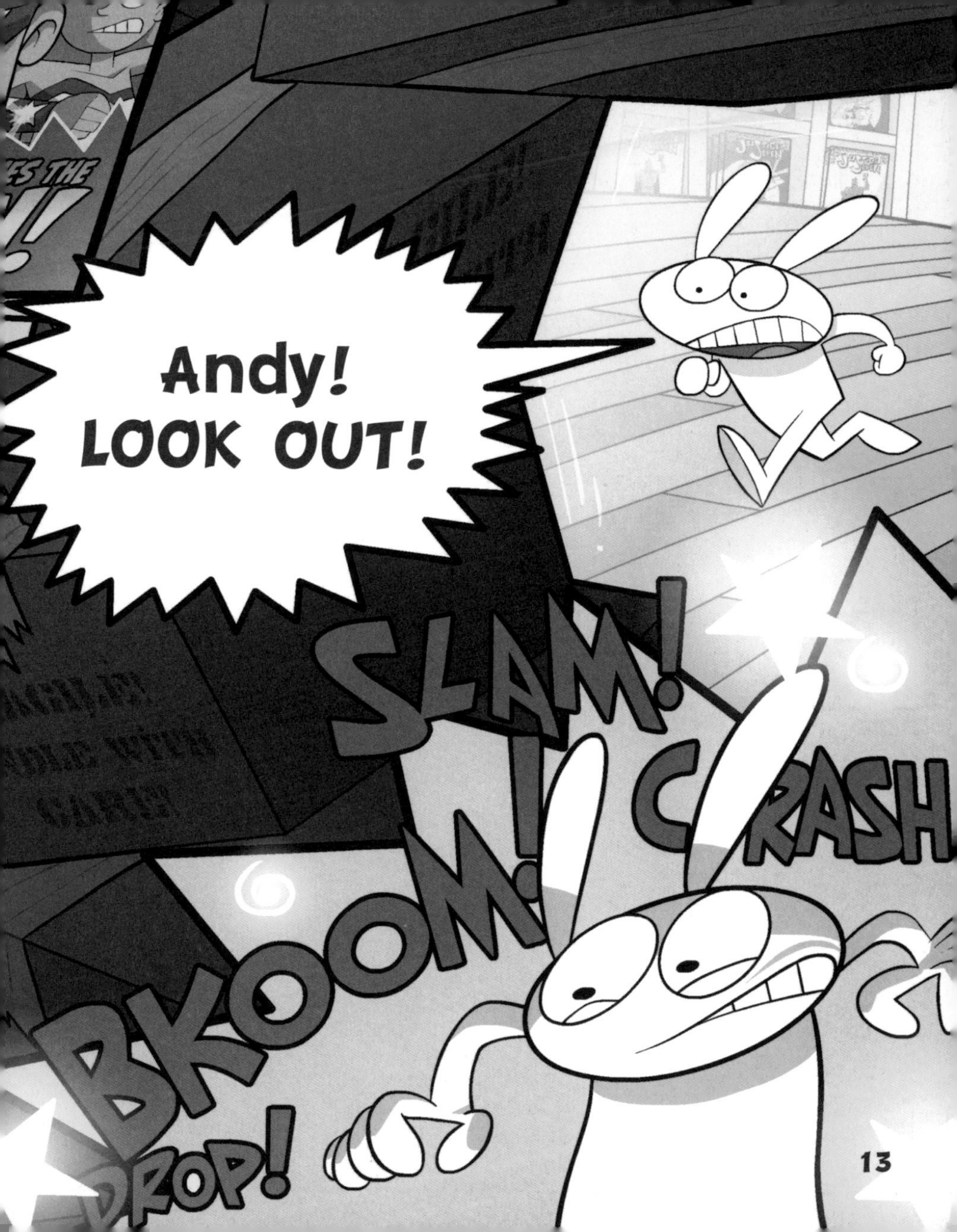
Andy! LOOK OUT!
SLAM!
CRASH
BKOOM!
DROP!

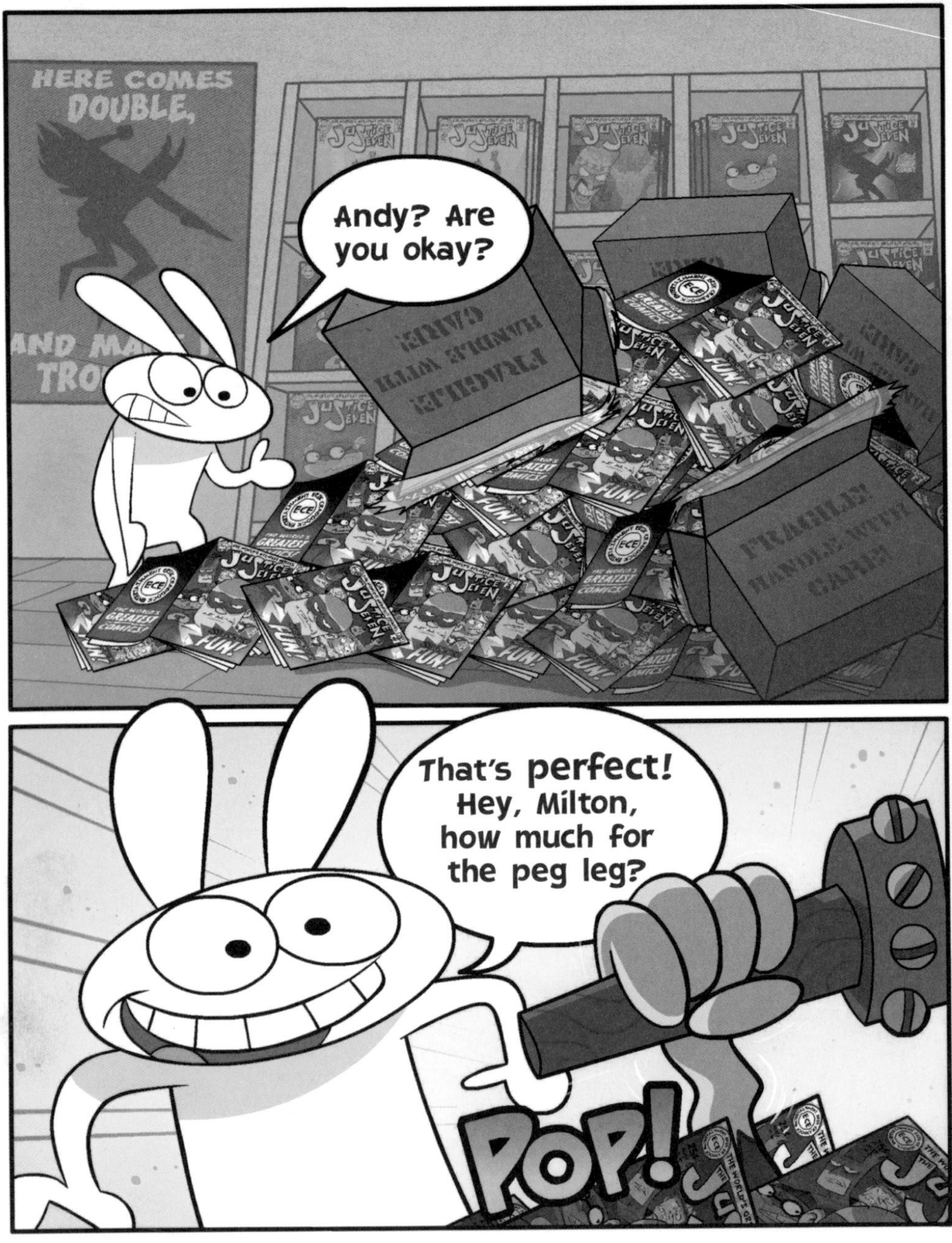
HERE COMES DOUBLE,
Andy? Are you okay?
FRAGILE! HANDLE WITH CARE!
That's perfect! Hey, Milton, how much for the peg leg?
POP!

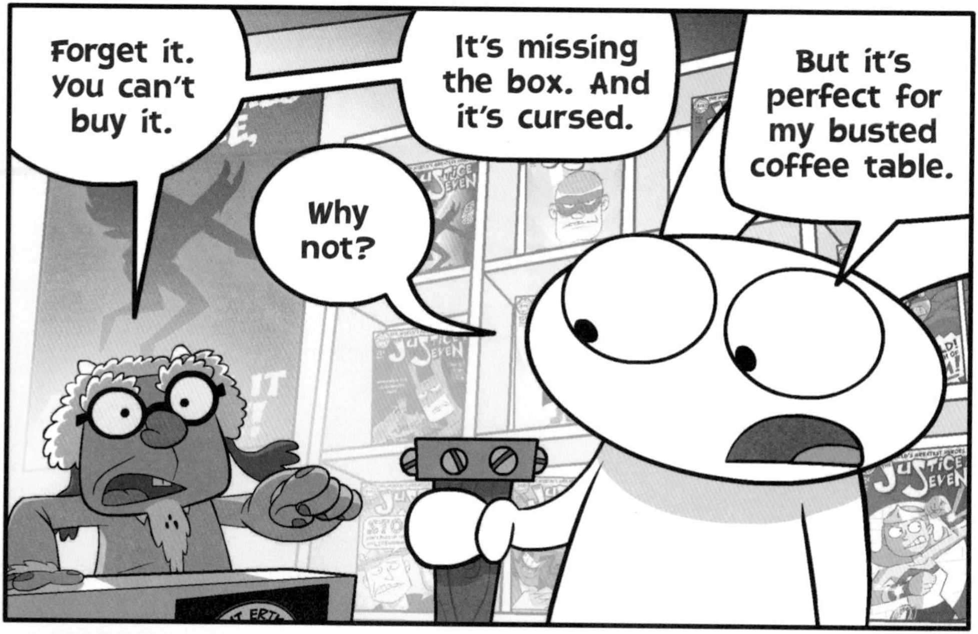
Forget it. You can't buy it.
Why not?
It's missing the box. And it's cursed.
But it's perfect for my busted coffee table.

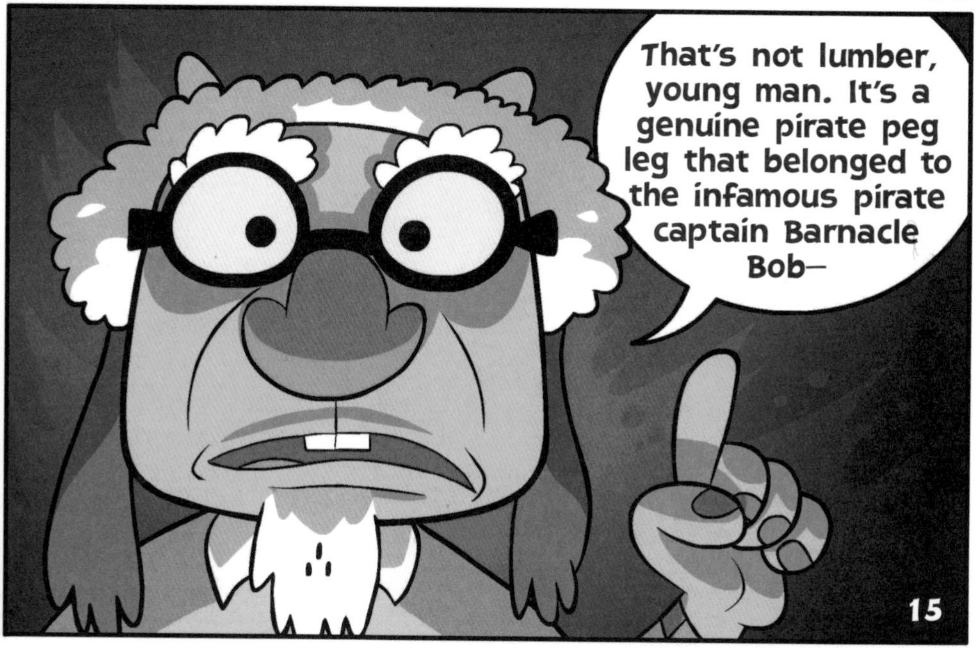
That's not lumber, young man. It's a genuine pirate peg leg that belonged to the infamous pirate captain Barnacle Bob—

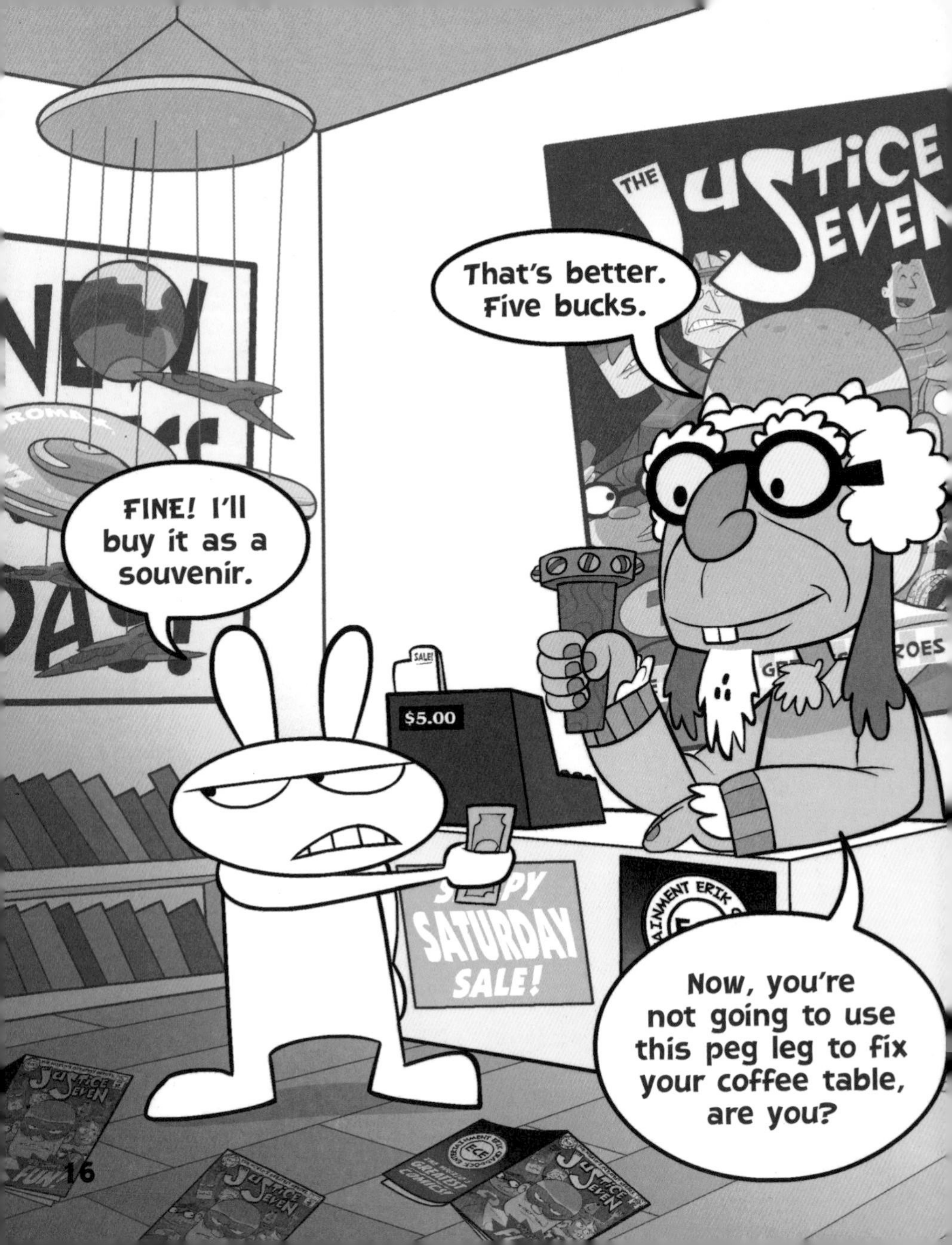
FINE! I'll buy it as a souvenir.
That's better. Five bucks.
$5.00
Now, you're not going to use this peg leg to fix your coffee table, are you?
SATURDAY SALE!

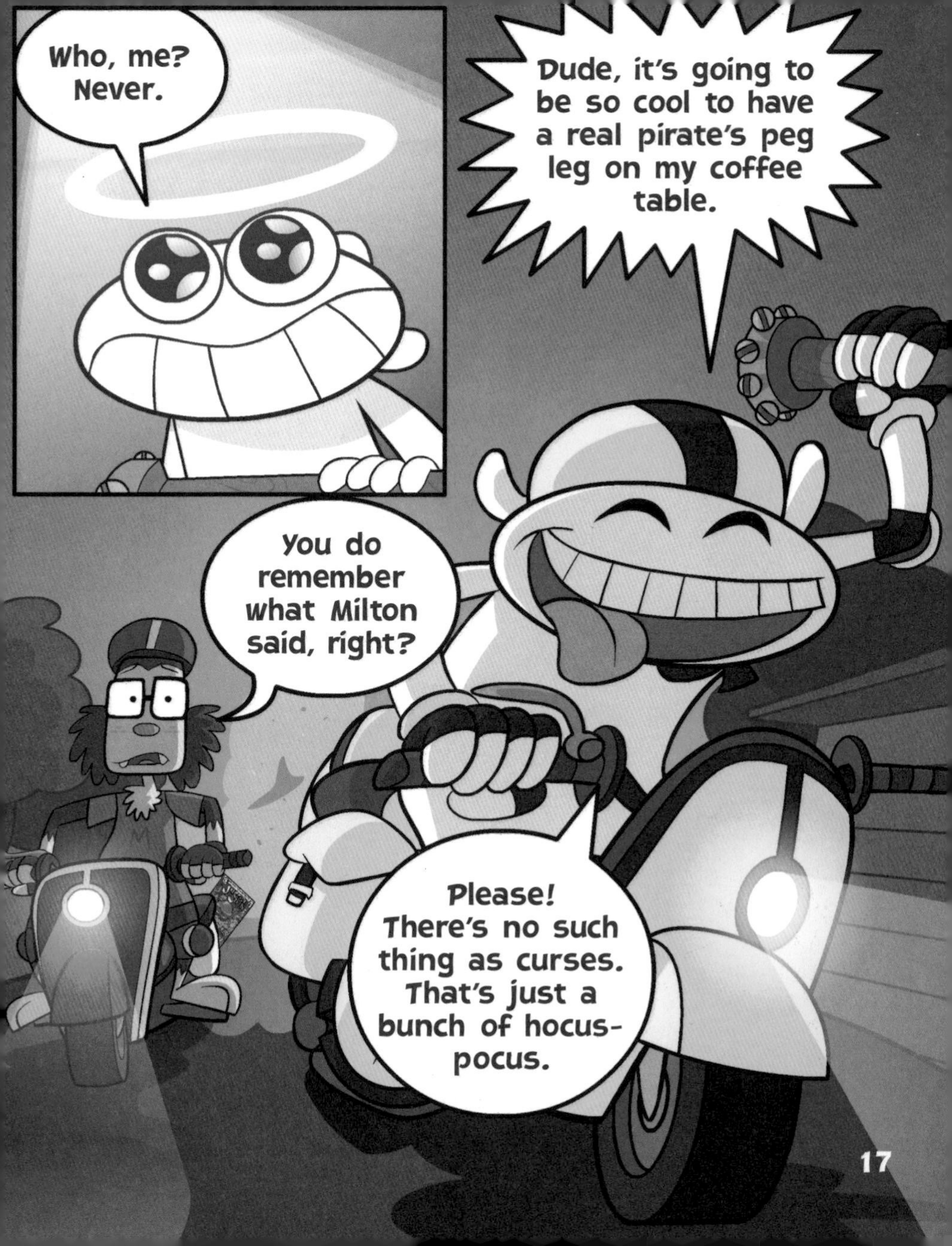
Who, me? Never.
Dude, it's going to be so cool to have a real pirate's peg leg on my coffee table.
You do remember what Milton said, right?
Please! There's no such thing as curses. That's just a bunch of hocus-pocus.

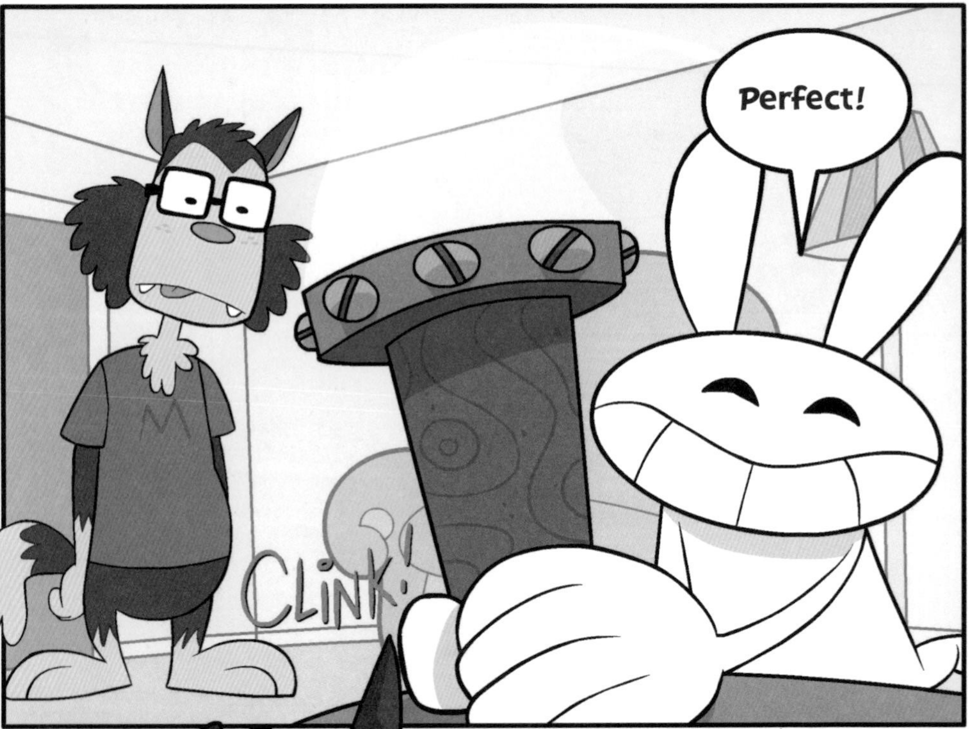
Perfect!
CLINK!

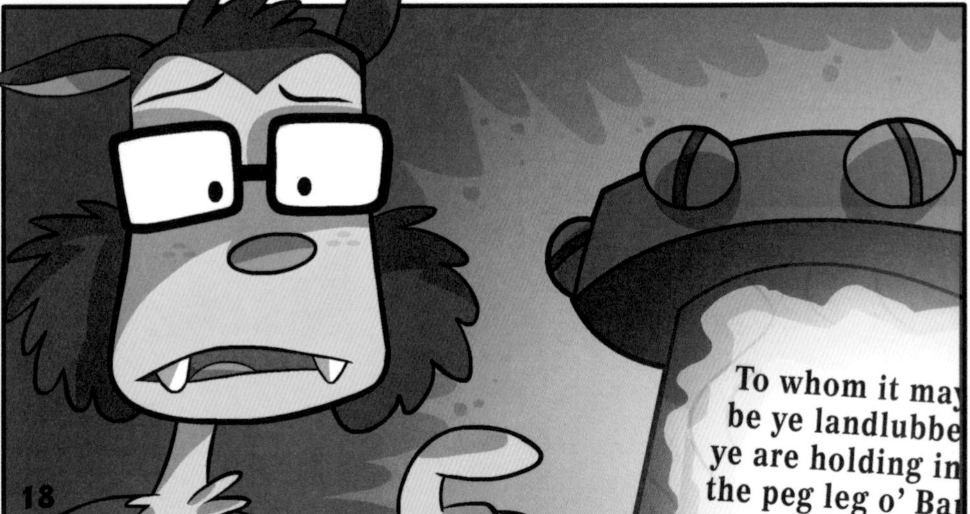
To whom it may
be ye landlubbe
ye are holding in
the peg leg o' Ba

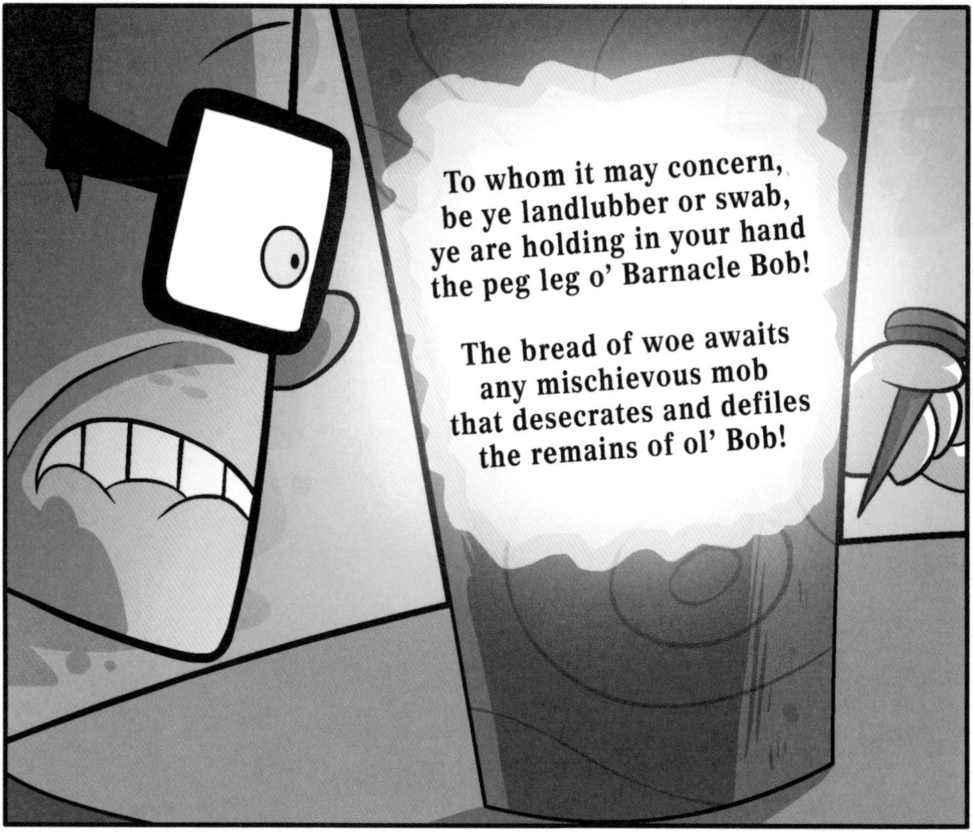
To whom it may concern, be ye landlubber or swab, ye are holding in your hand the peg leg o' Barnacle Bob!
The bread of woe awaits any mischievous mob that desecrates and defiles the remains of ol' Bob!

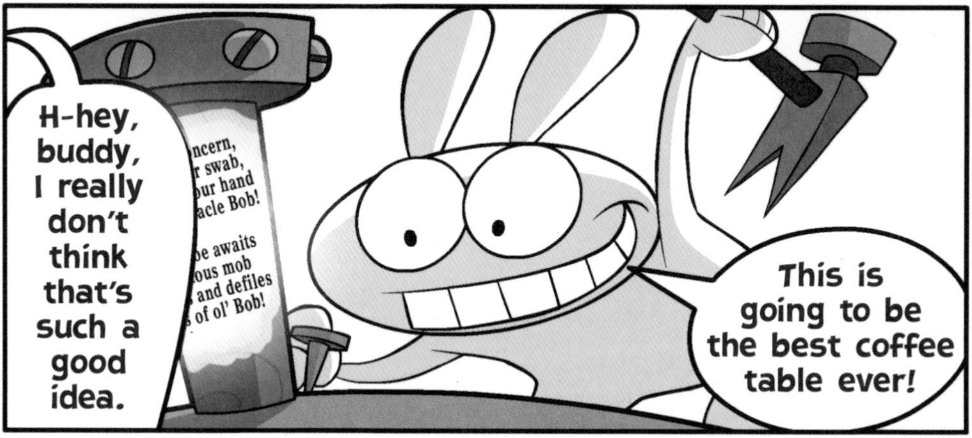
H-hey, buddy, I really don't think that's such a good idea.
This is going to be the best coffee table ever!

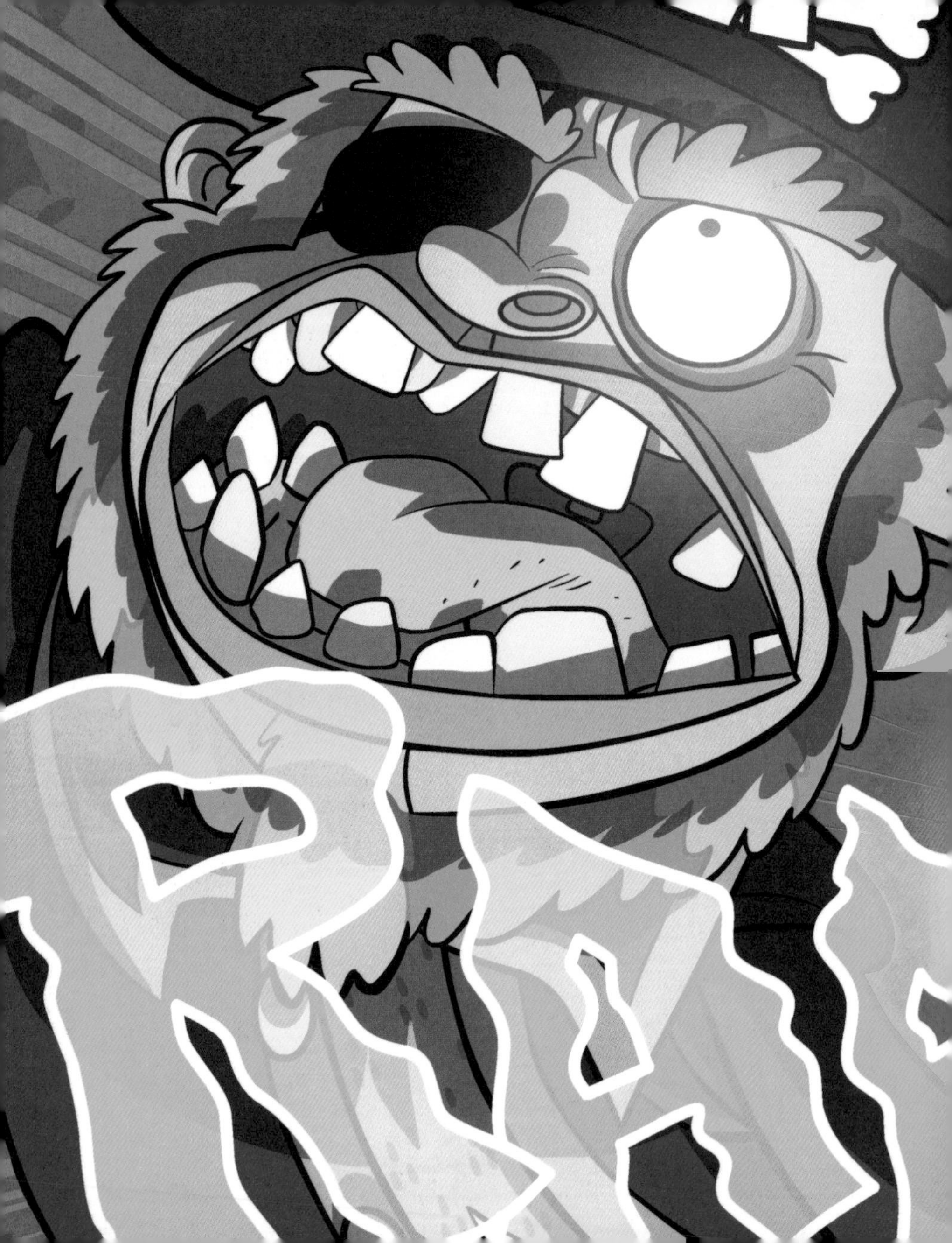

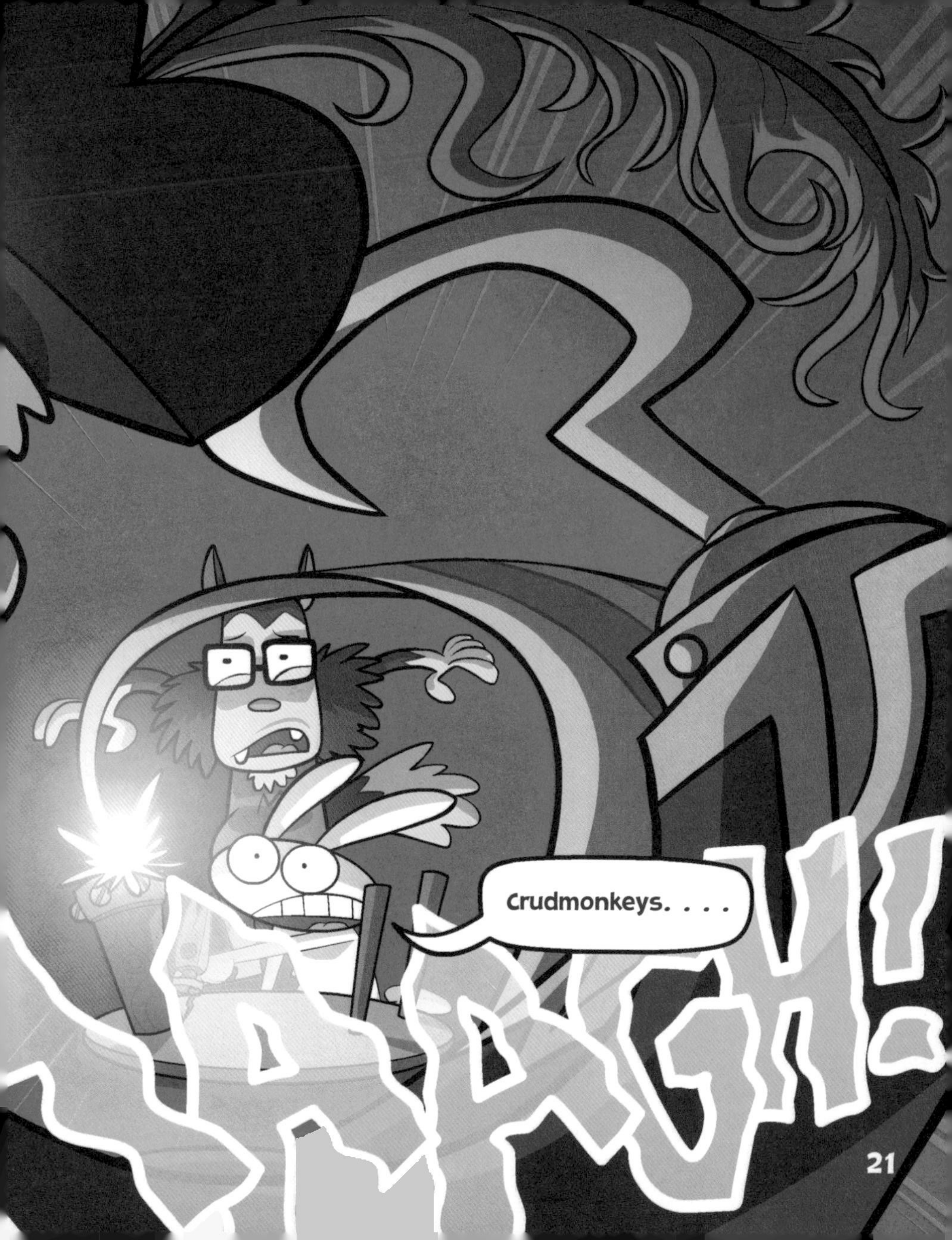
Crudmonkeys. . . .

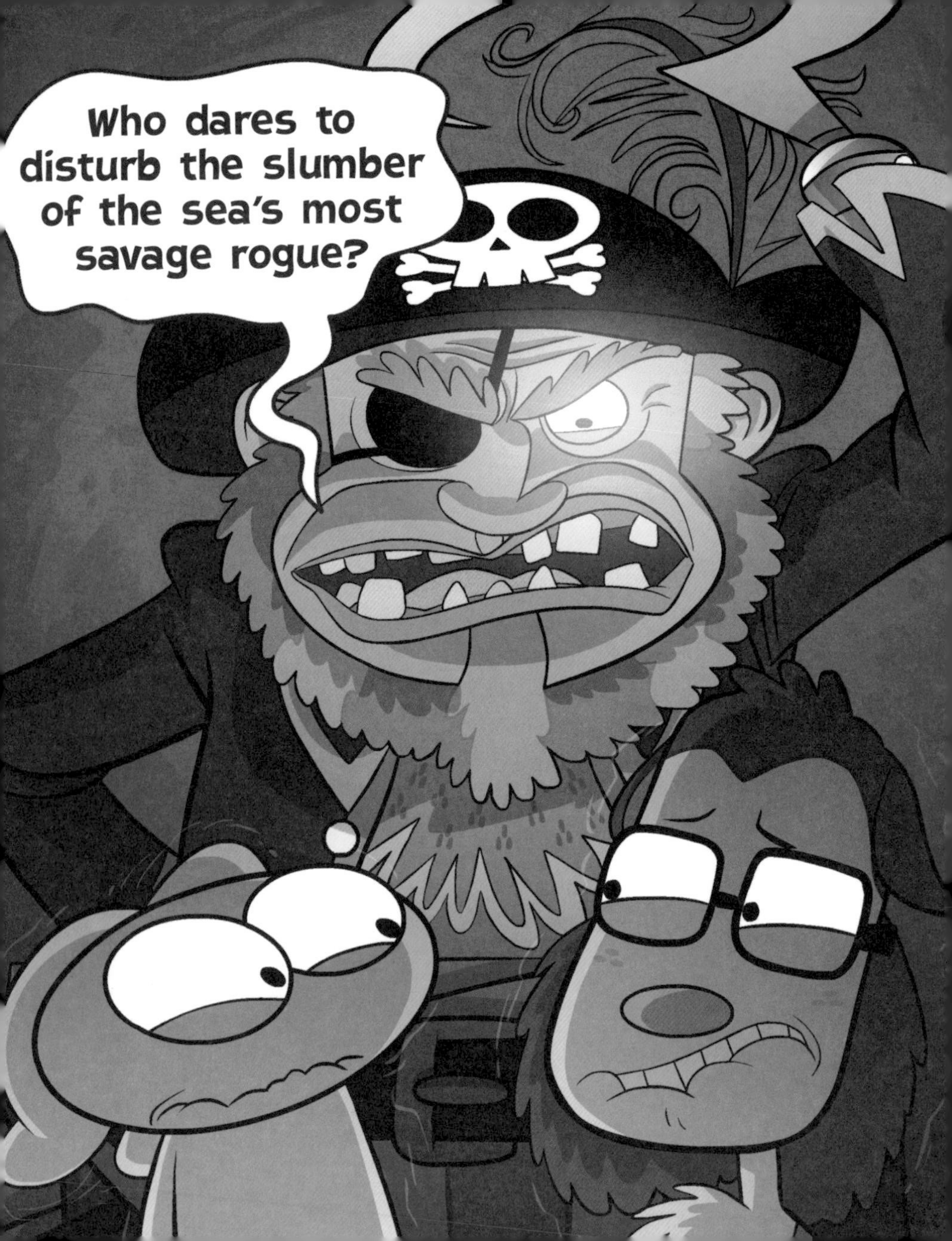
Who dares to disturb the slumber of the sea's most savage rogue?

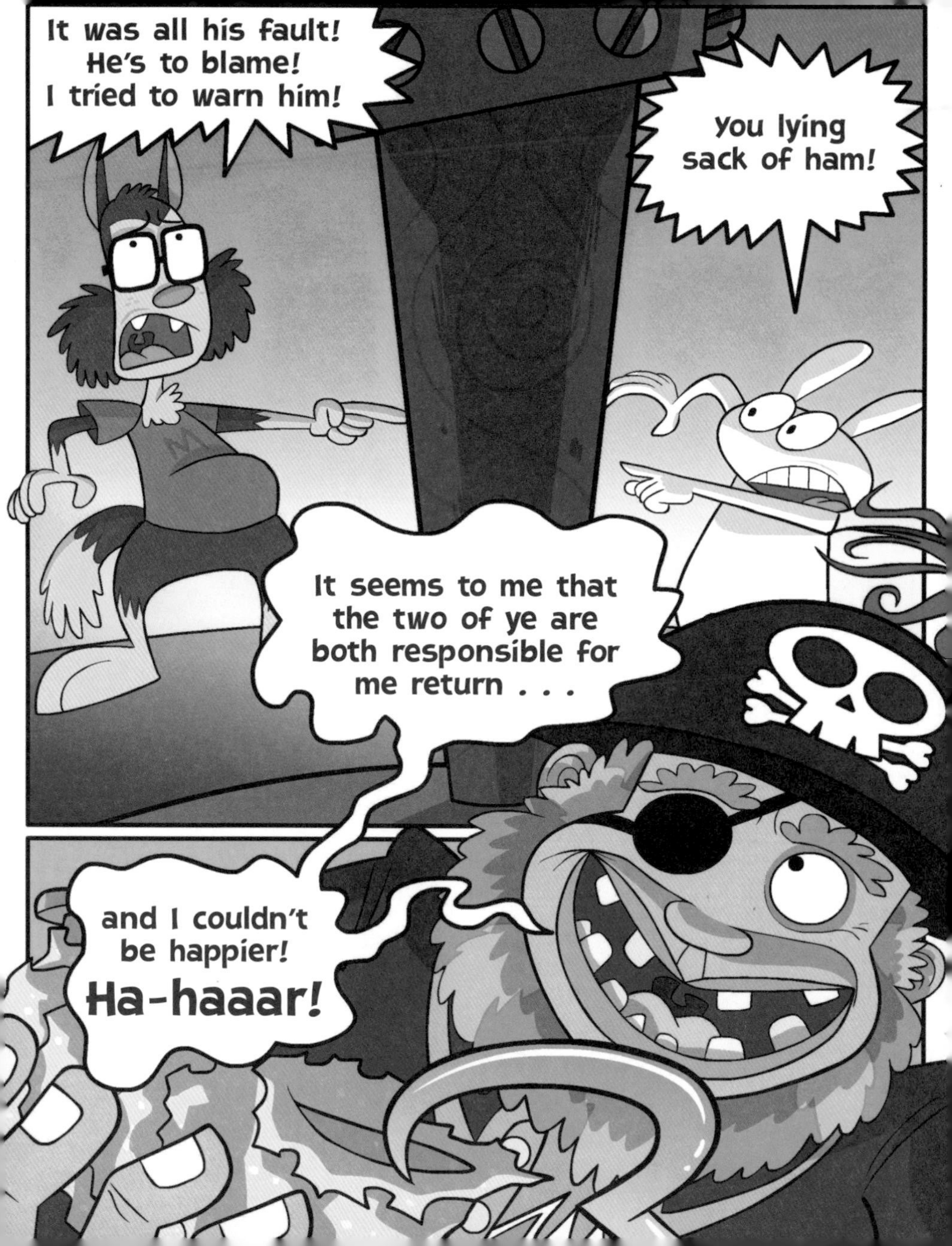
It was all his fault! He's to blame! I tried to warn him!
You lying sack of ham!
It seems to me that the two of ye are both responsible for me return . . .
and I couldn't be happier!
Ha-haaar!

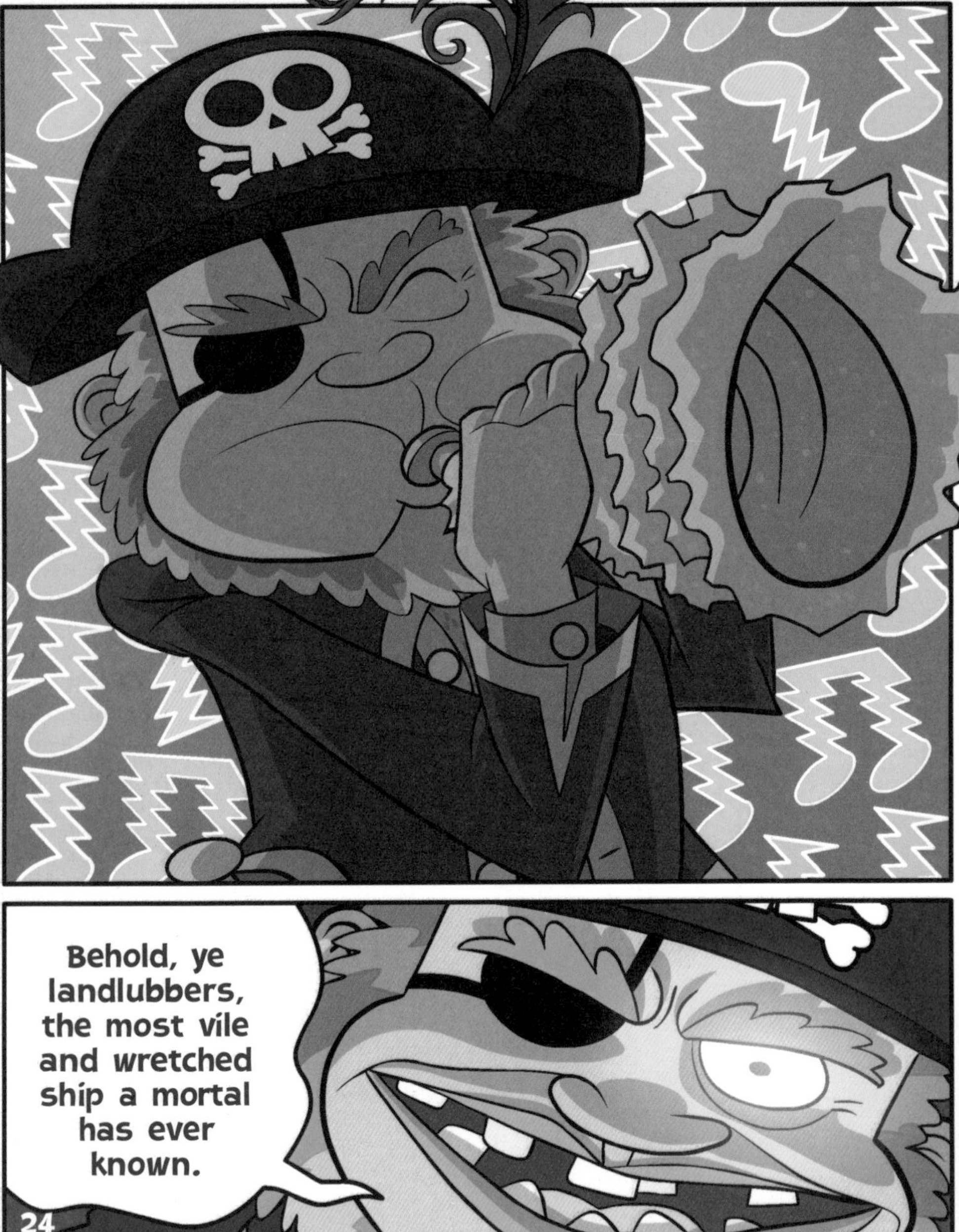
Behold, ye landlubbers, the most vile and wretched ship a mortal has ever known.

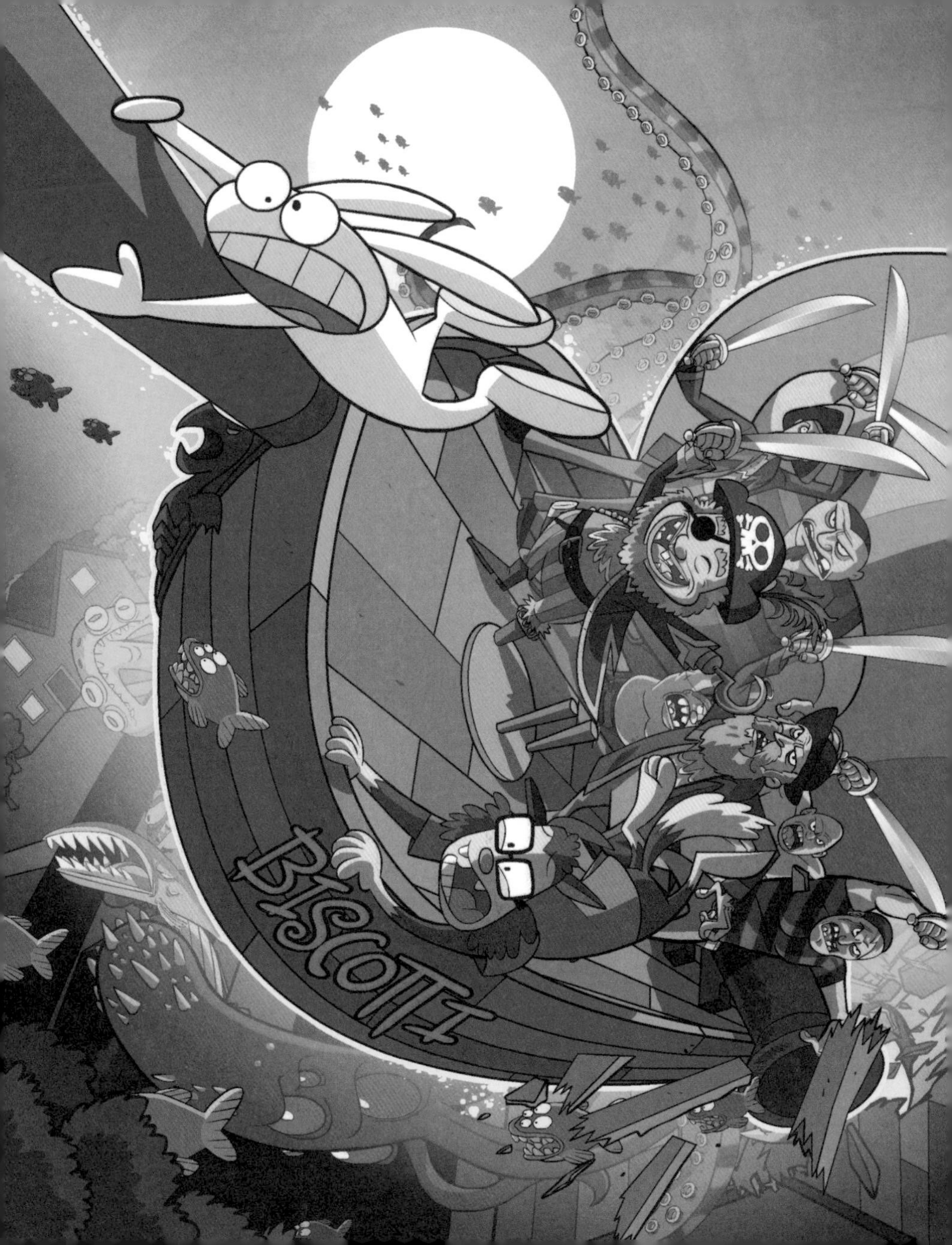
BISCOTTI

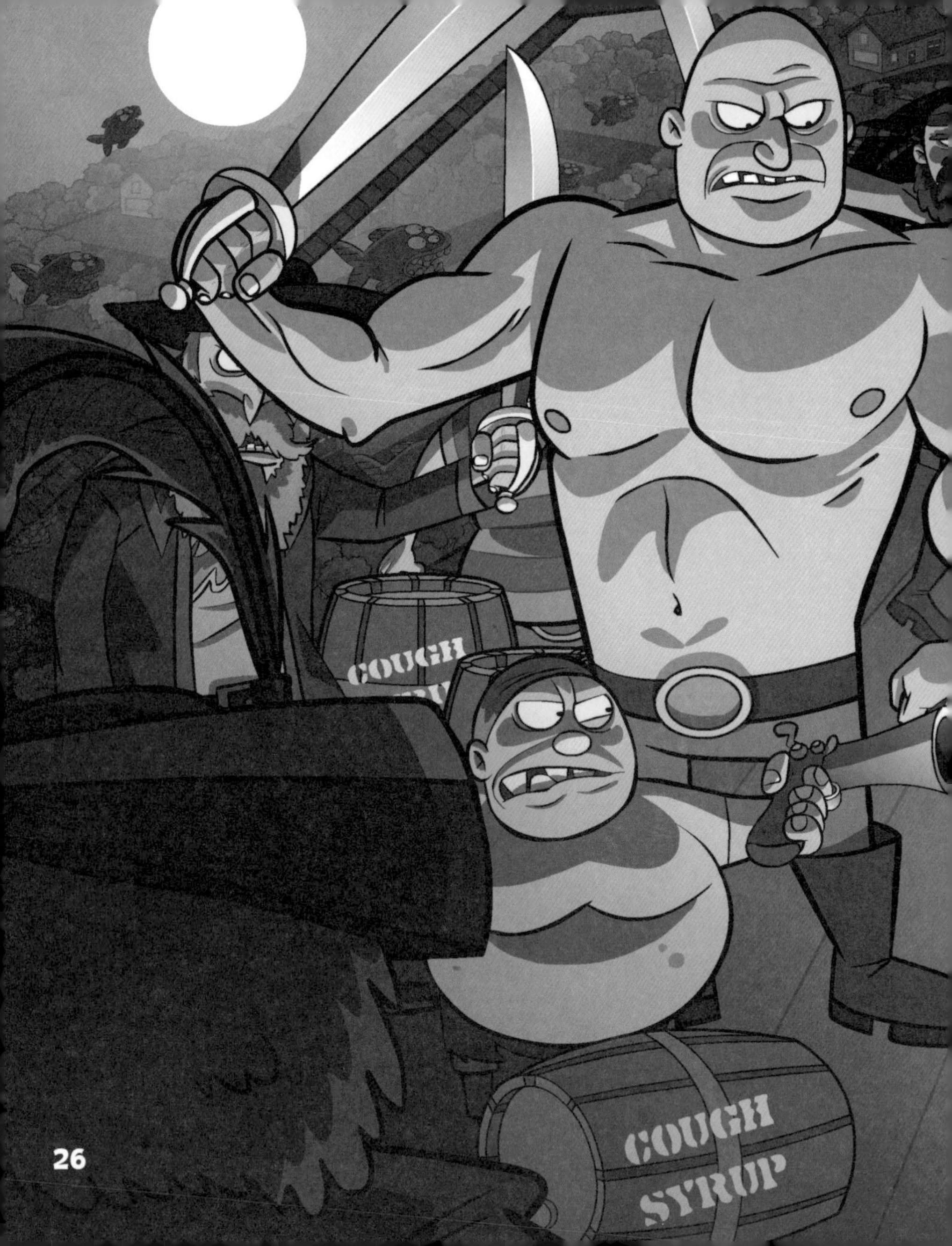
COUGH
COUGH
SYRUP

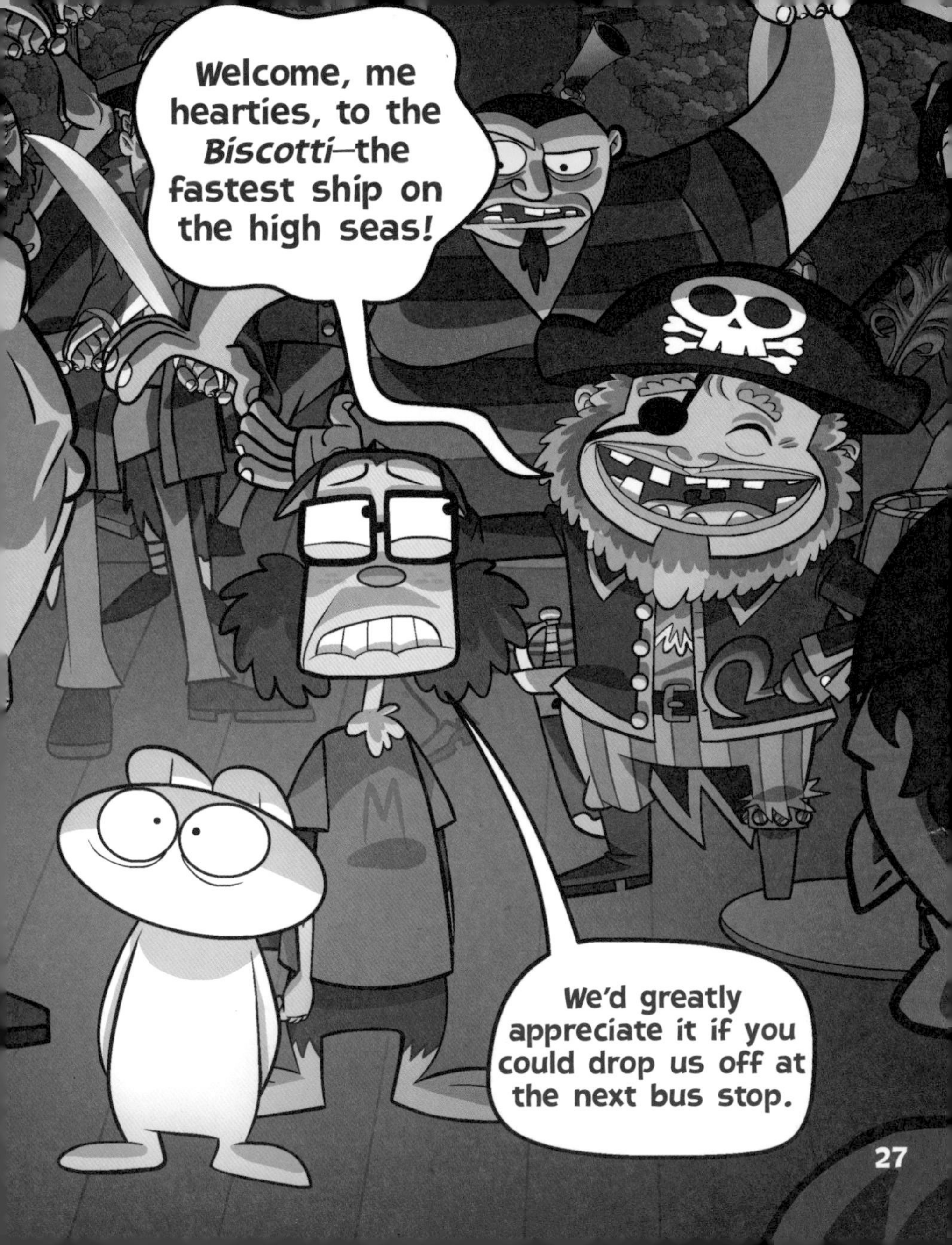
Welcome, me hearties, to the *Biscotti*—the fastest ship on the high seas!
We'd greatly appreciate it if you could drop us off at the next bus stop.

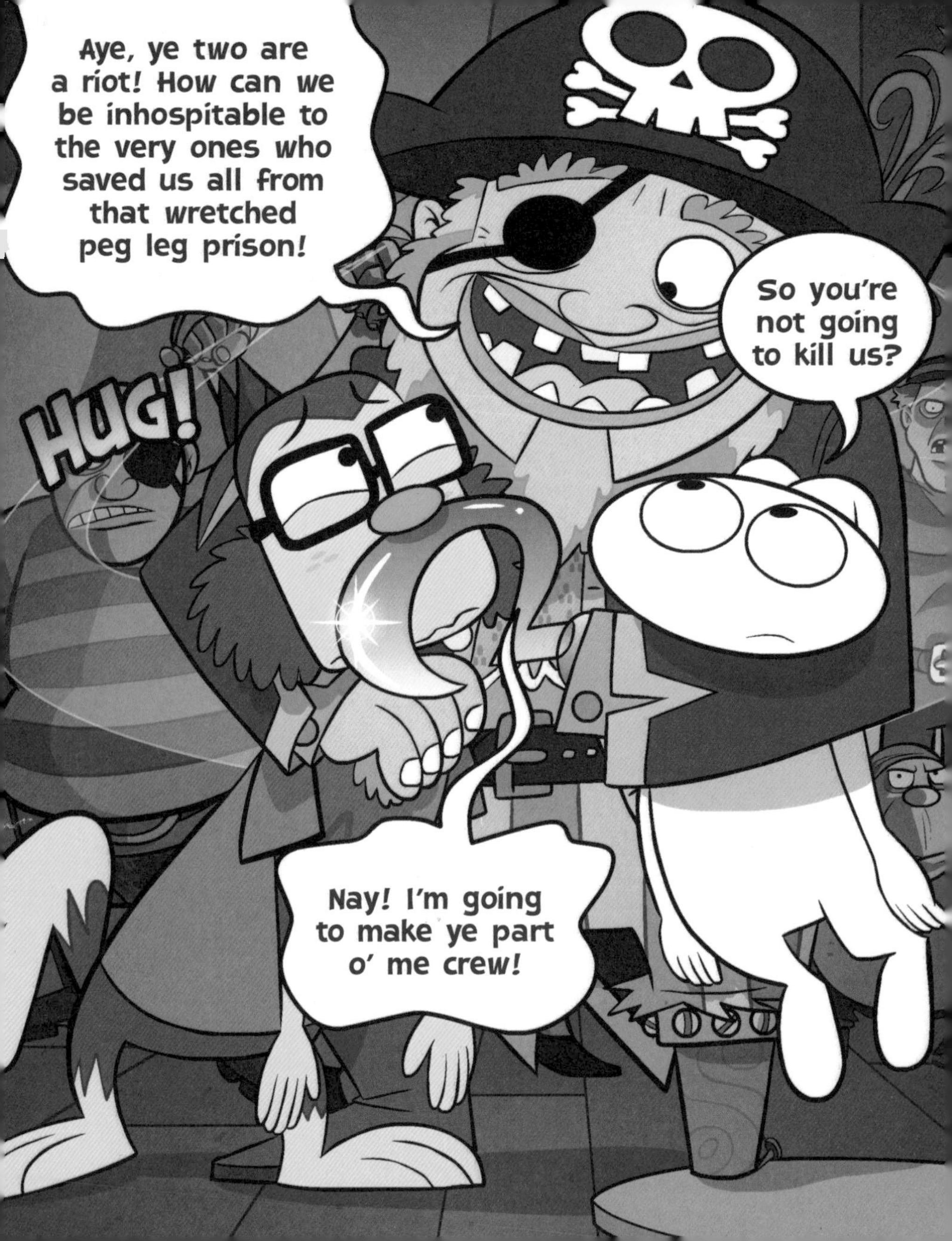
Aye, ye two are a riot! How can we be inhospitable to the very ones who saved us all from that wretched peg leg prison!
HUG!
So you're not going to kill us?
Nay! I'm going to make ye part o' me crew!

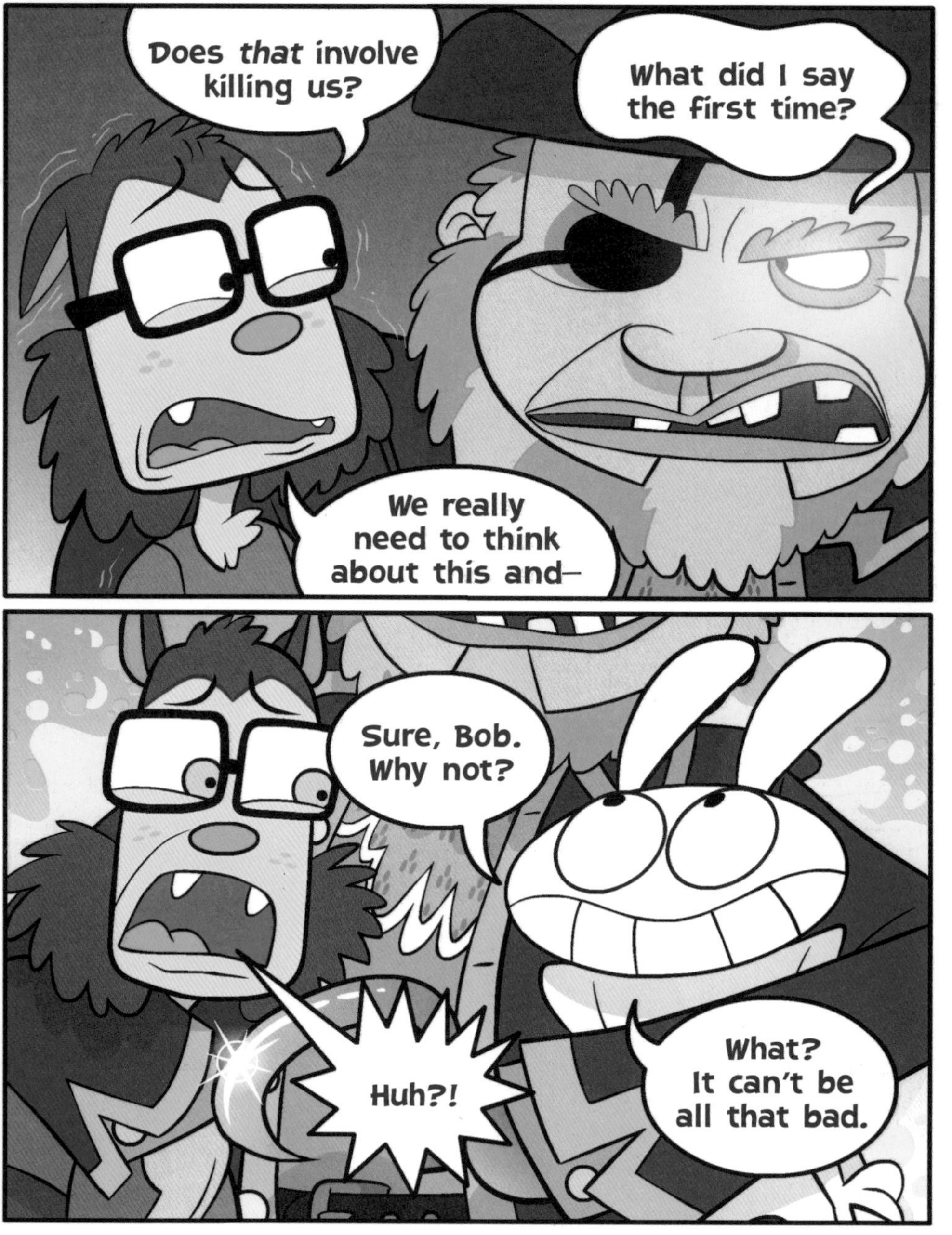
Does *that* involve killing us?
What did I say the first time?
We really need to think about this and—
Sure, Bob. Why not?
Huh?!
What? It can't be all that bad.

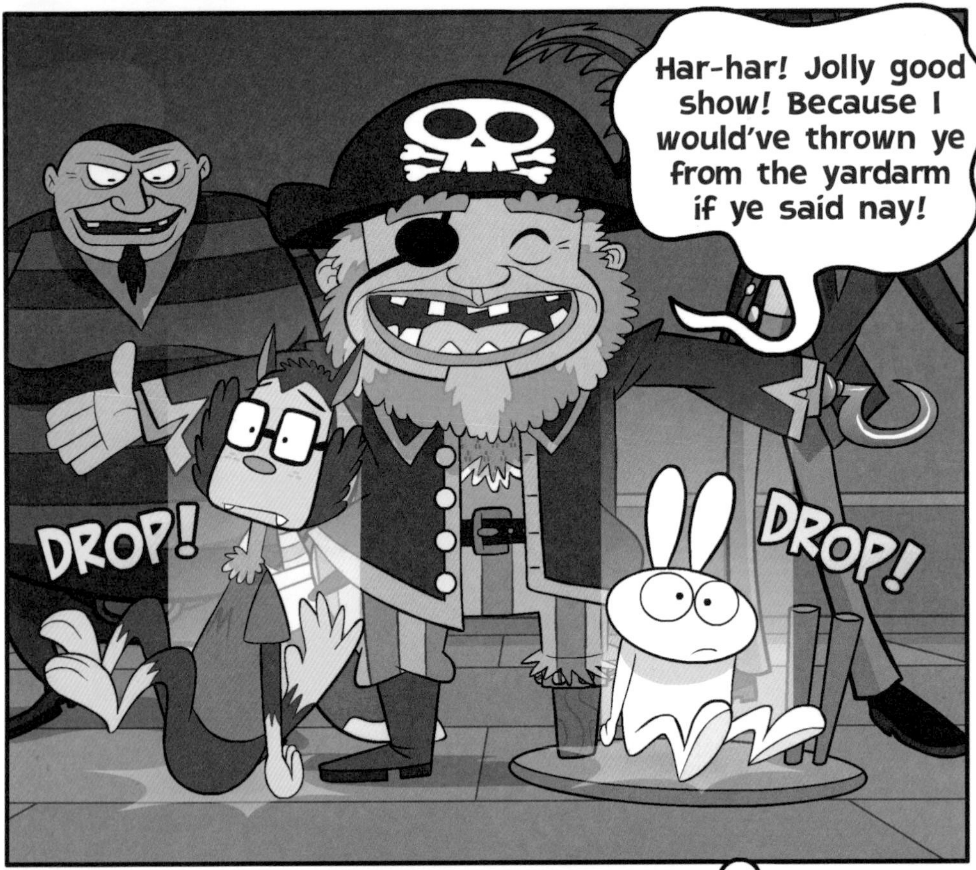
Har-har! Jolly good show! Because I would've thrown ye from the yardarm if ye said nay!
DROP!
DROP!

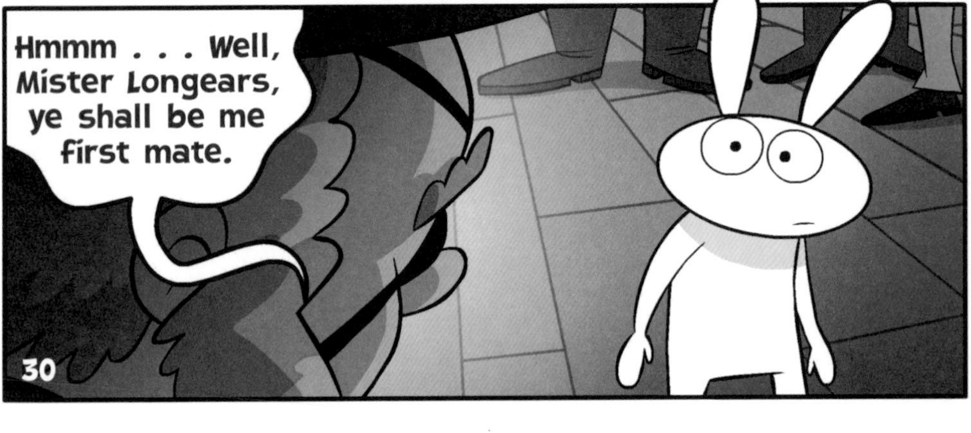
Hmmm . . . Well, Mister Longears, ye shall be me first mate.

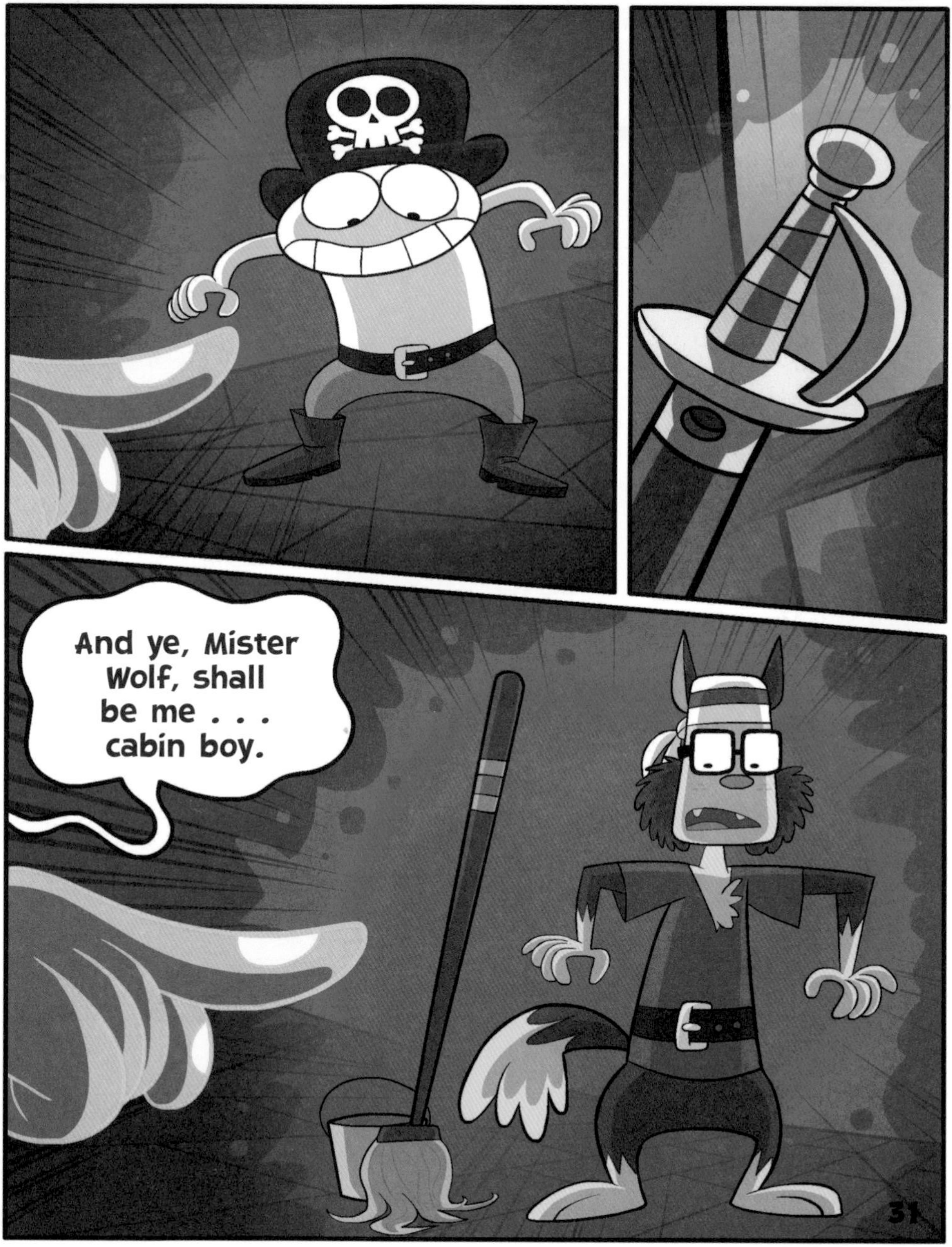
And ye, Mister Wolf, shall be me . . . cabin boy.

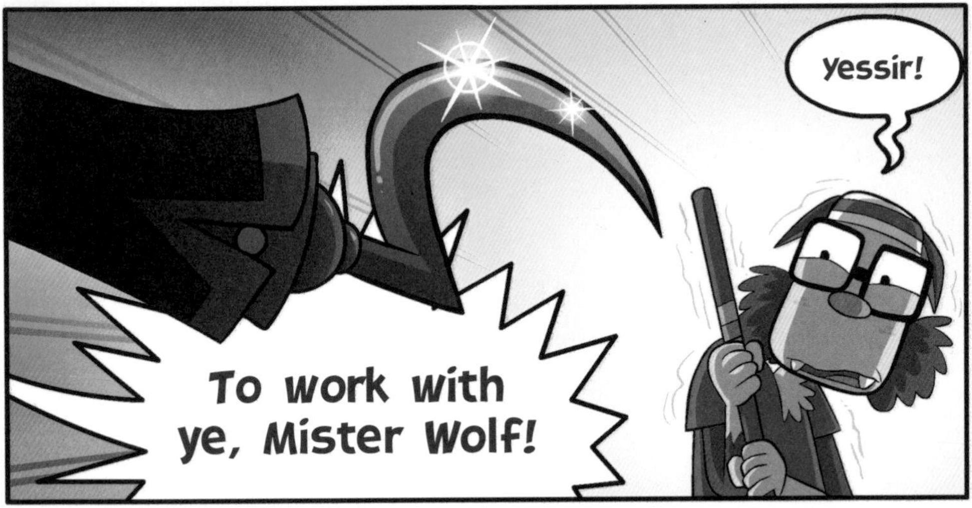
Yessir!
To work with ye, Mister Wolf!

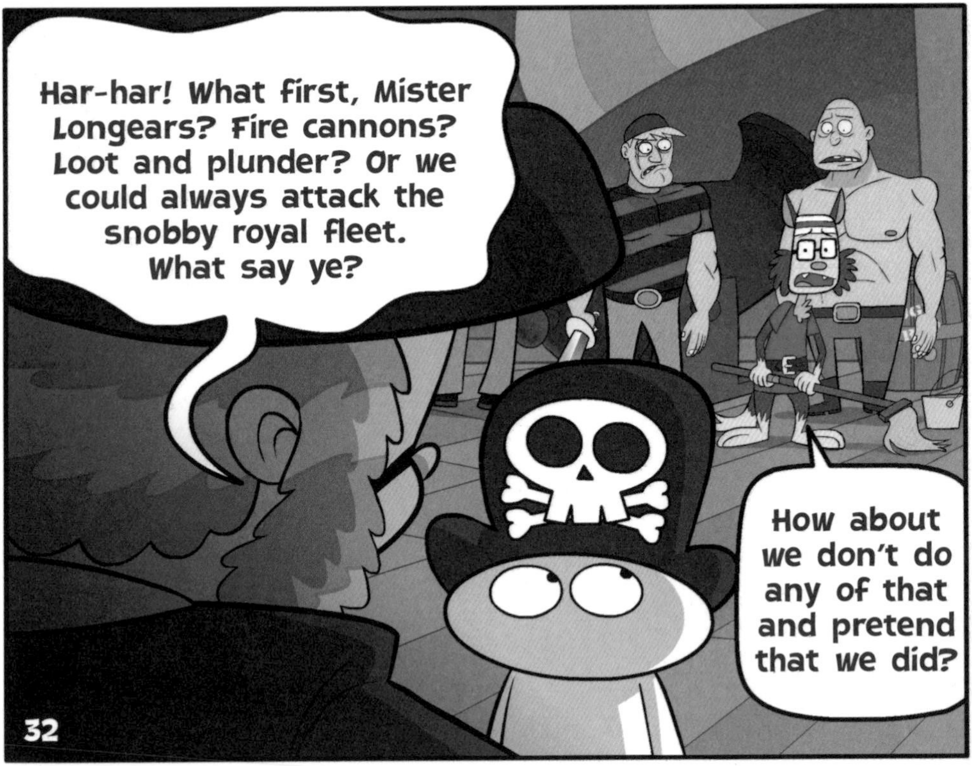
Har-har! What first, Mister Longears? Fire cannons? Loot and plunder? Or we could always attack the snobby royal fleet. What say ye?
How about we don't do any of that and pretend that we did?

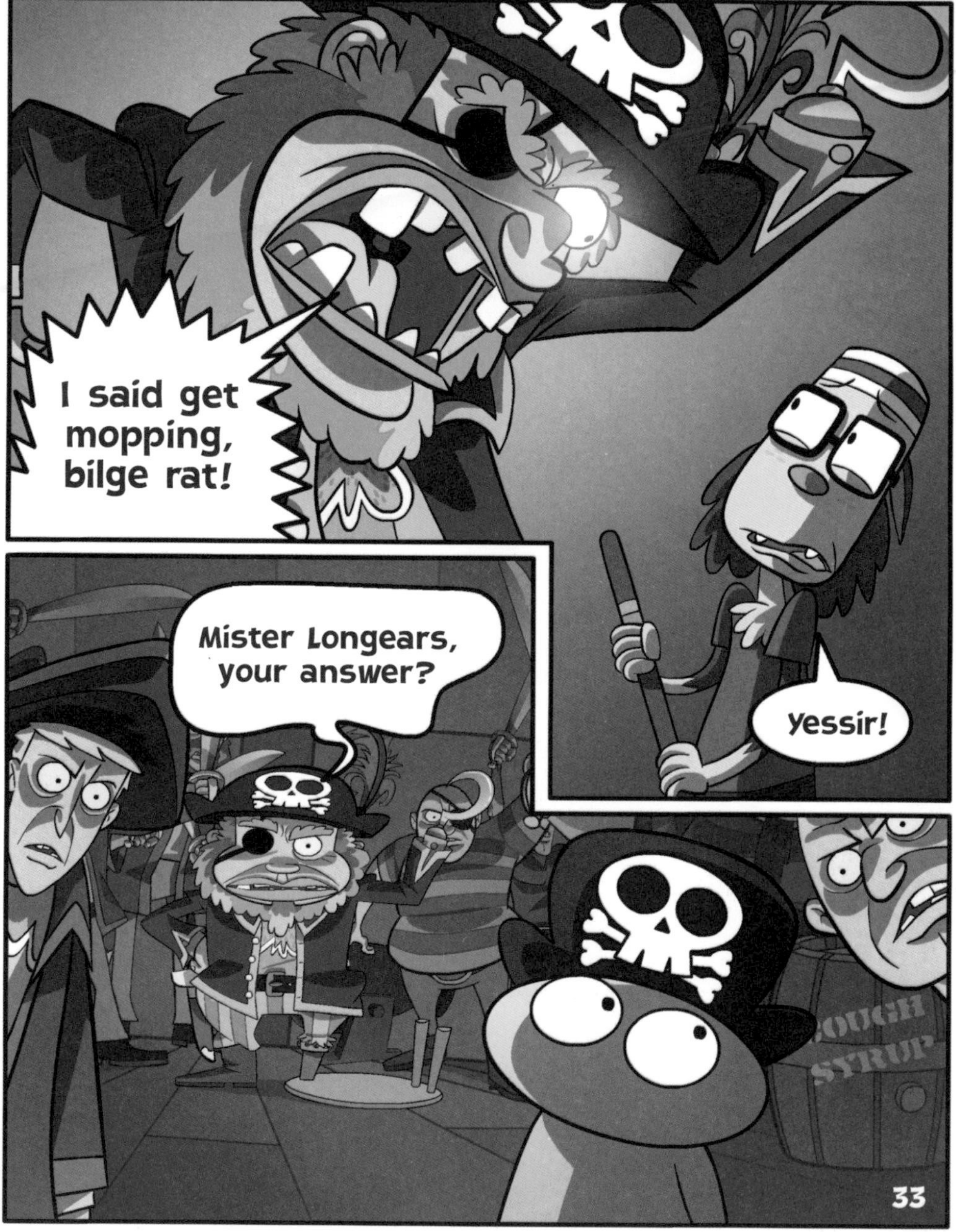
I said get mopping, bilge rat!
Yessir!
Mister Longears, your answer?

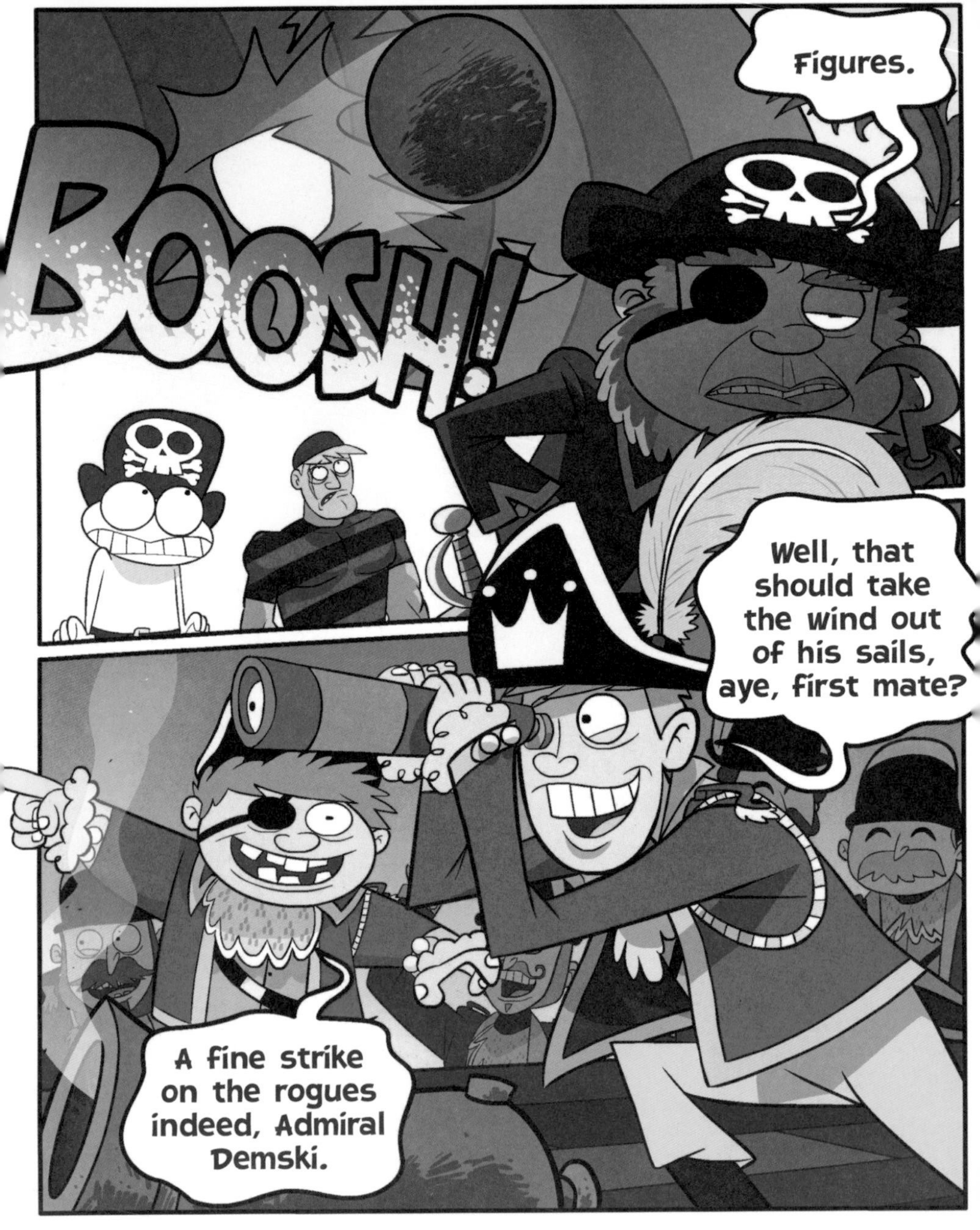
BOOSH!
Figures.
Well, that should take the wind out of his sails, aye, first mate?
A fine strike on the rogues indeed, Admiral Demski.

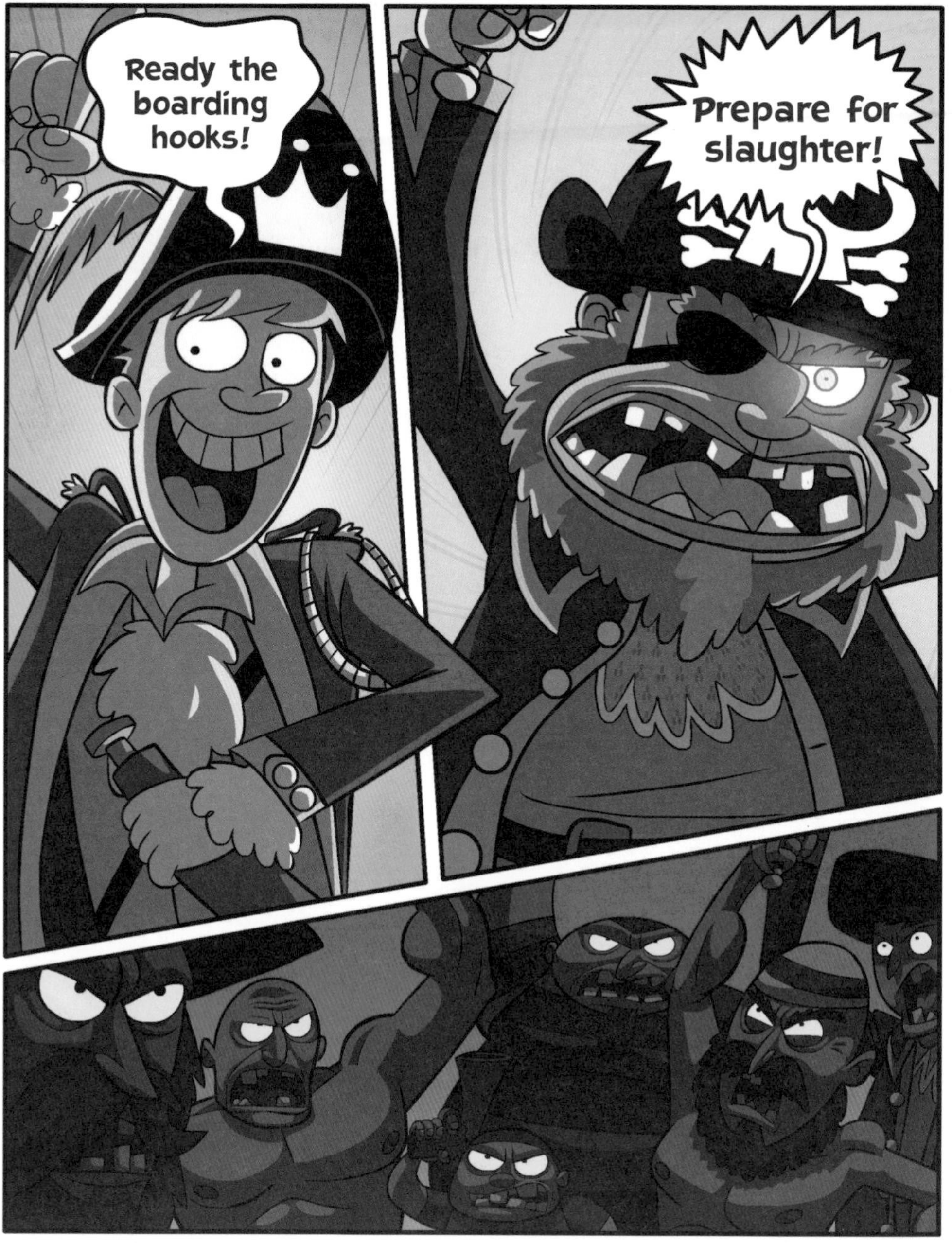
Ready the boarding hooks!
Prepare for slaughter!

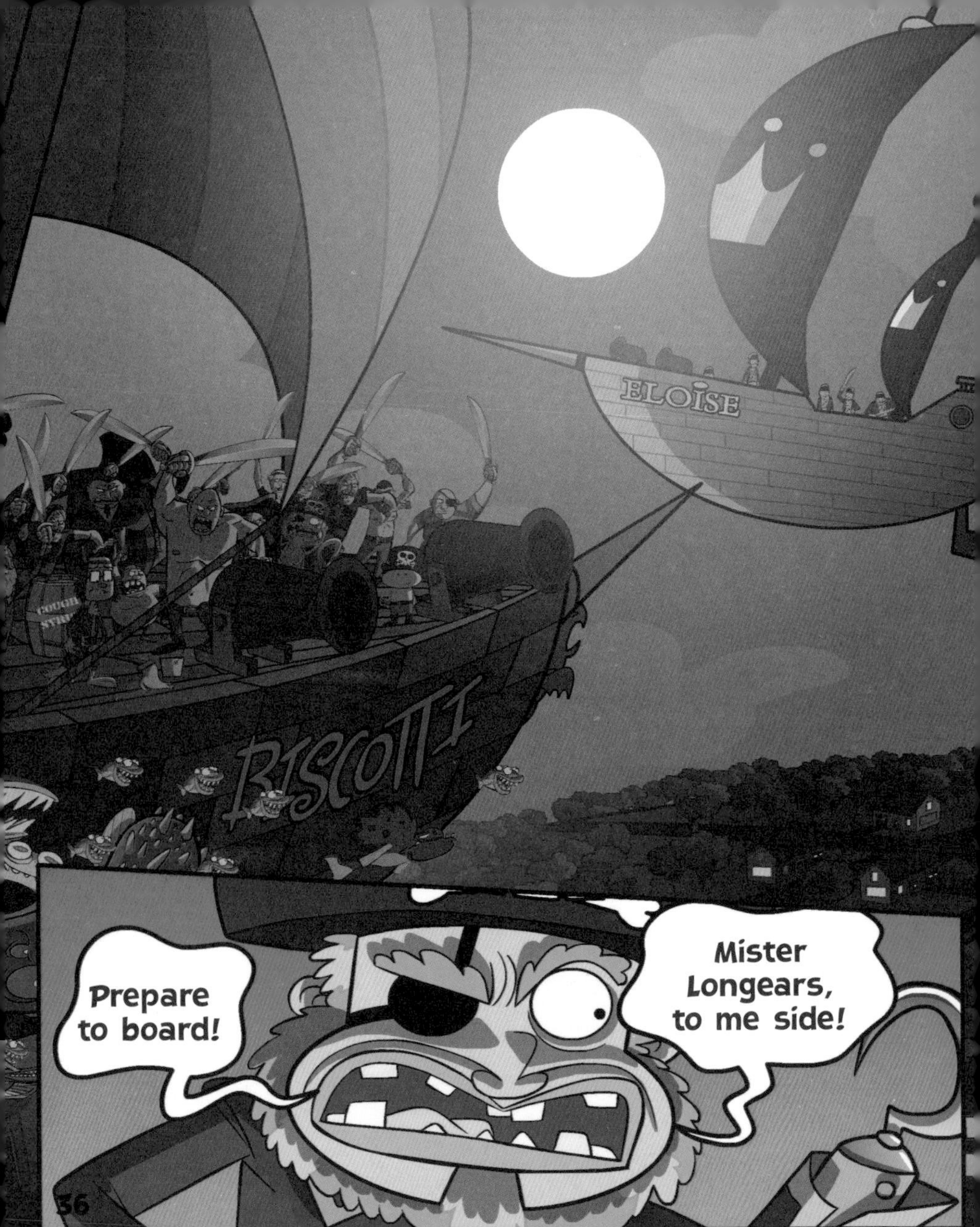
ELOISE
BISCOTTI
Prepare to board!
Mister Longears, to me side!

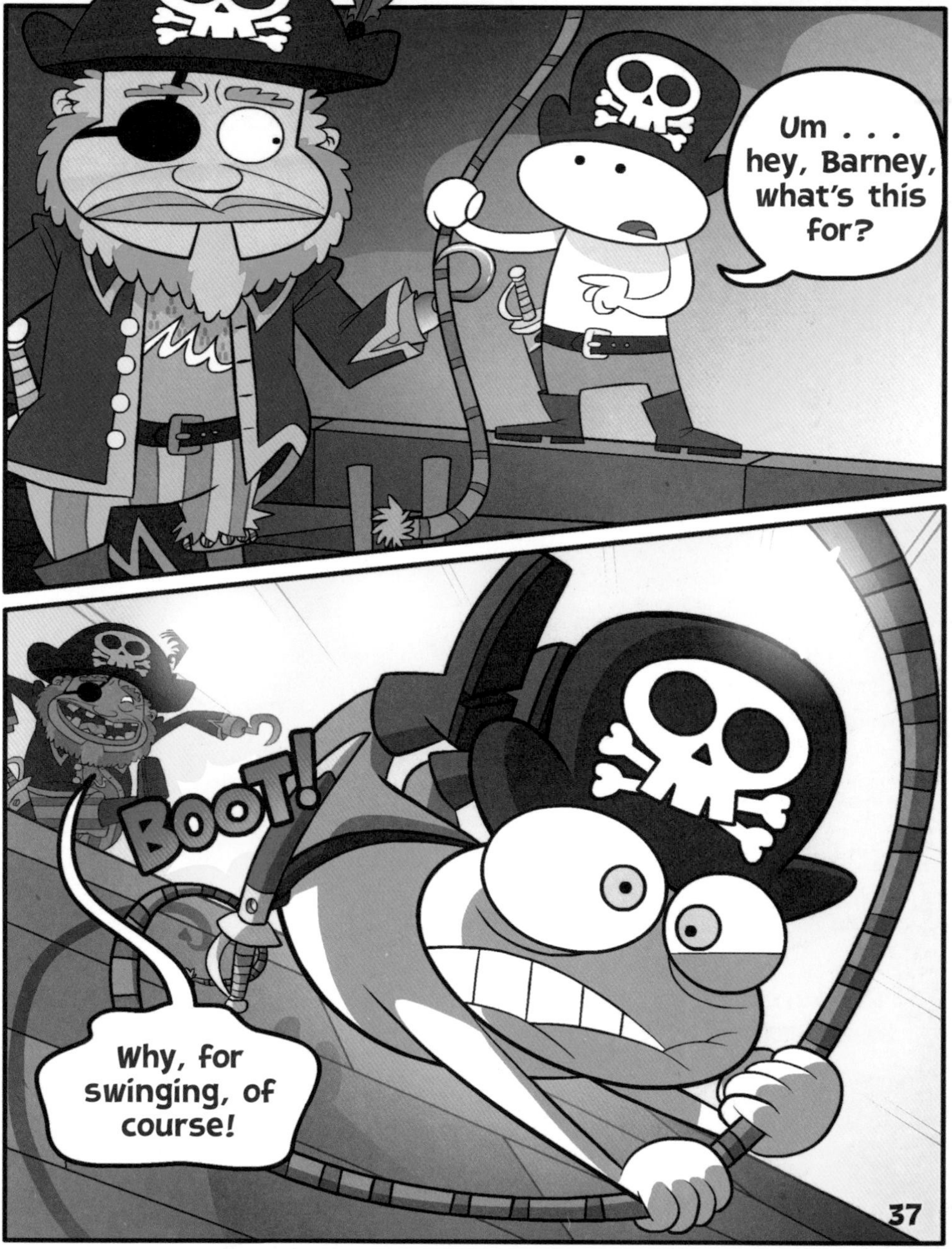
Um . . . hey, Barney, what's this for?
BOOT!
Why, for swinging, of course!

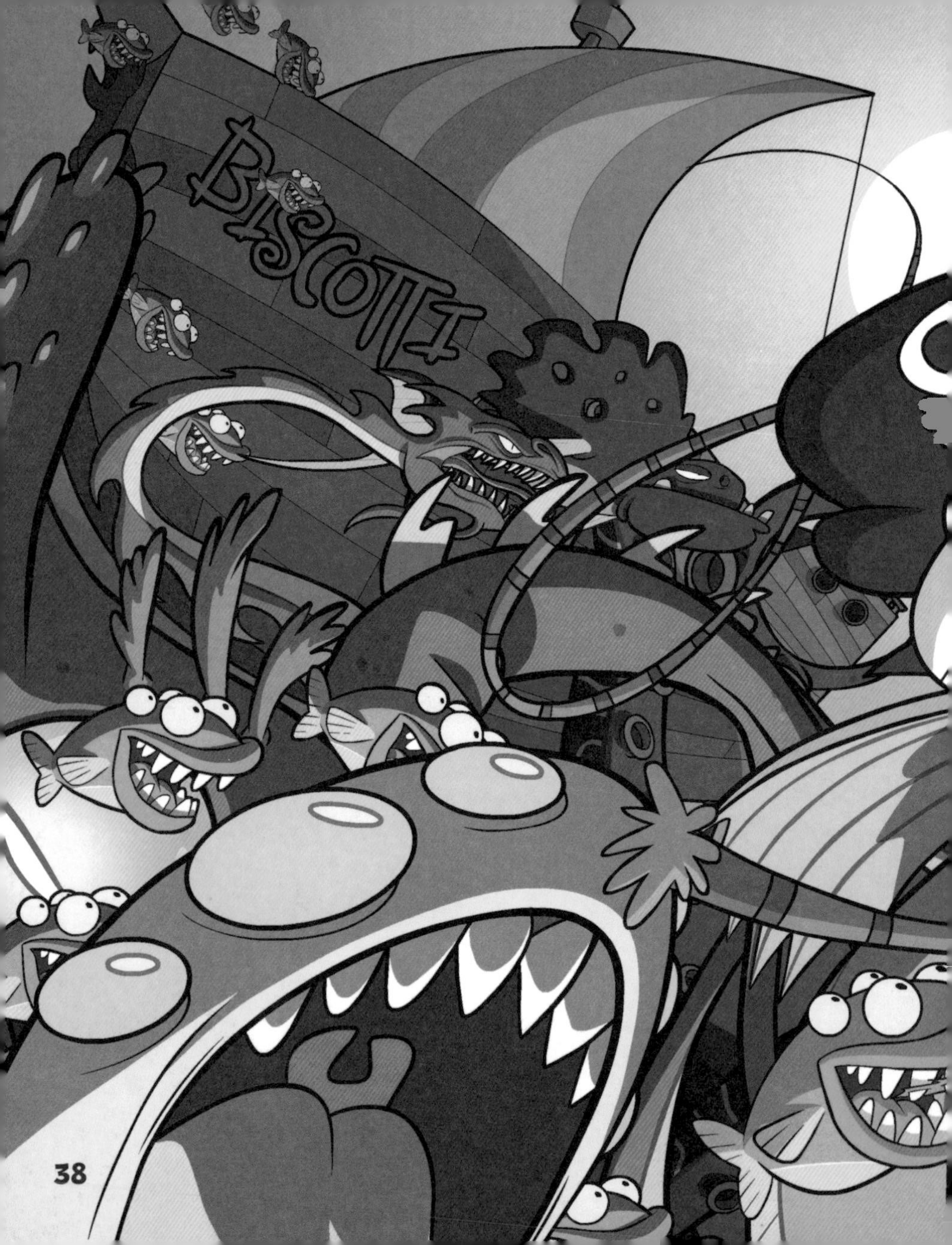
BISCOTTI

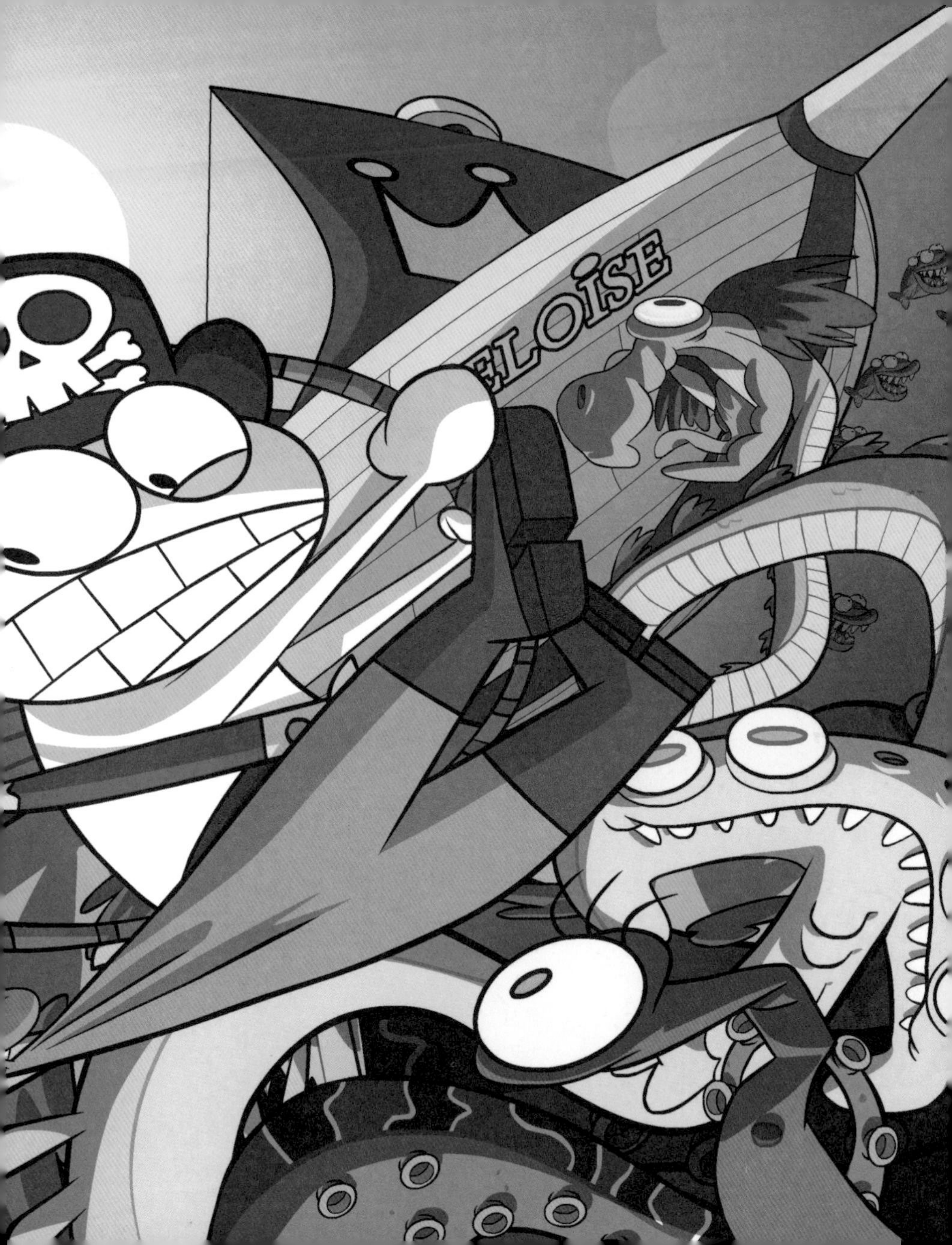
ELOISE

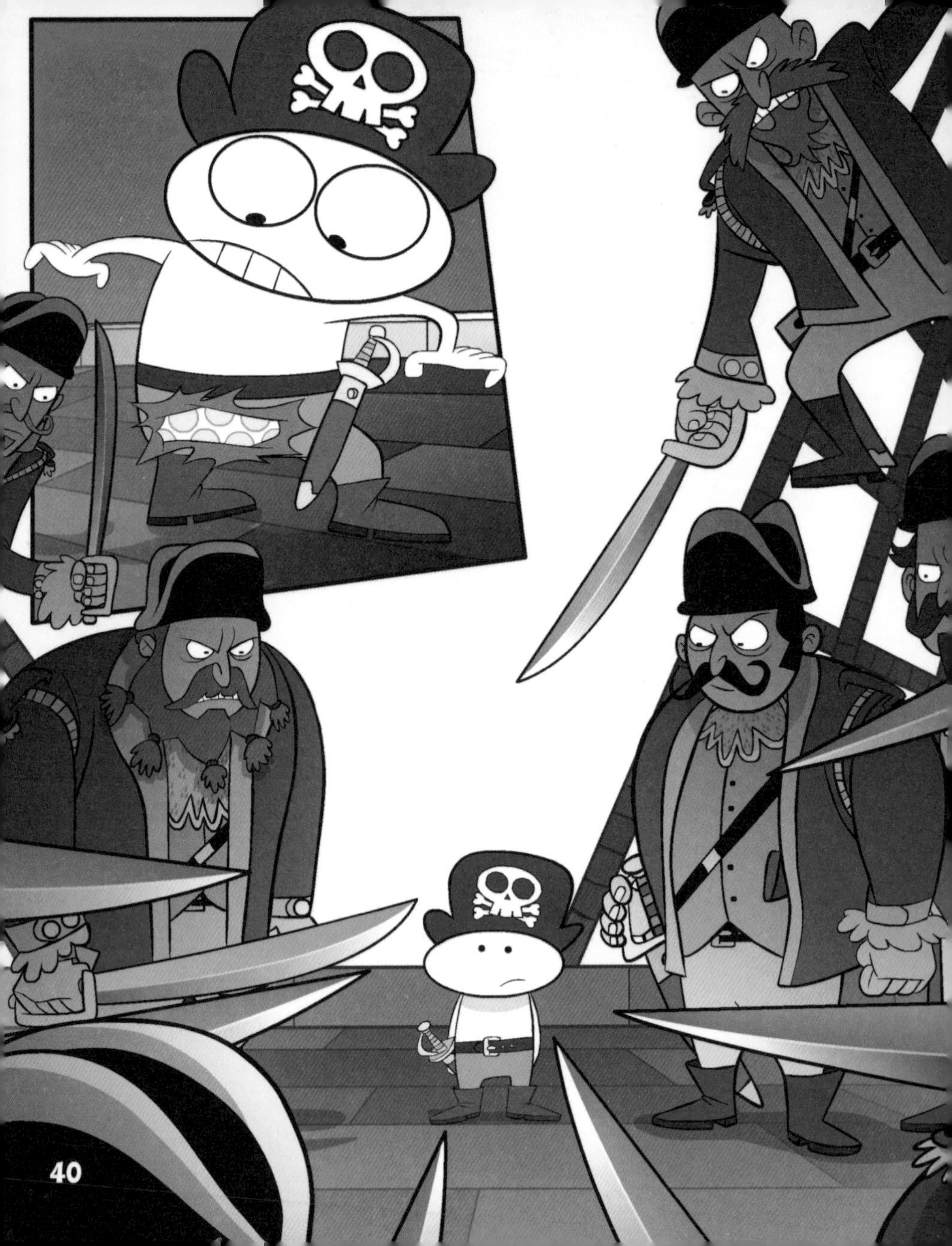

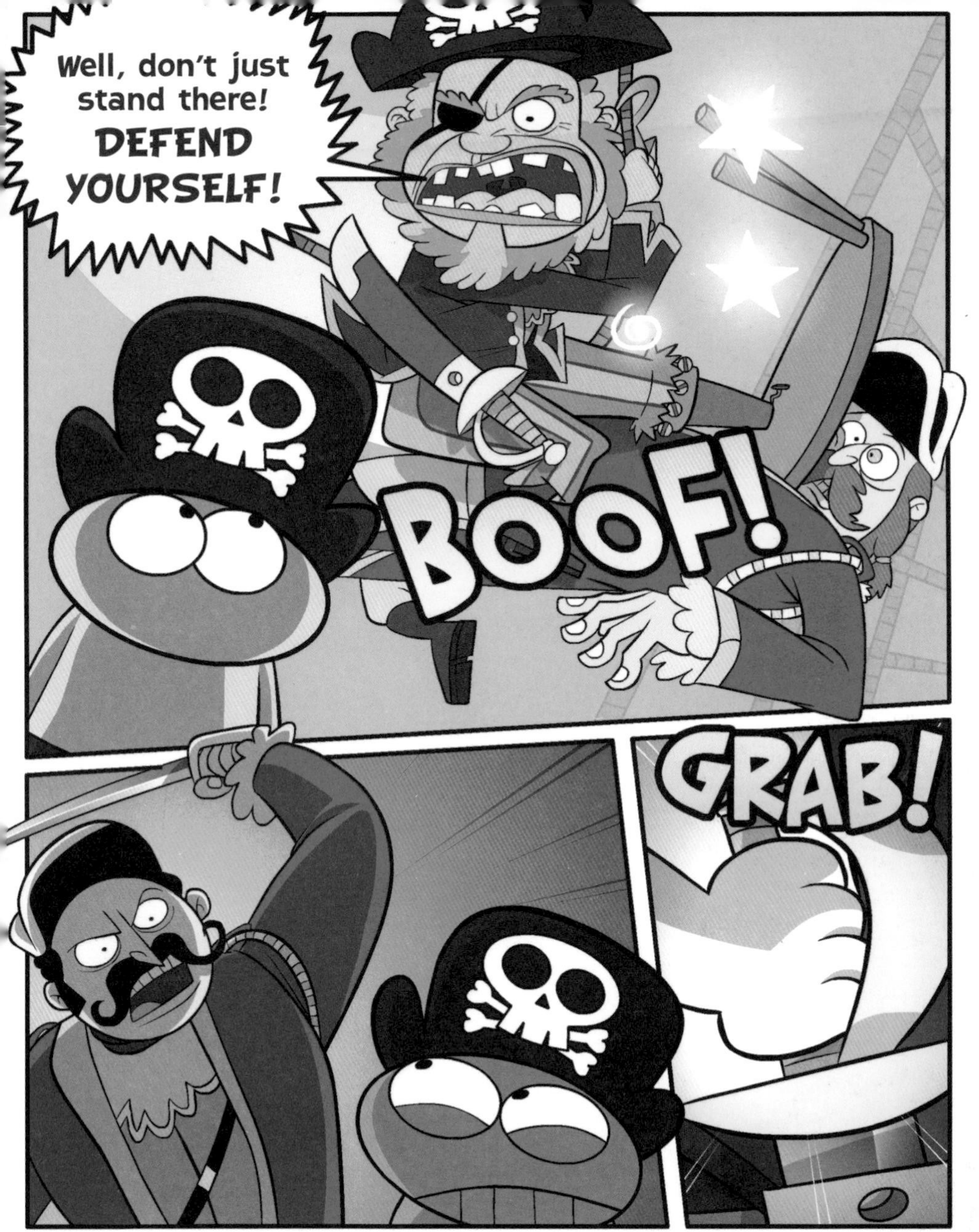
Well, don't just stand there! DEFEND YOURSELF!
BOOF!
GRAB!

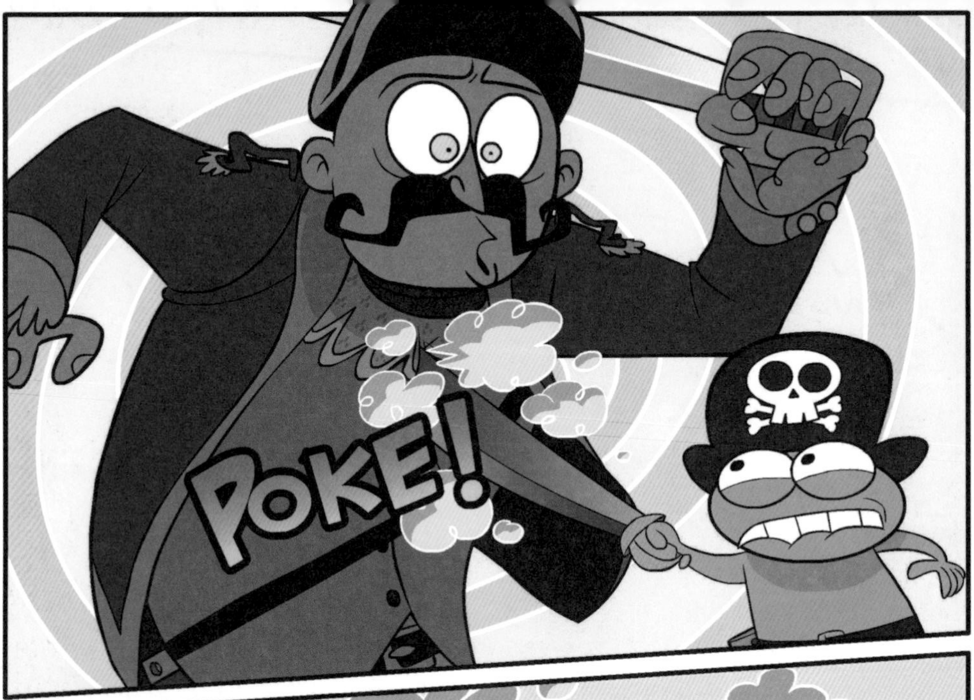
POKE!
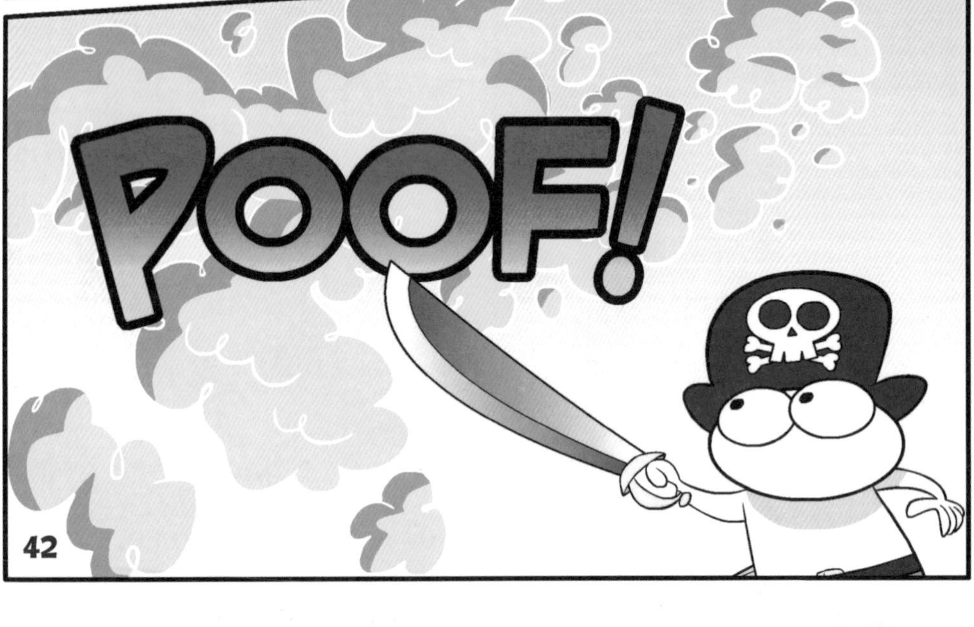
POOF!

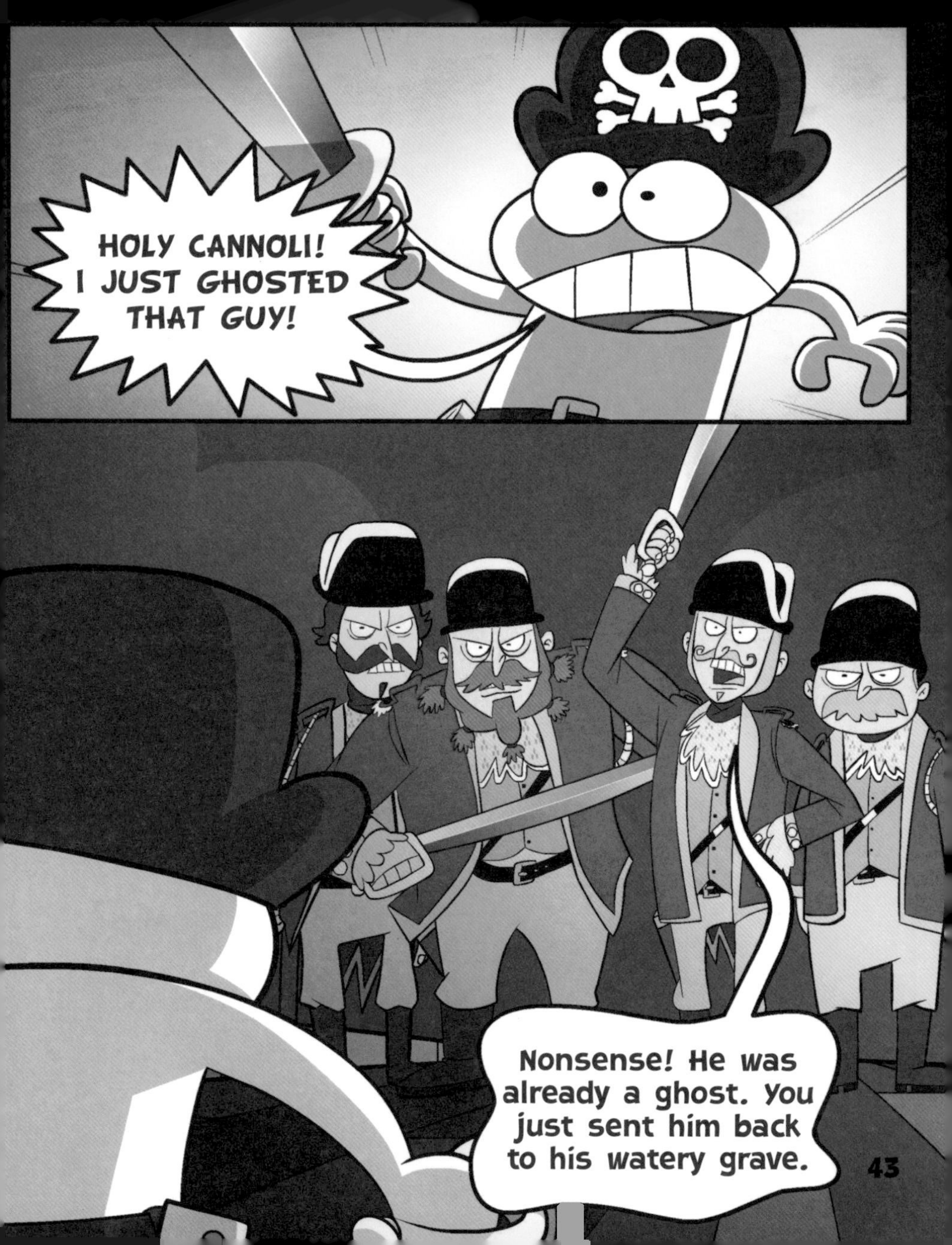
HOLY CANNOLI! I JUST GHOSTED THAT GUY!
Nonsense! He was already a ghost. You just sent him back to his watery grave.

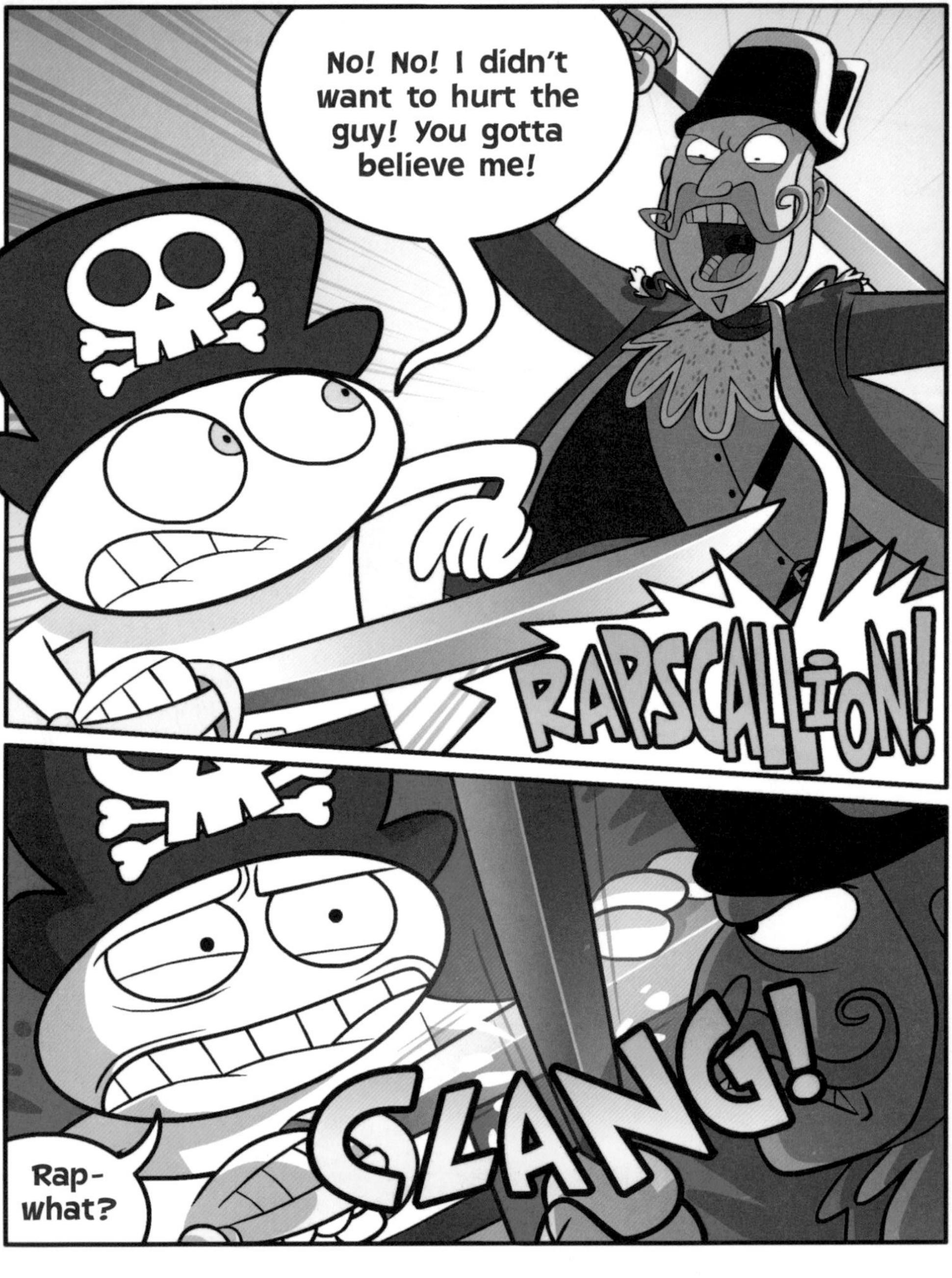
No! No! I didn't want to hurt the guy! You gotta believe me!
RAPSCALLION!
CLANG!
Rap-what?

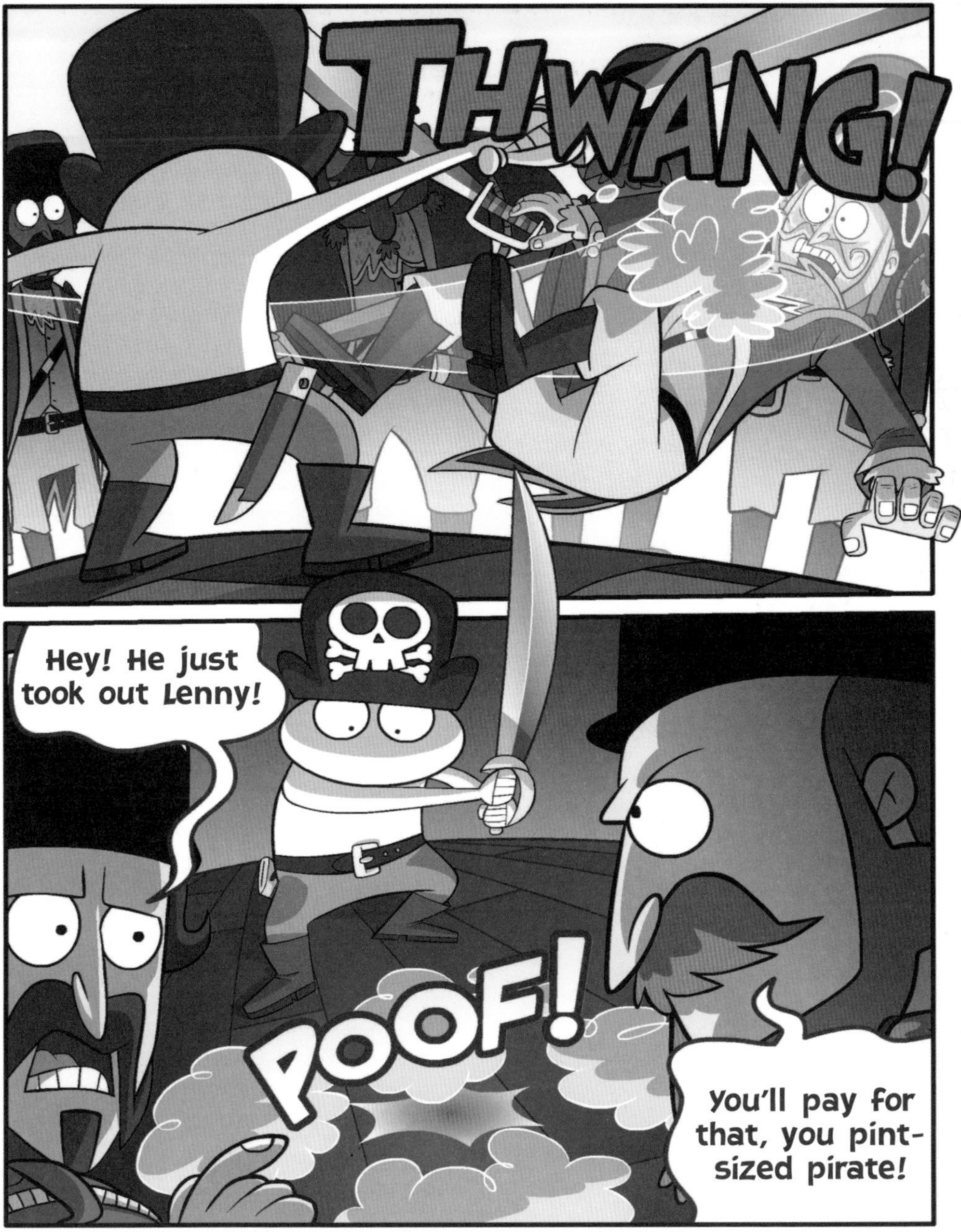
THWANG!
Hey! He just took out Lenny!
POOF!
You'll pay for that, you pint-sized pirate!

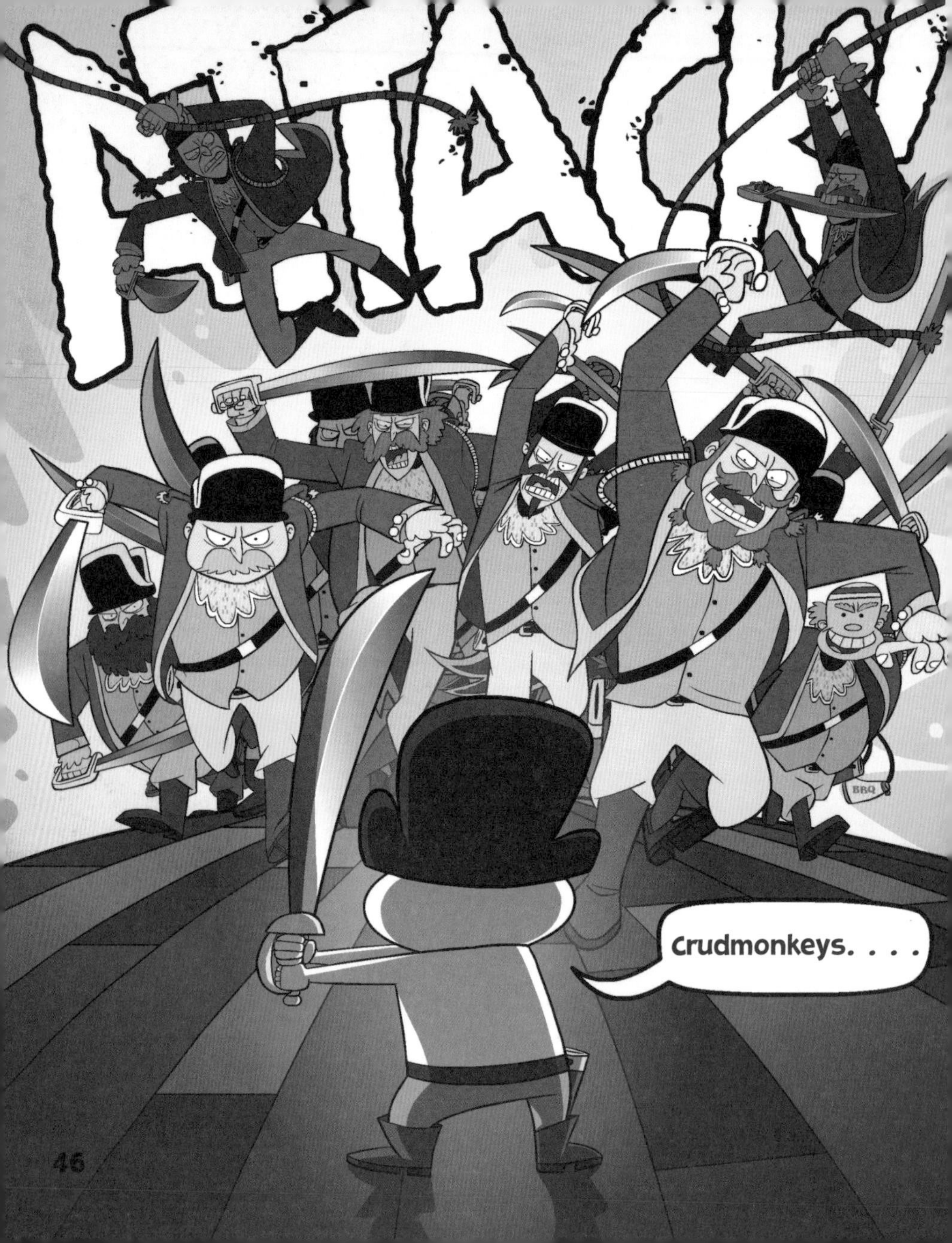
ATTACK!
Crudmonkeys. . . .

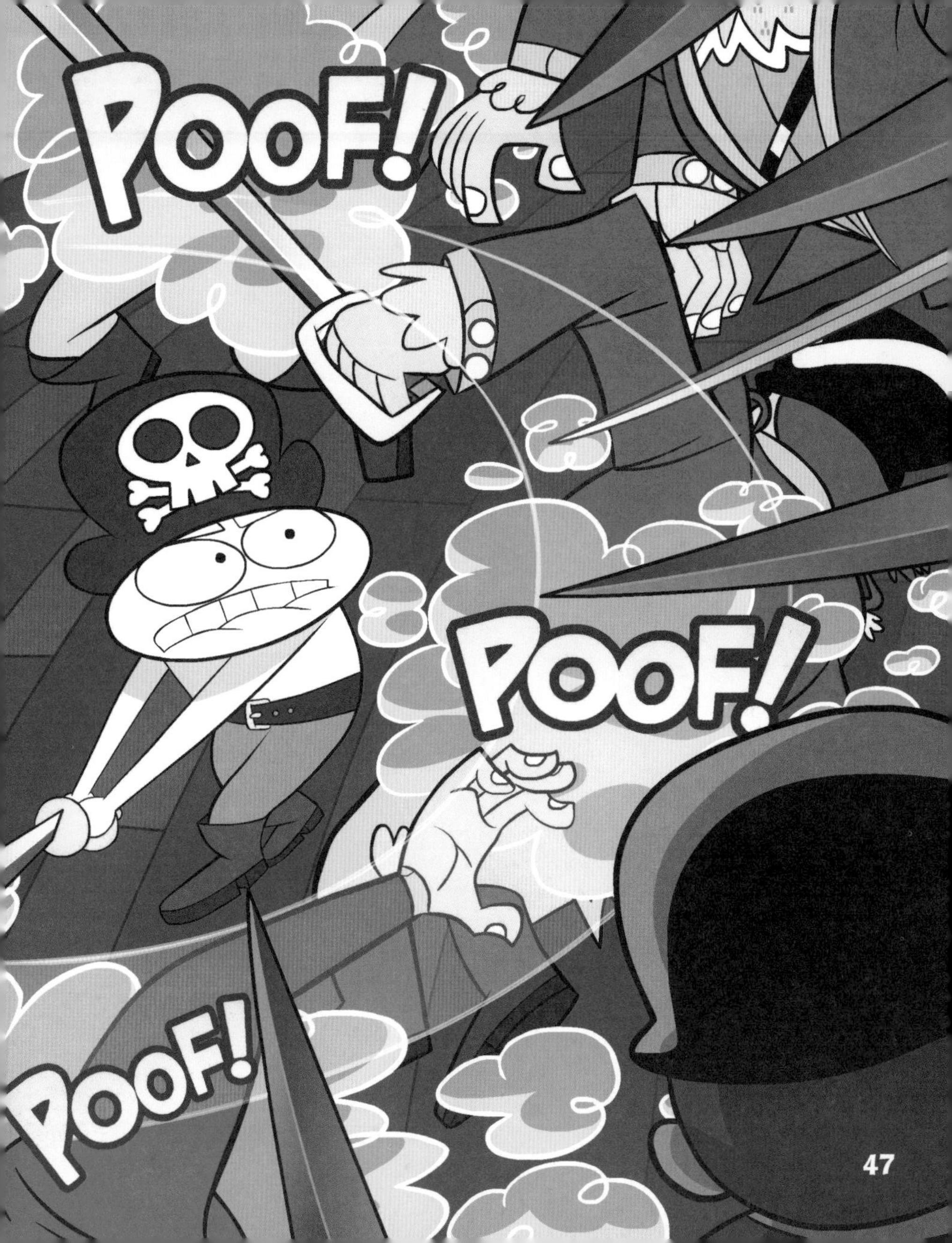
POOF!
POOF!
POOF!

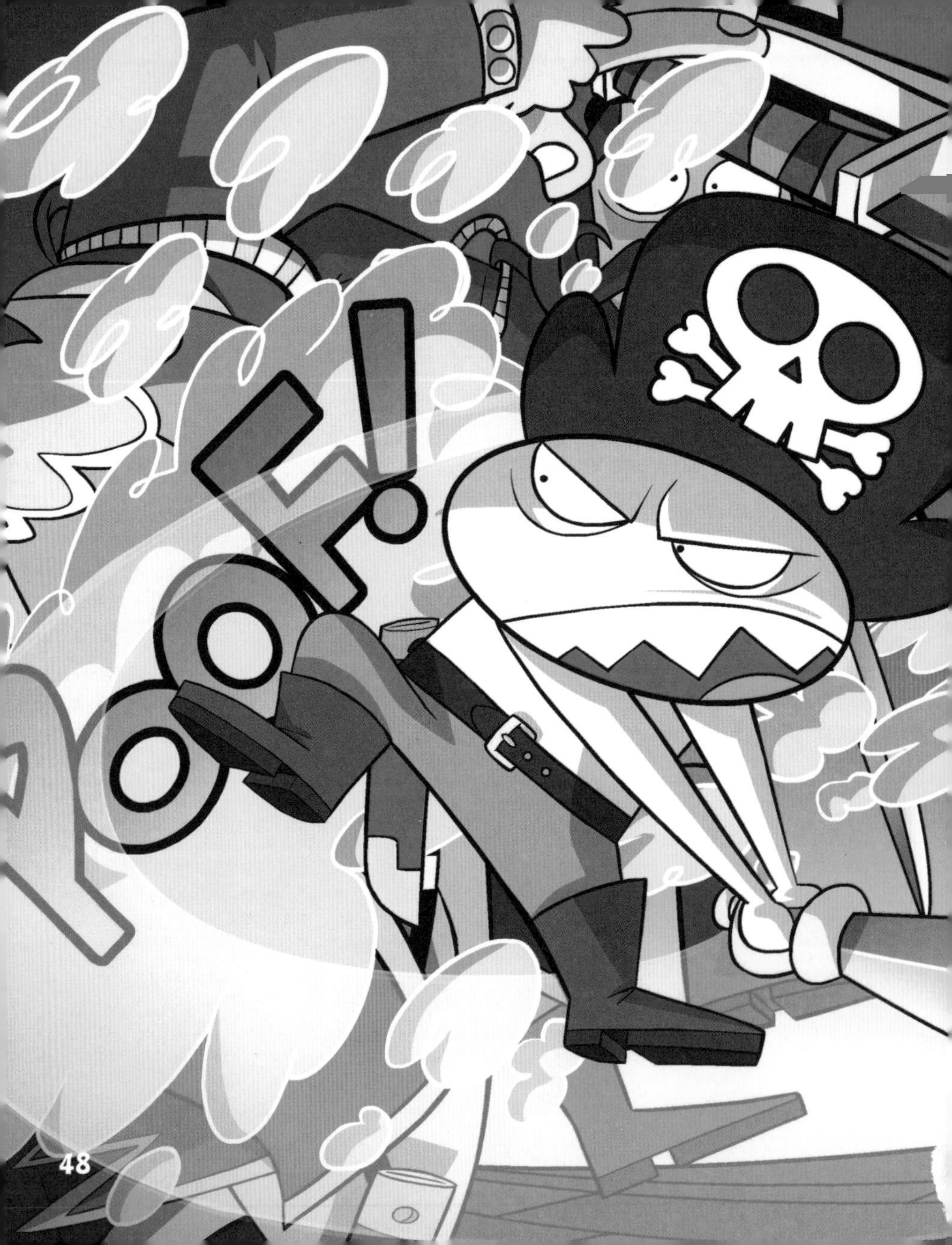
POOF!

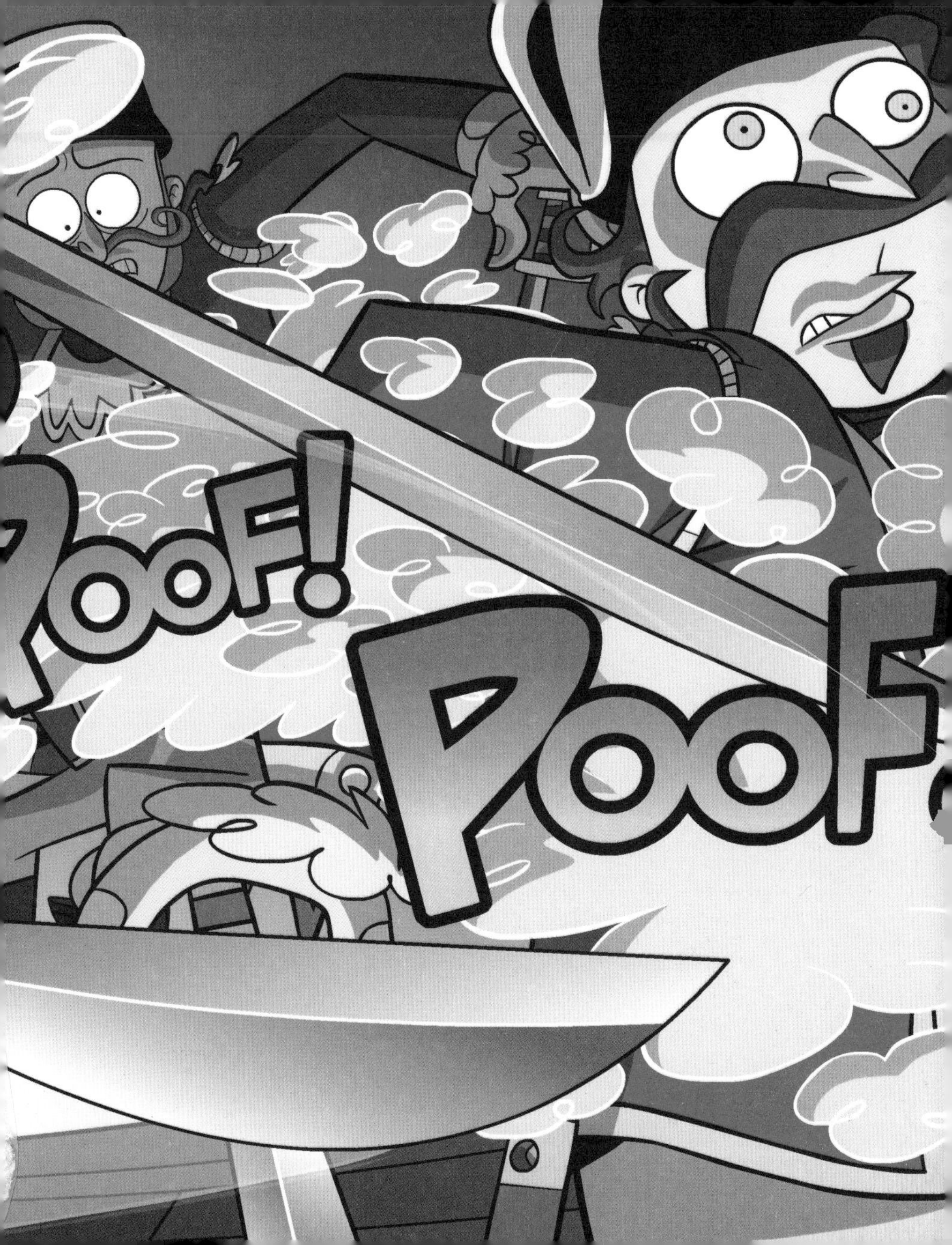
POOF!
POOF!

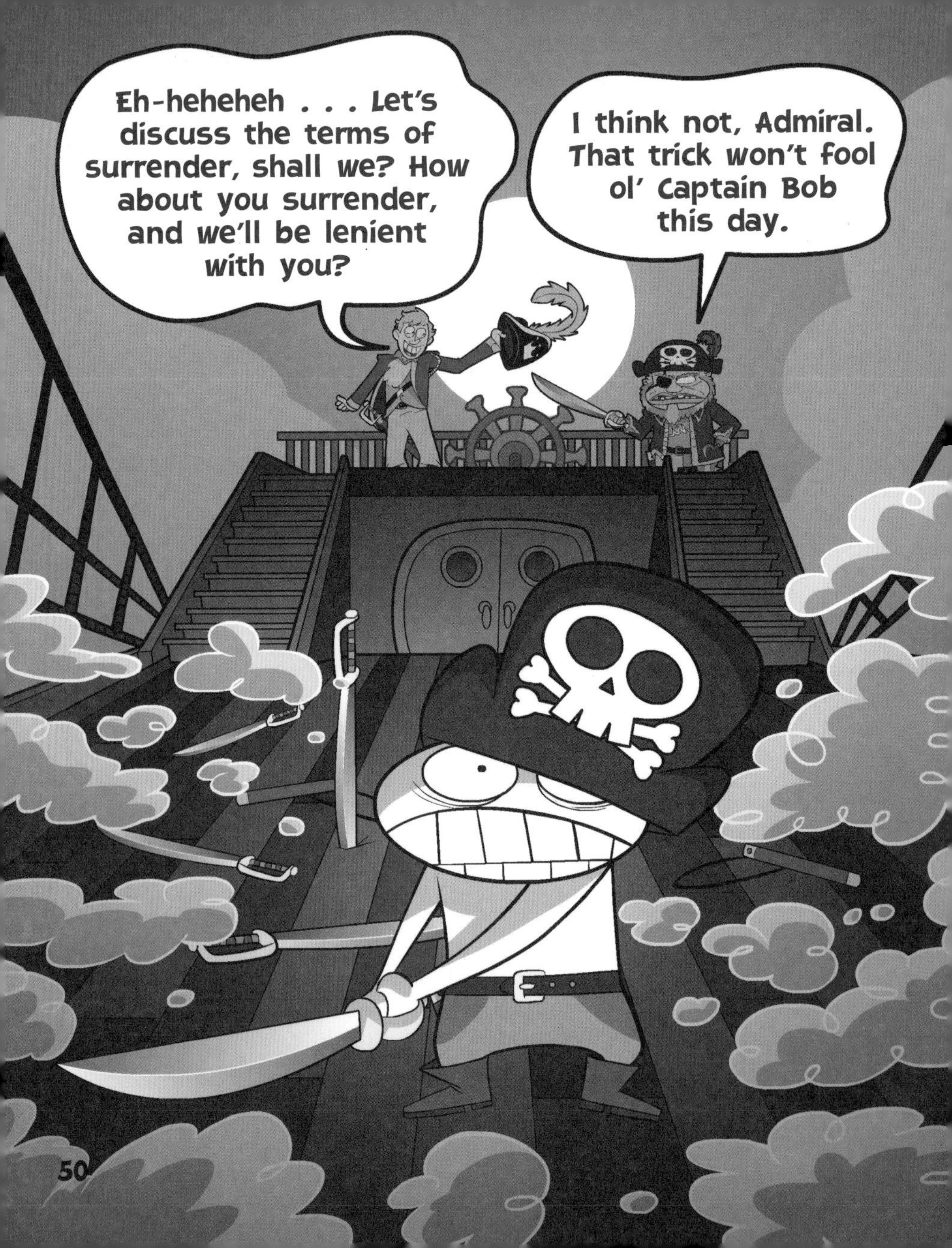
Eh-heheheh . . . Let's discuss the terms of surrender, shall we? How about you surrender, and we'll be lenient with you?
I think not, Admiral. That trick won't fool ol' Captain Bob this day.

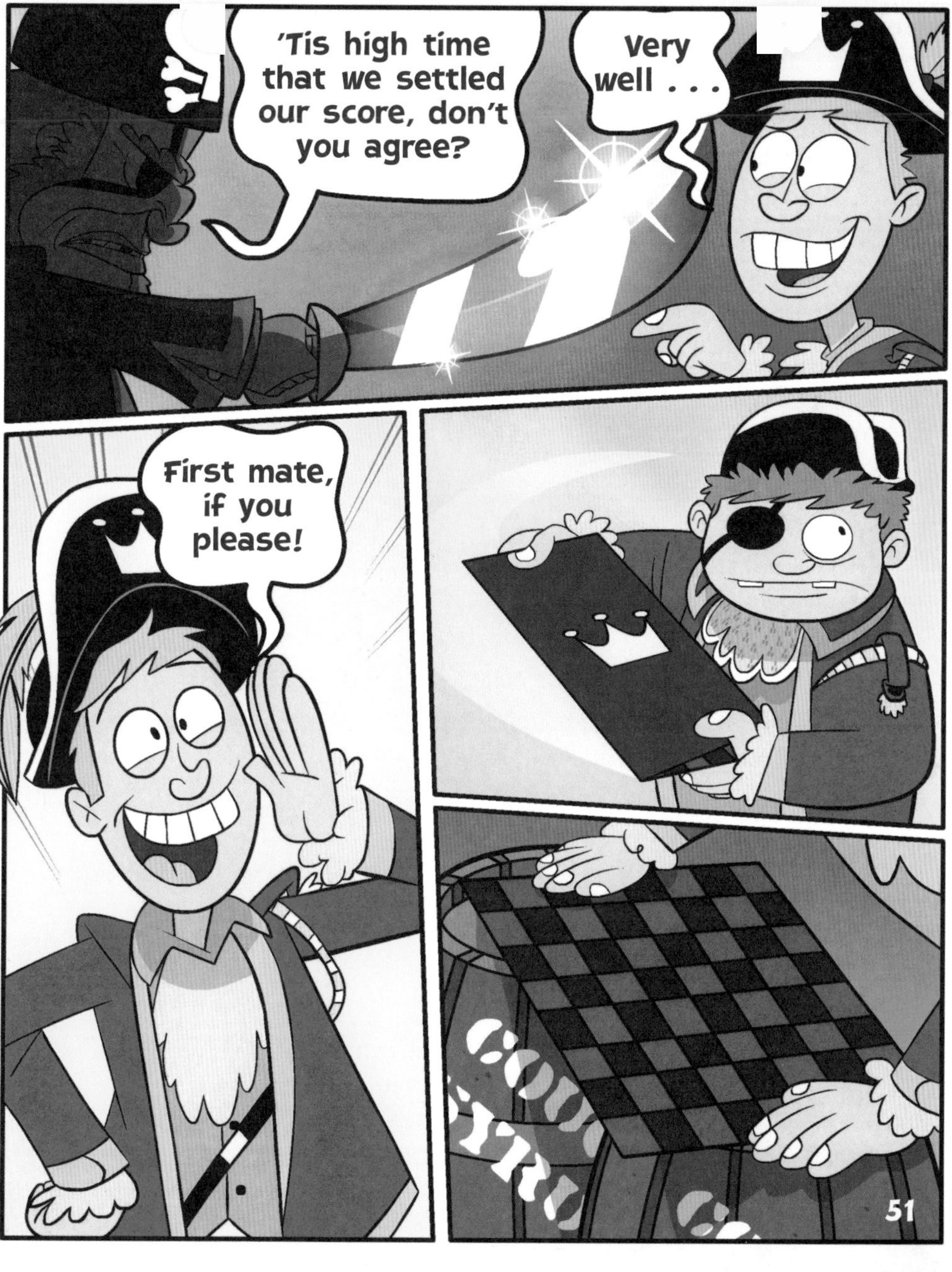
'Tis high time that we settled our score, don't you agree?
Very well . . .
First mate, if you please!

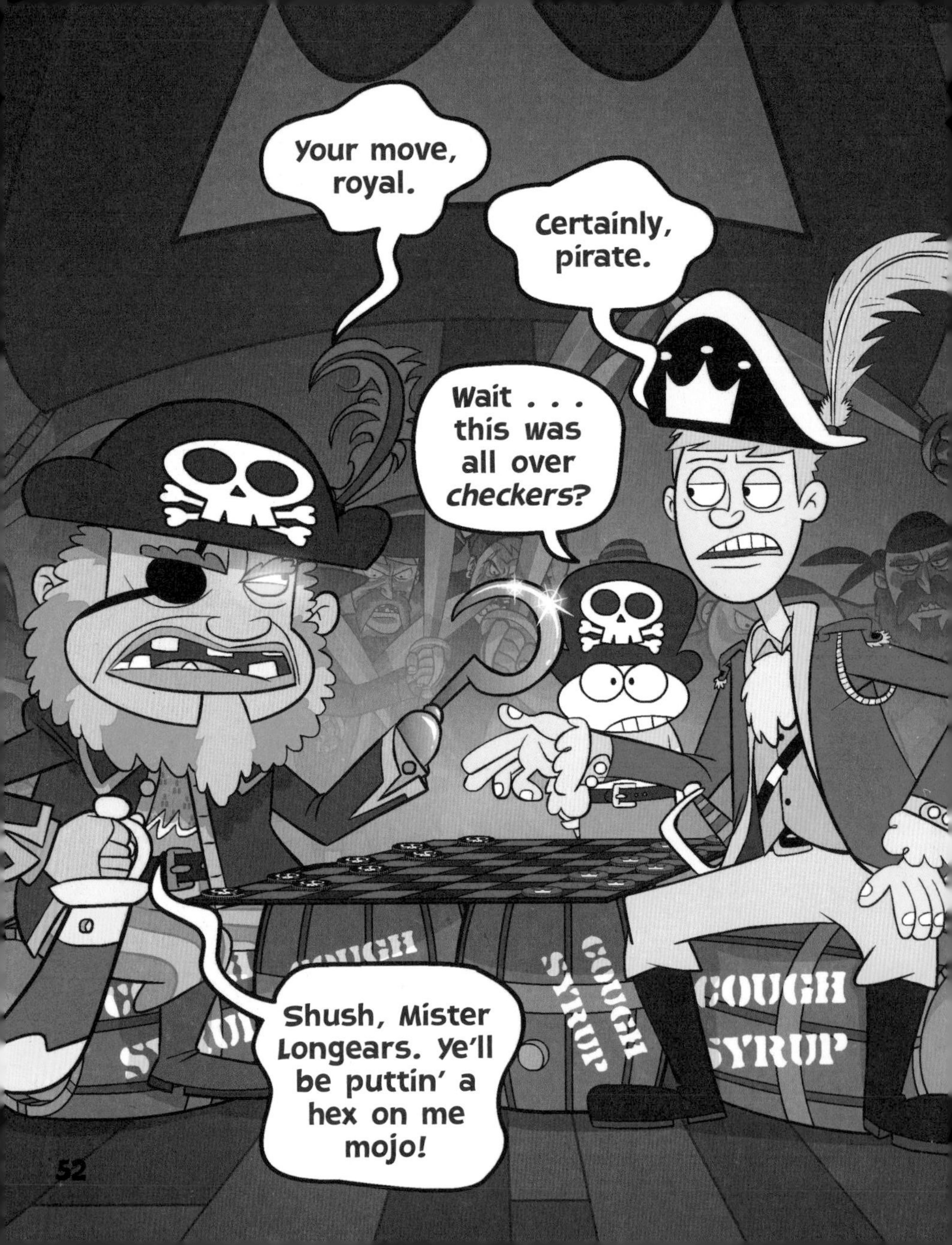
Your move, royal.
Certainly, pirate.
Wait . . . this was all over *checkers*?
COUGH SYRUP
COUGH SYRUP
Shush, Mister Longears. Ye'll be puttin' a hex on me mojo!

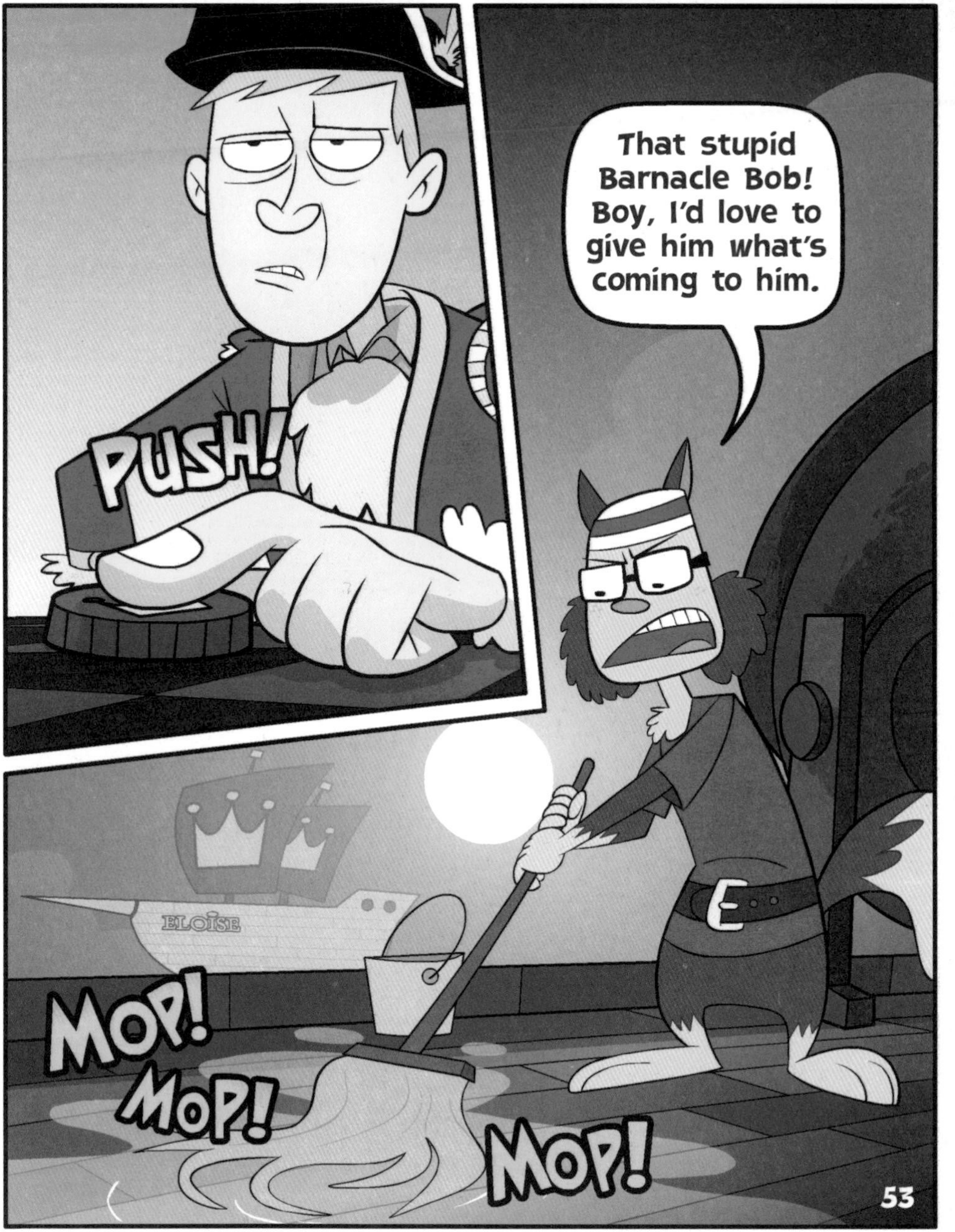
PUSH!
That stupid Barnacle Bob! Boy, I'd love to give him what's coming to him.
ELOISE
MOP!
MOP!
MOP!

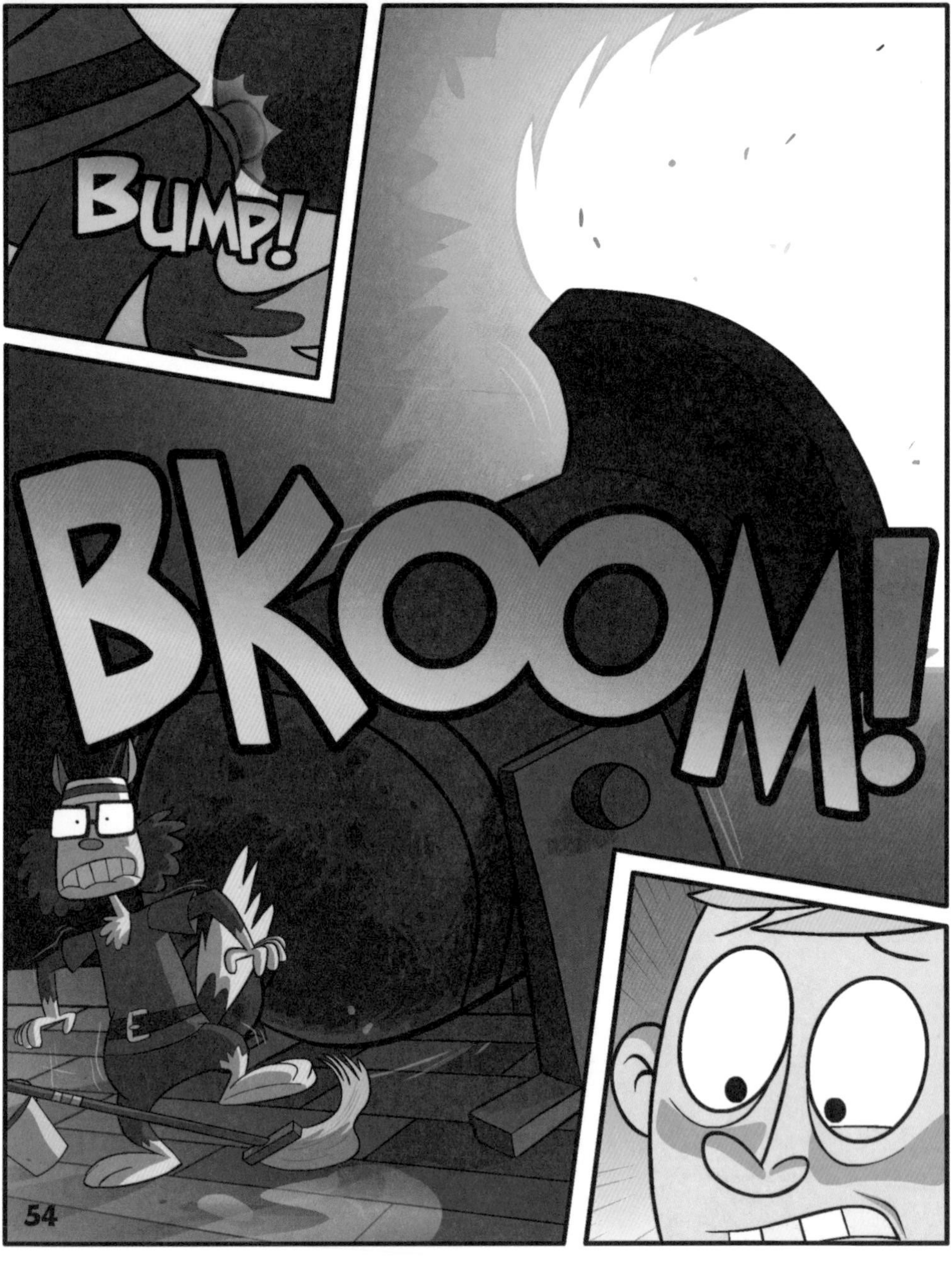
BUMP!
BKOOM!

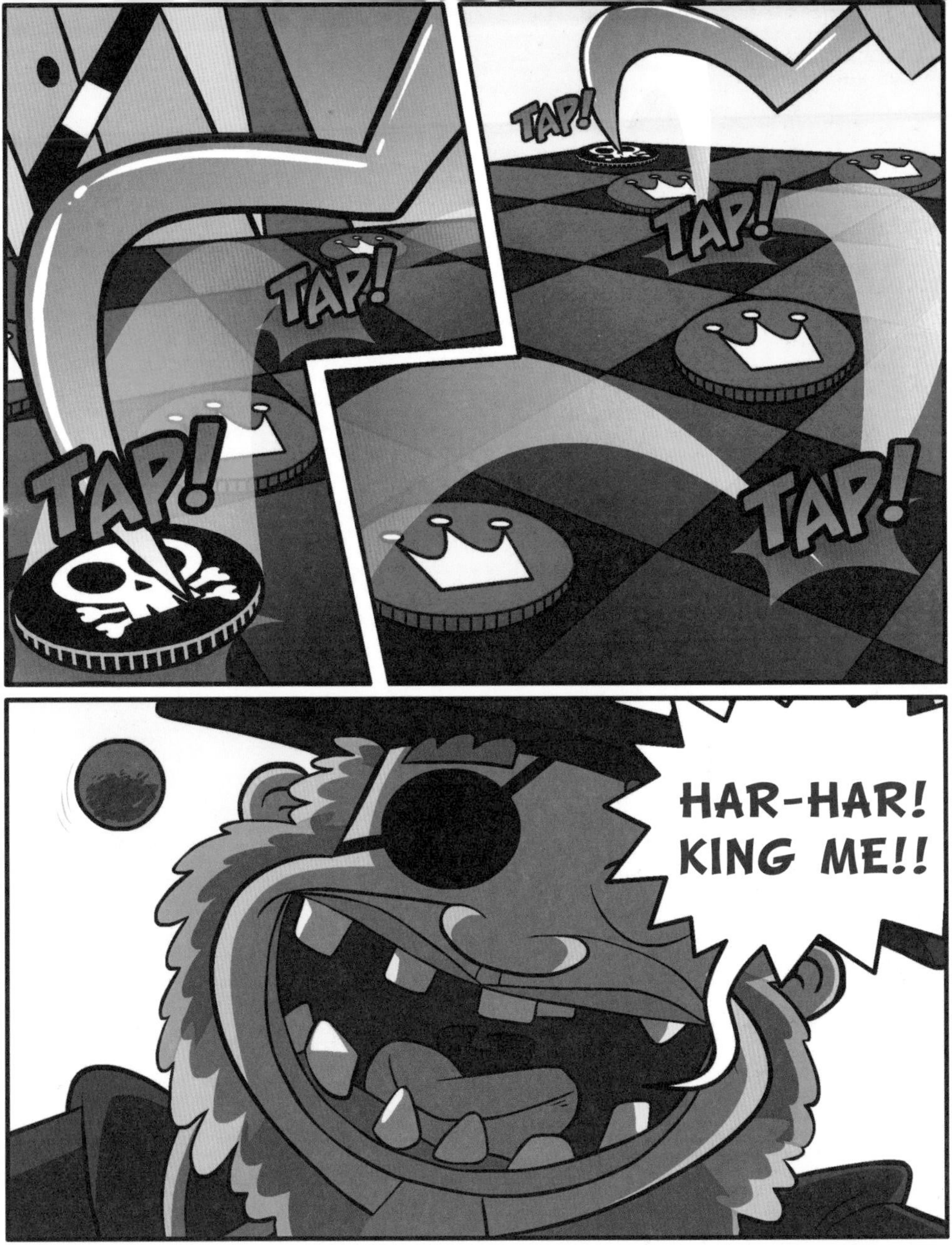
TAP!
TAP!
TAP!
TAP!
TAP!
HAR-HAR!
KING ME!!

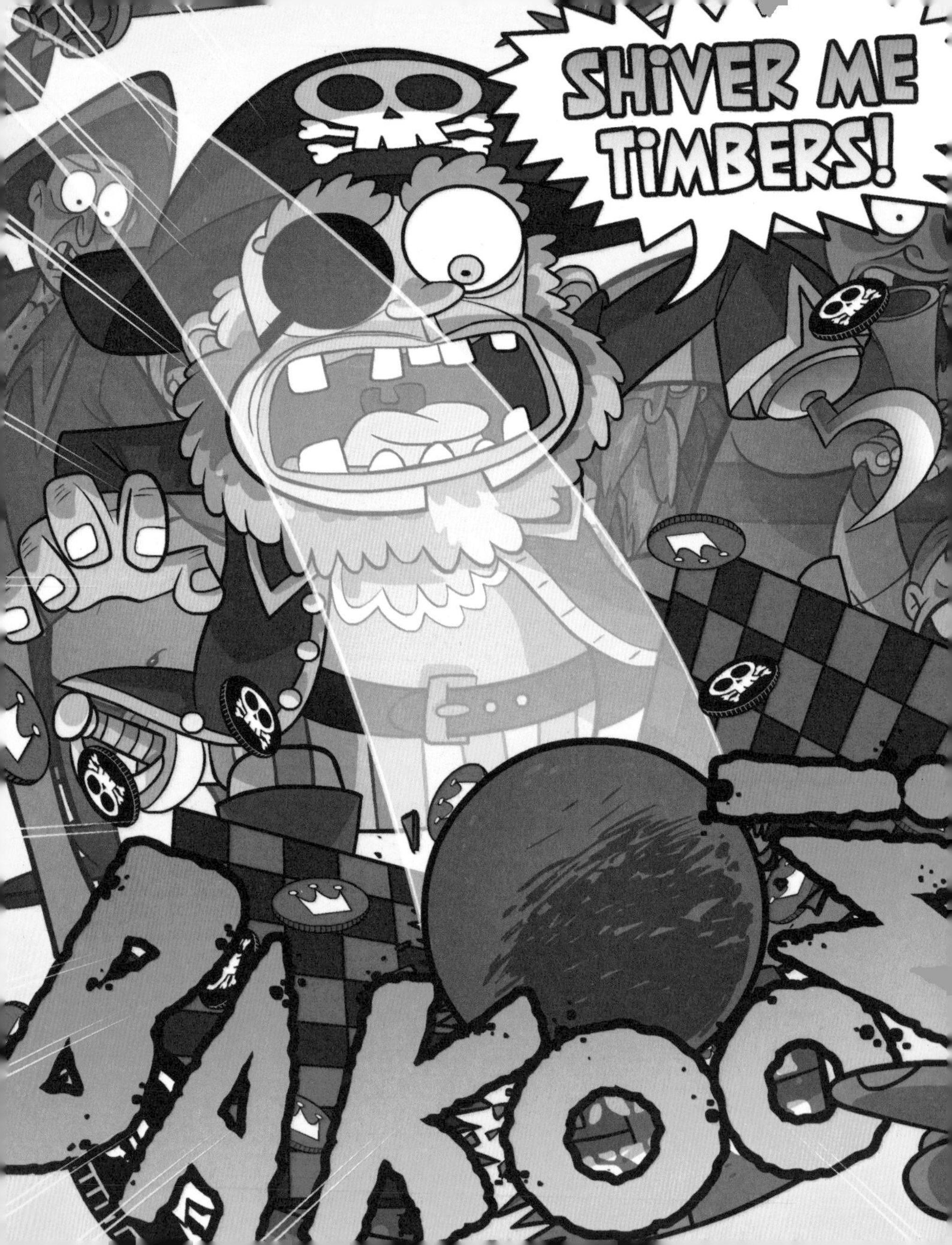
SHIVER ME TIMBERS!

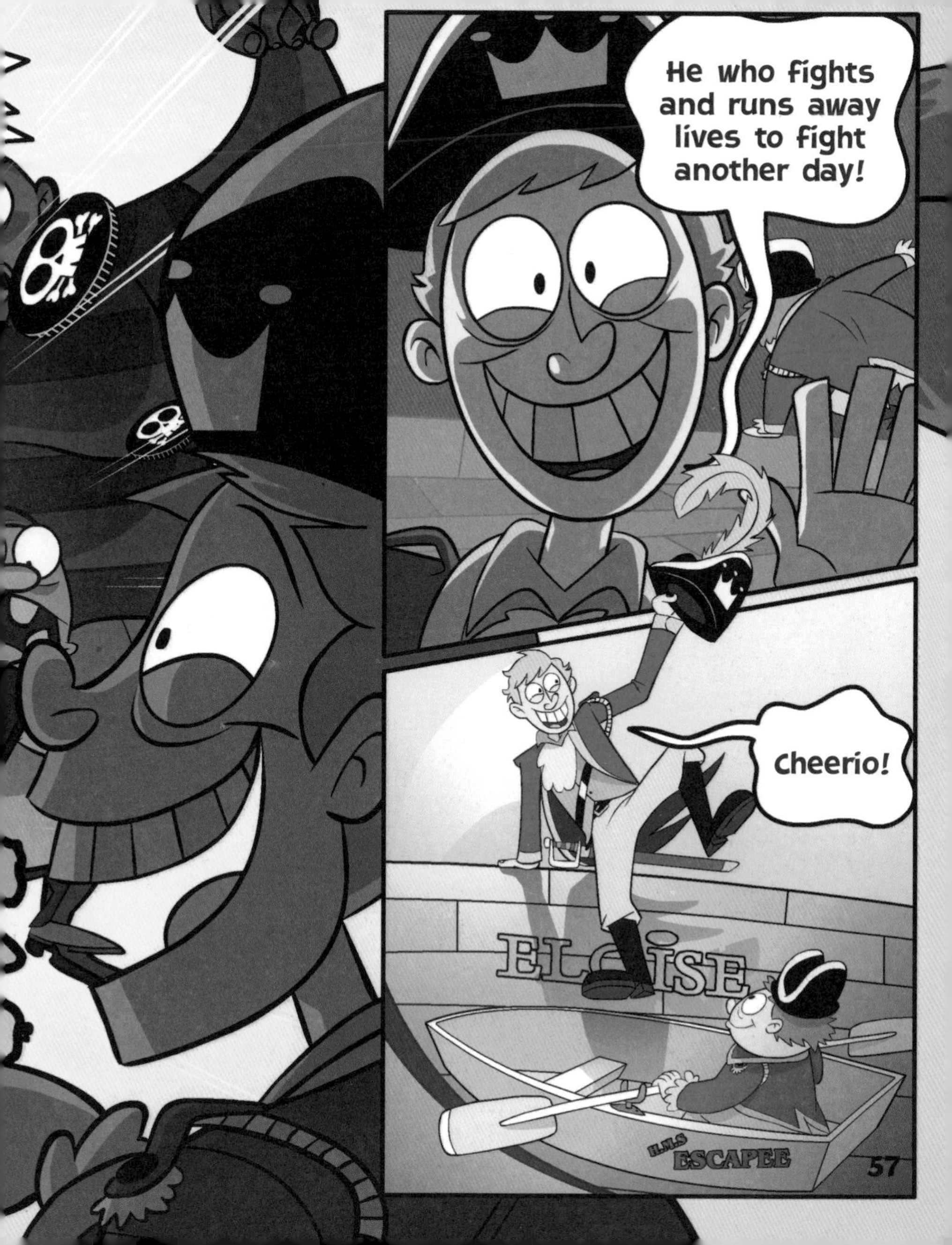
He who fights and runs away lives to fight another day!
Cheerio!
ELOISE
H.M.S
ESCAPEE

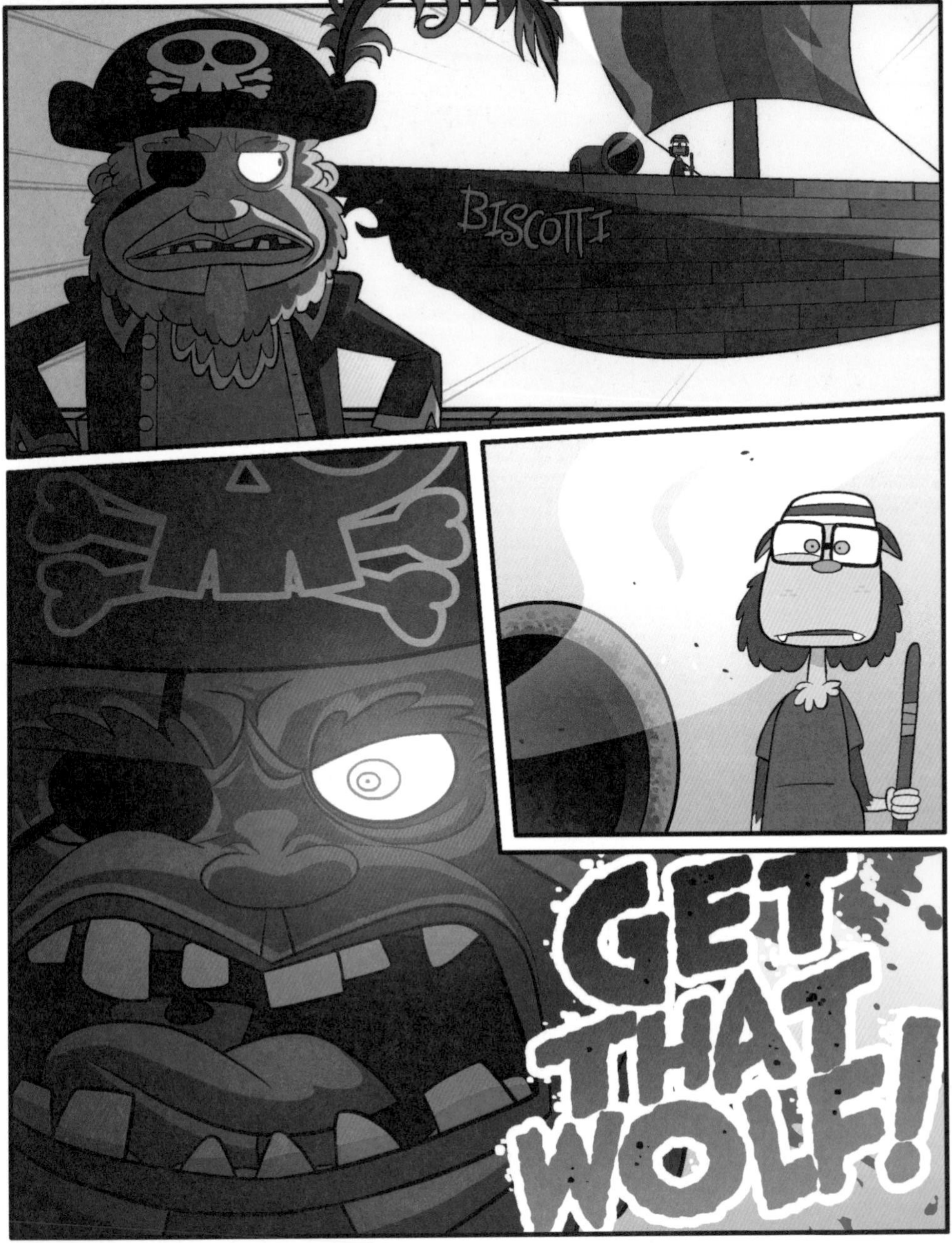
BISCOTTI
GET THAT WOLF!

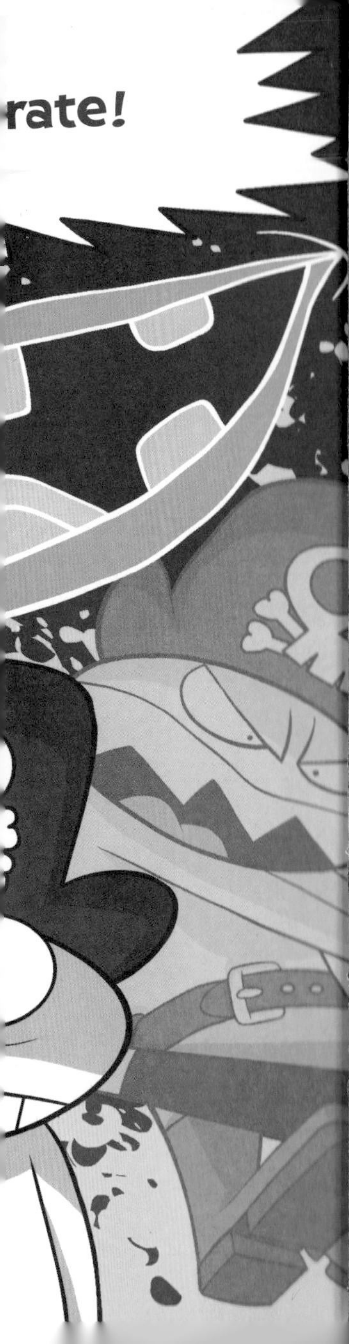
rate!

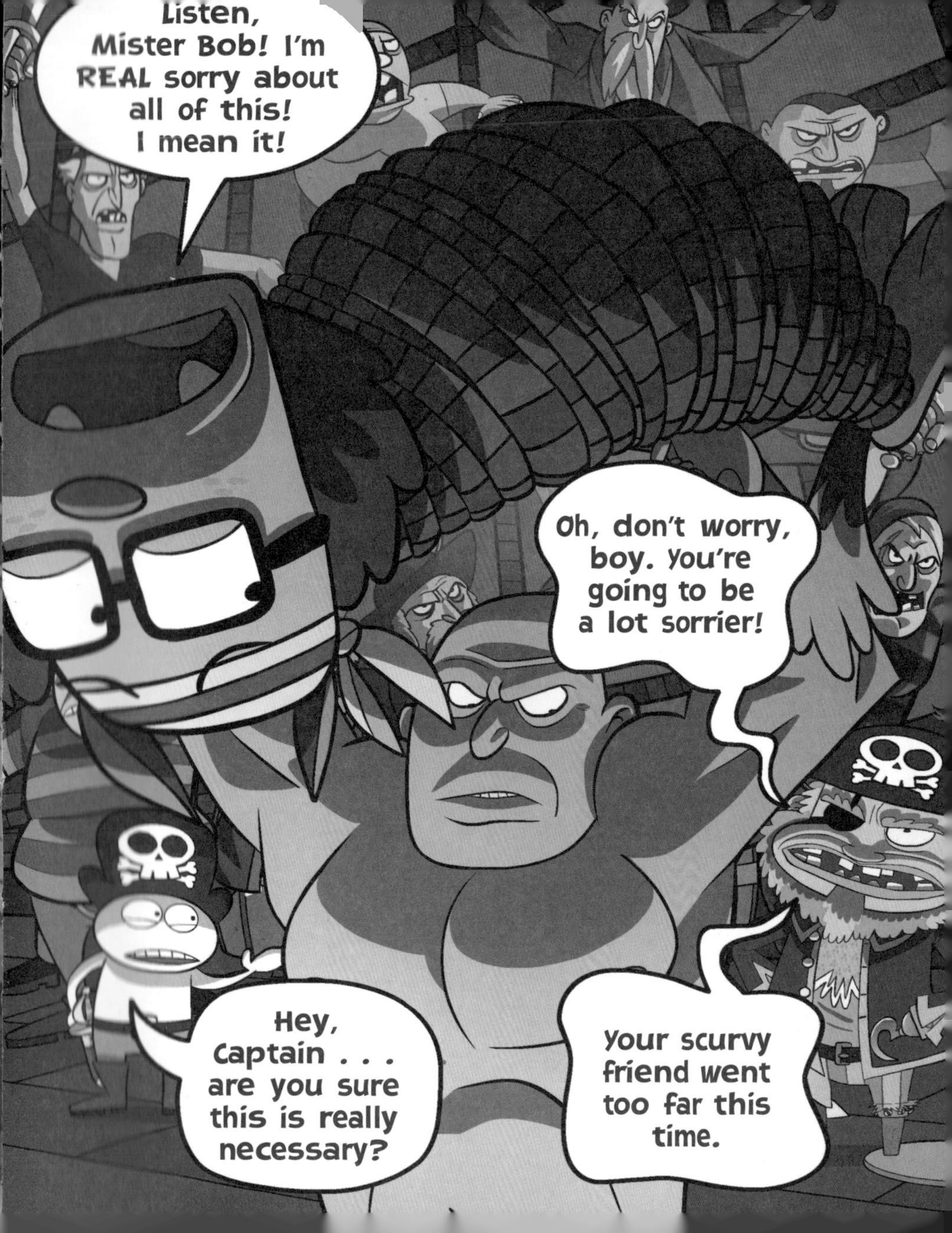
Listen, Mister Bob! I'm REAL sorry about all of this! I mean it!
Oh, don't worry, boy. You're going to be a lot sorrier!
Hey, Captain . . . are you sure this is really necessary?
Your scurvy friend went too far this time.

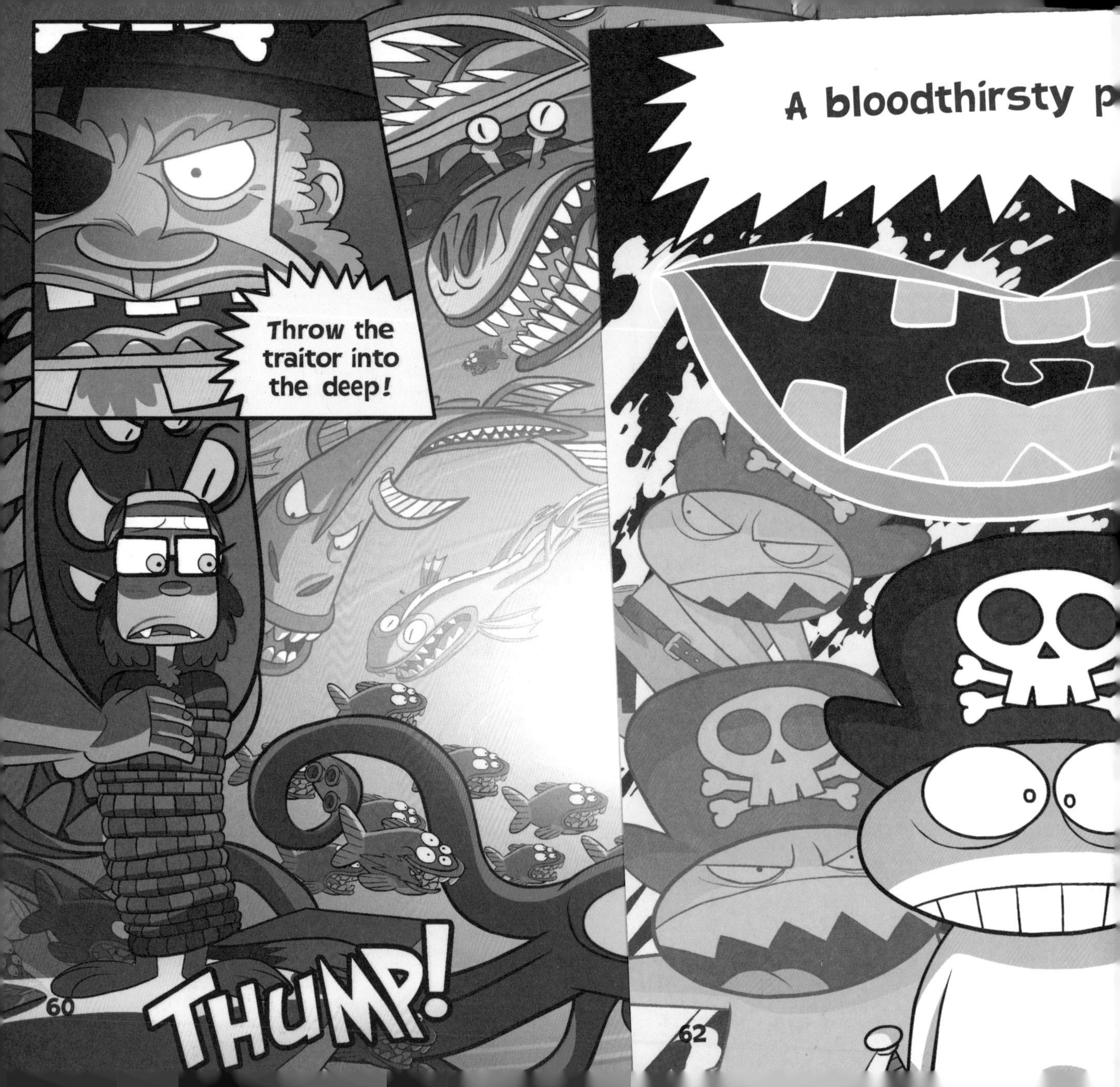
Throw the traitor into the deep!
THUMP!
A bloodthirsty p

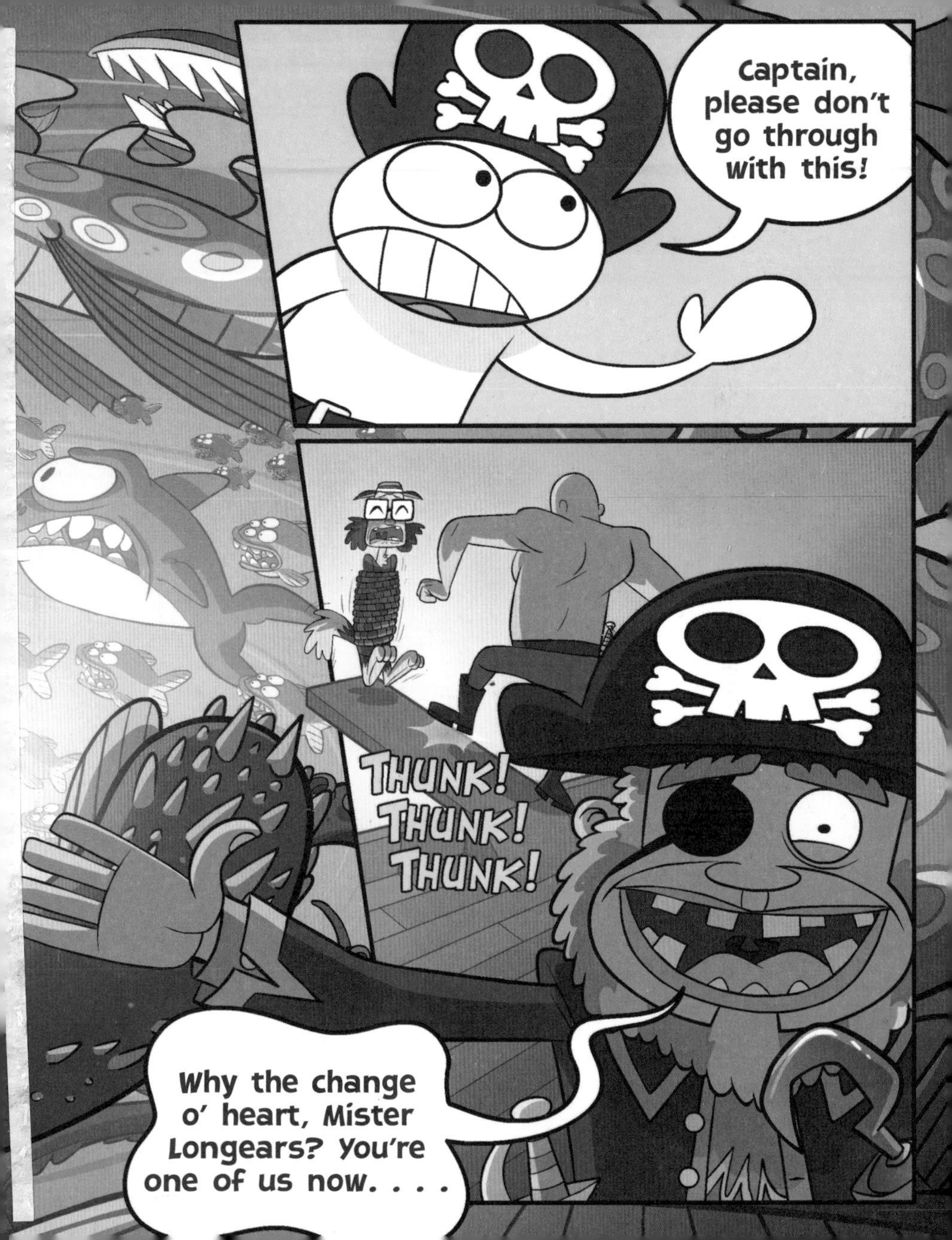
Captain, please don't go through with this!
THUNK! THUNK! THUNK!
Why the change o' heart, Mister Longears? You're one of us now. . . .

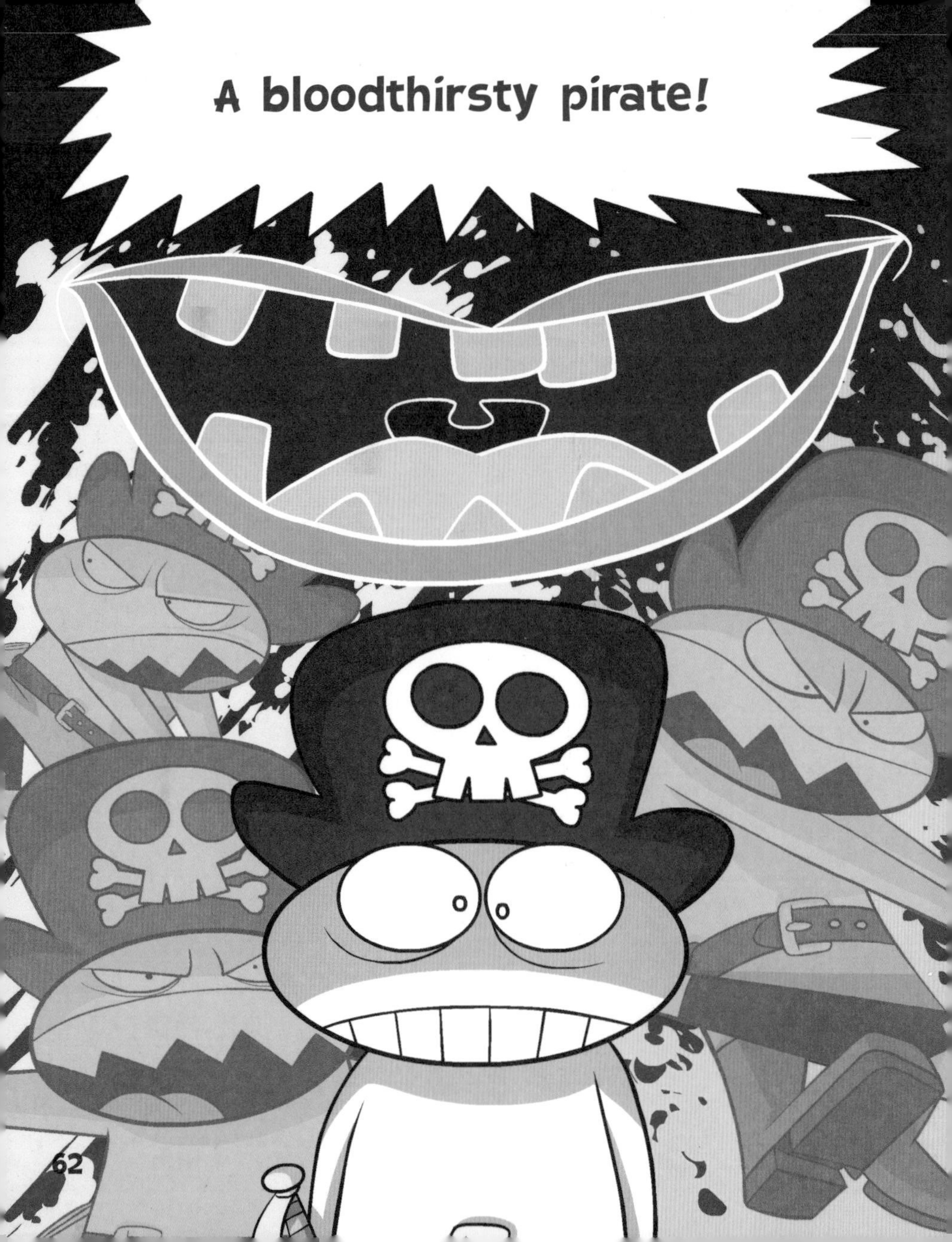
A bloodthirsty pirate!

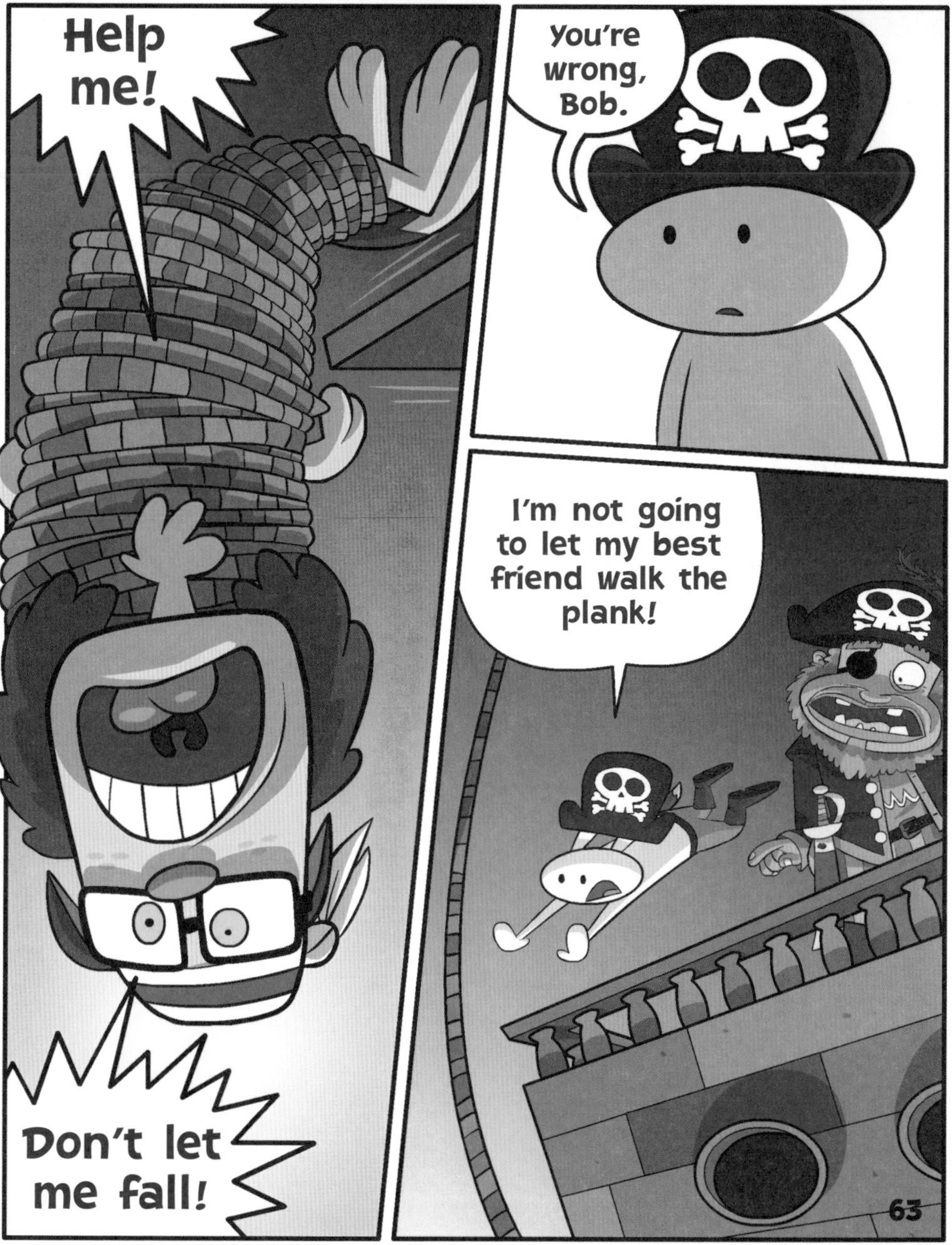
Help me!
Don't let me fall!
You're wrong, Bob.
I'm not going to let my best friend walk the plank!

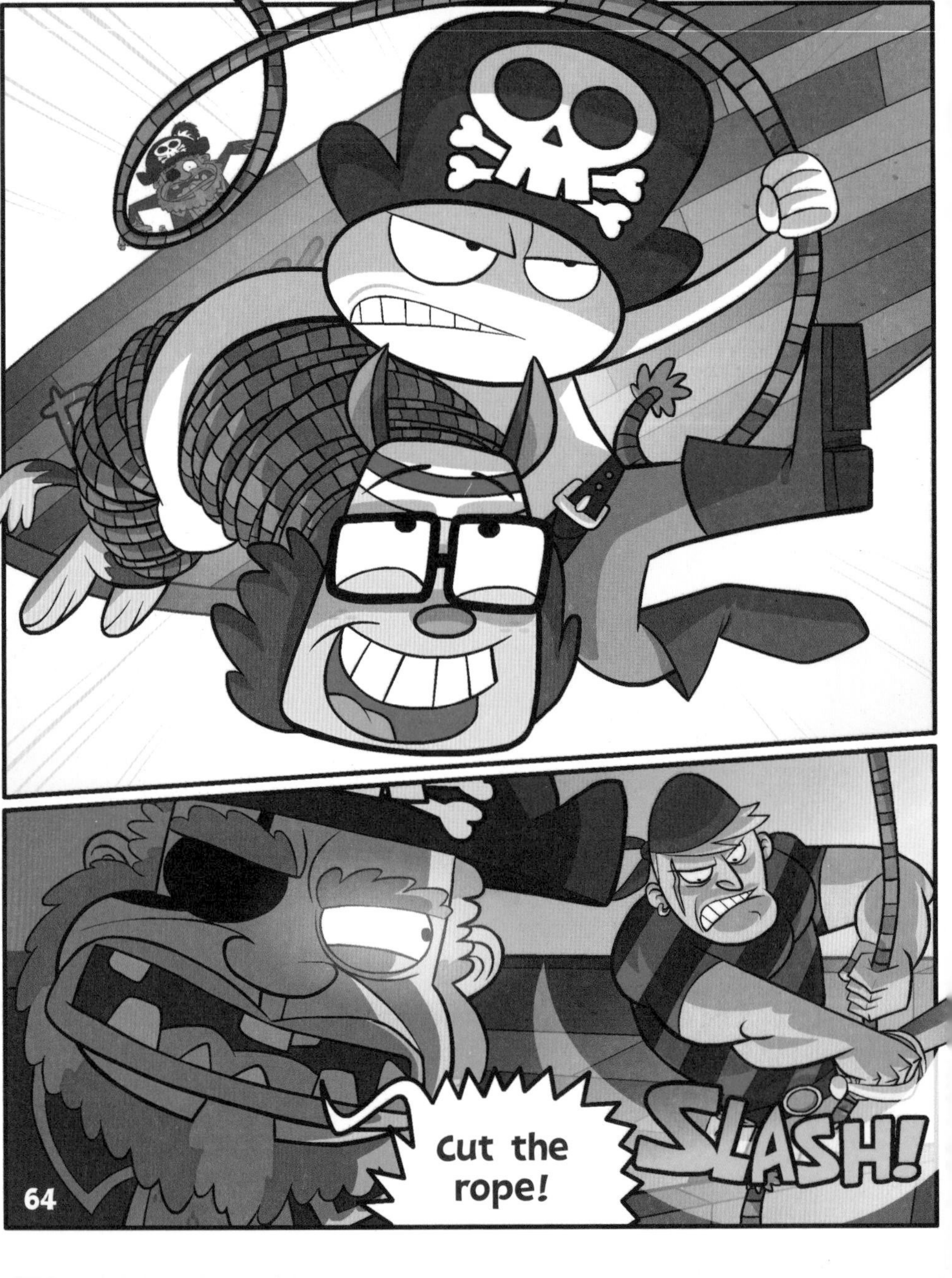
Cut the rope!
SLASH!

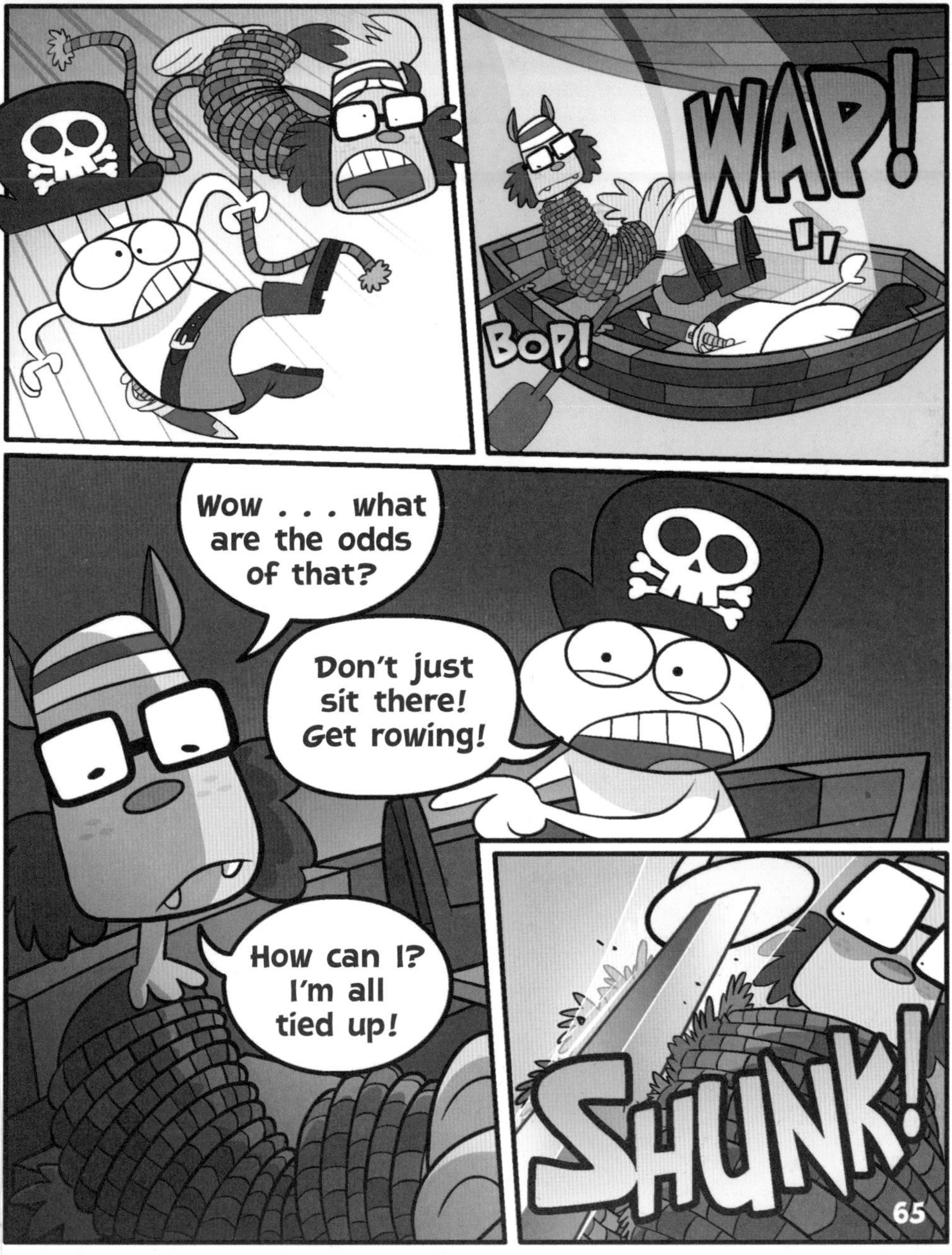

WAP!
BOP!
Wow . . . what are the odds of that?
Don't just sit there! Get rowing!
How can I? I'm all tied up!
SHUNK!

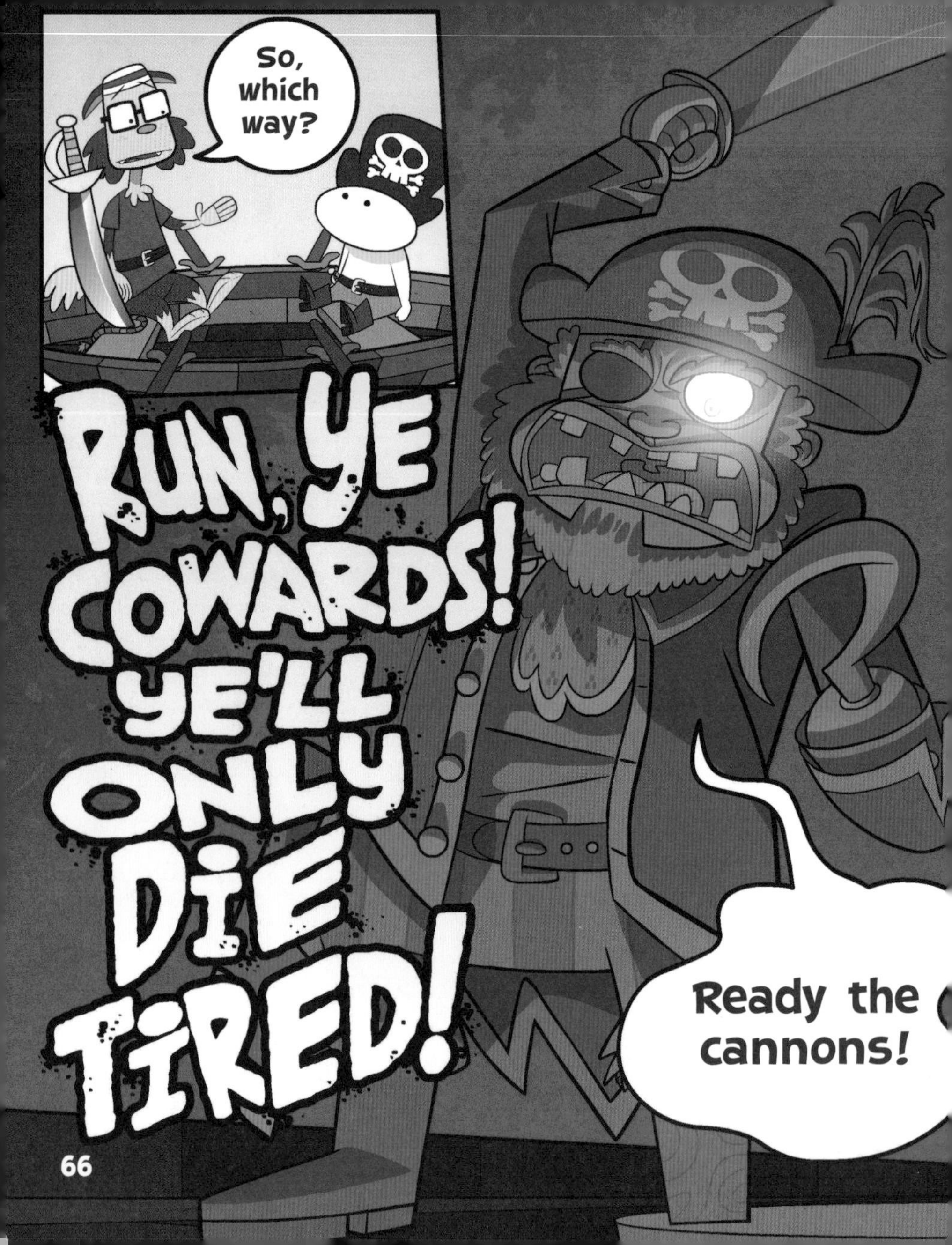
So, which way?
RUN, YE COWARDS! YE'LL ONLY DIE TIRED!
Ready the cannons!

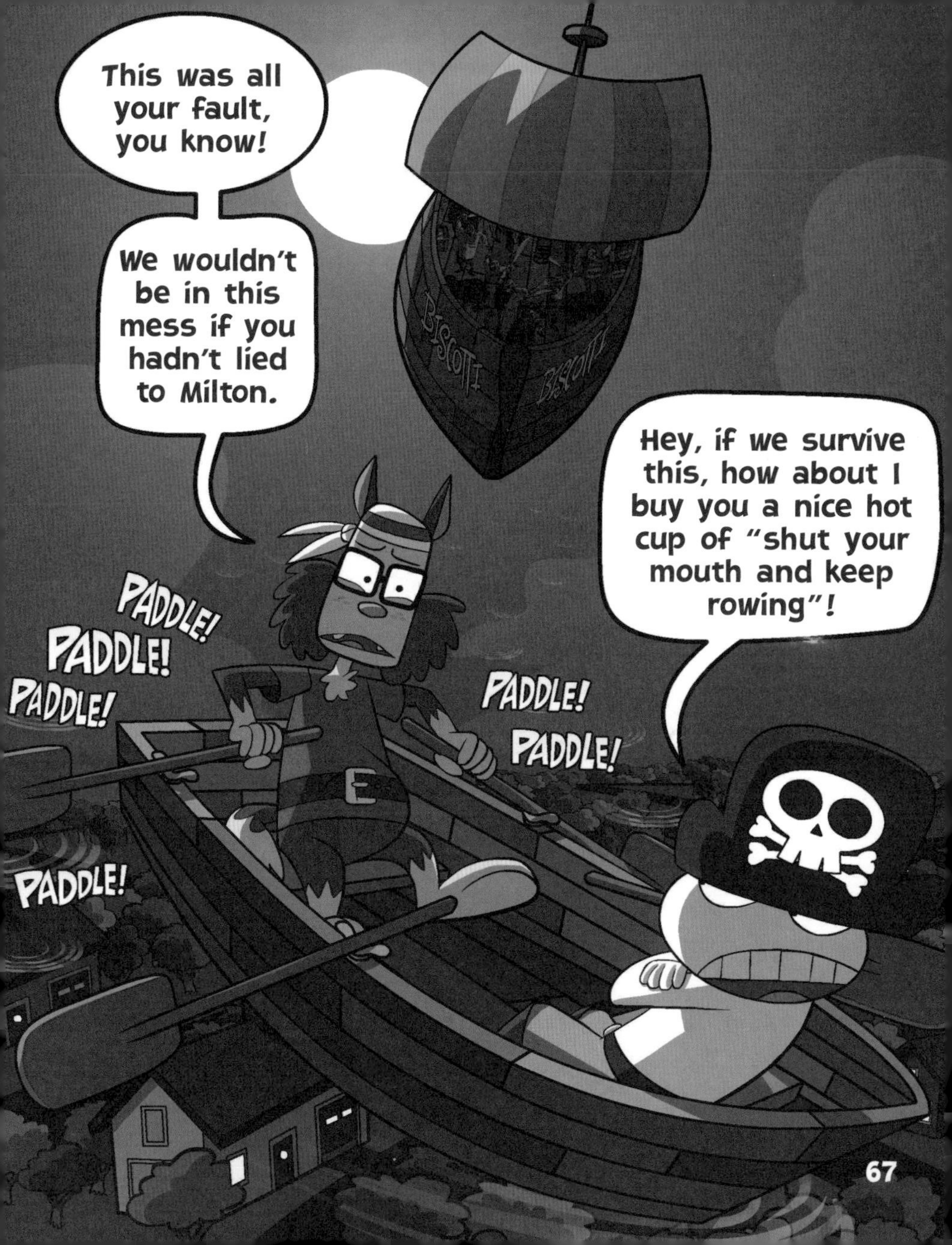
This was all your fault, you know!
We wouldn't be in this mess if you hadn't lied to Milton.
BISCOTTI
BISCOTTI
PADDLE!
PADDLE!
PADDLE!
PADDLE!
PADDLE!
PADDLE!
Hey, if we survive this, how about I buy you a nice hot cup of "shut your mouth and keep rowing"!
E

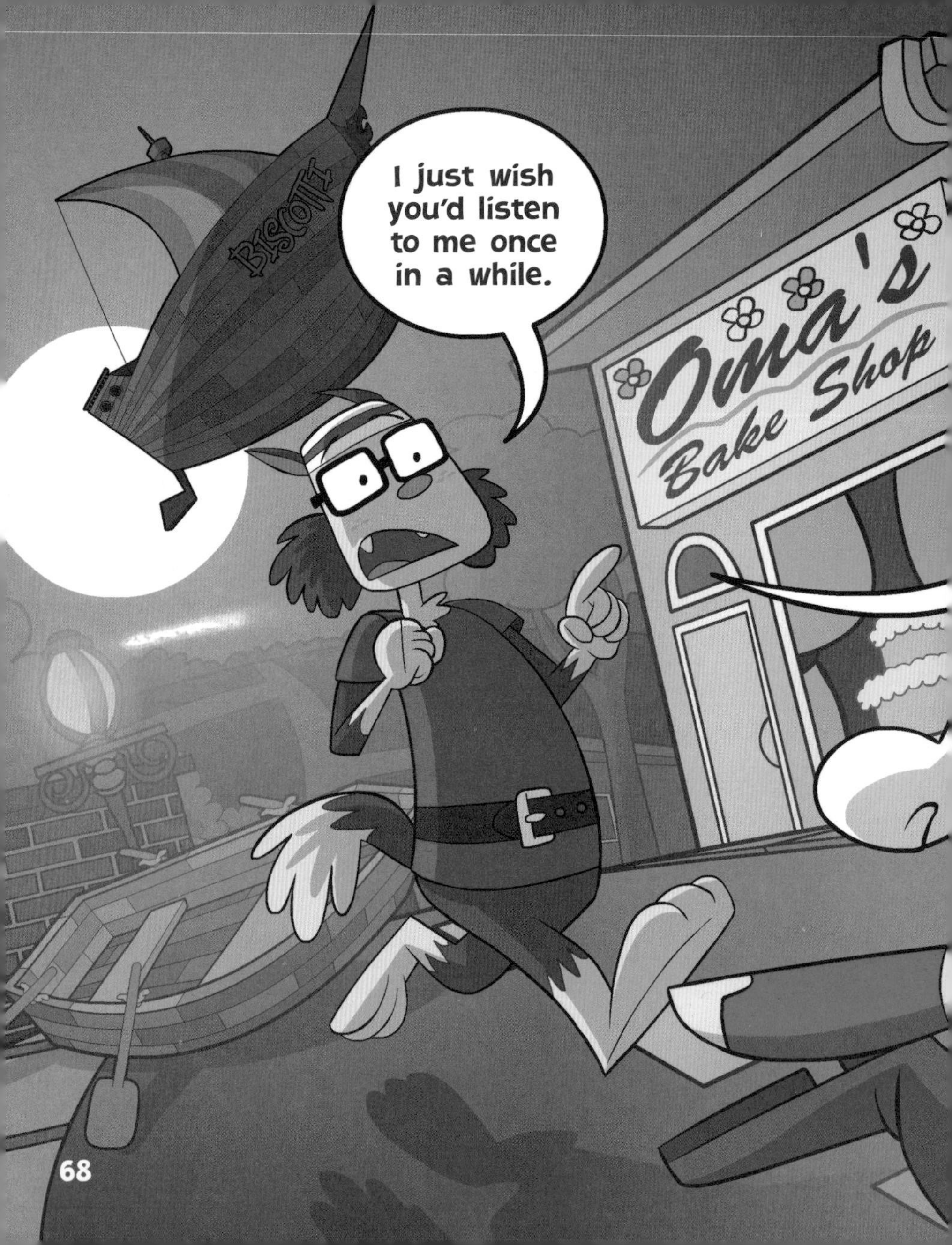
BISCOTTI
I just wish you'd listen to me once in a while.
Oma's
Bake Shop

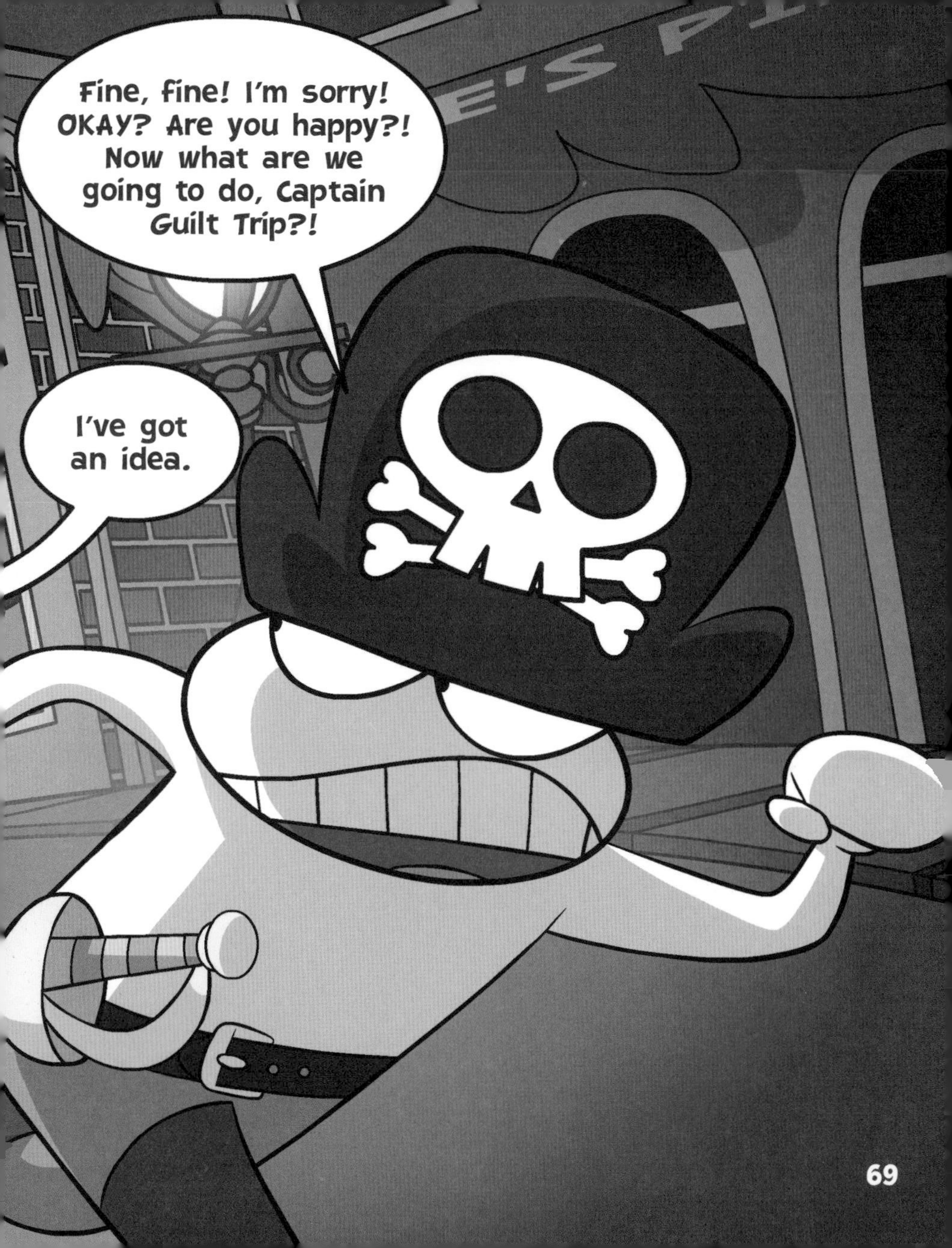
Fine, fine! I'm sorry! OKAY? Are you happy?! Now what are we going to do, Captain Guilt Trip?!
I've got an idea.

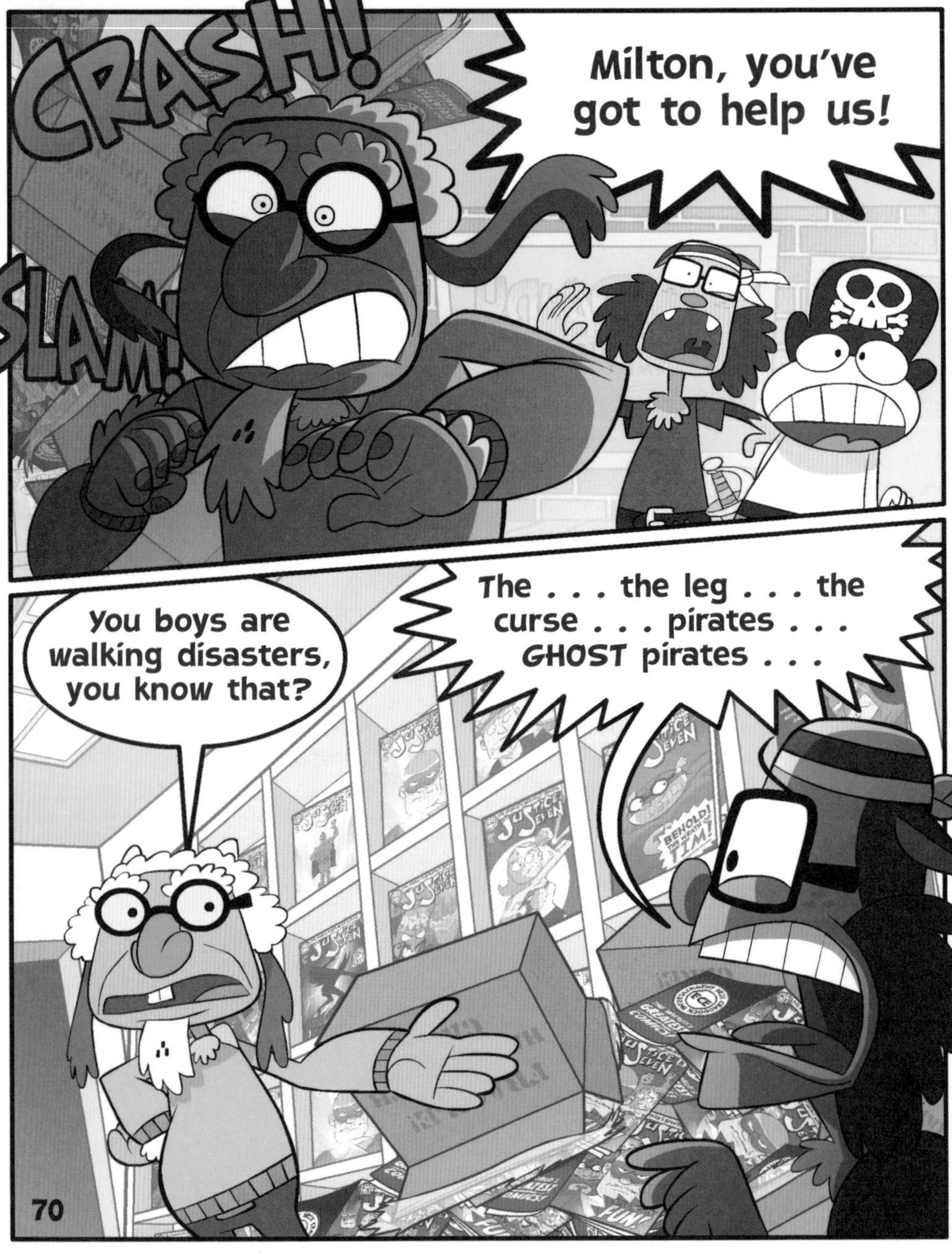
CRASH!
Milton, you've got to help us!
SLAM!
You boys are walking disasters, you know that?
The . . . the leg . . . the curse . . . pirates . . . *GHOST* pirates . . .
JUSTICE SEVEN
BEHOLD! THE WRATH OF TIM!

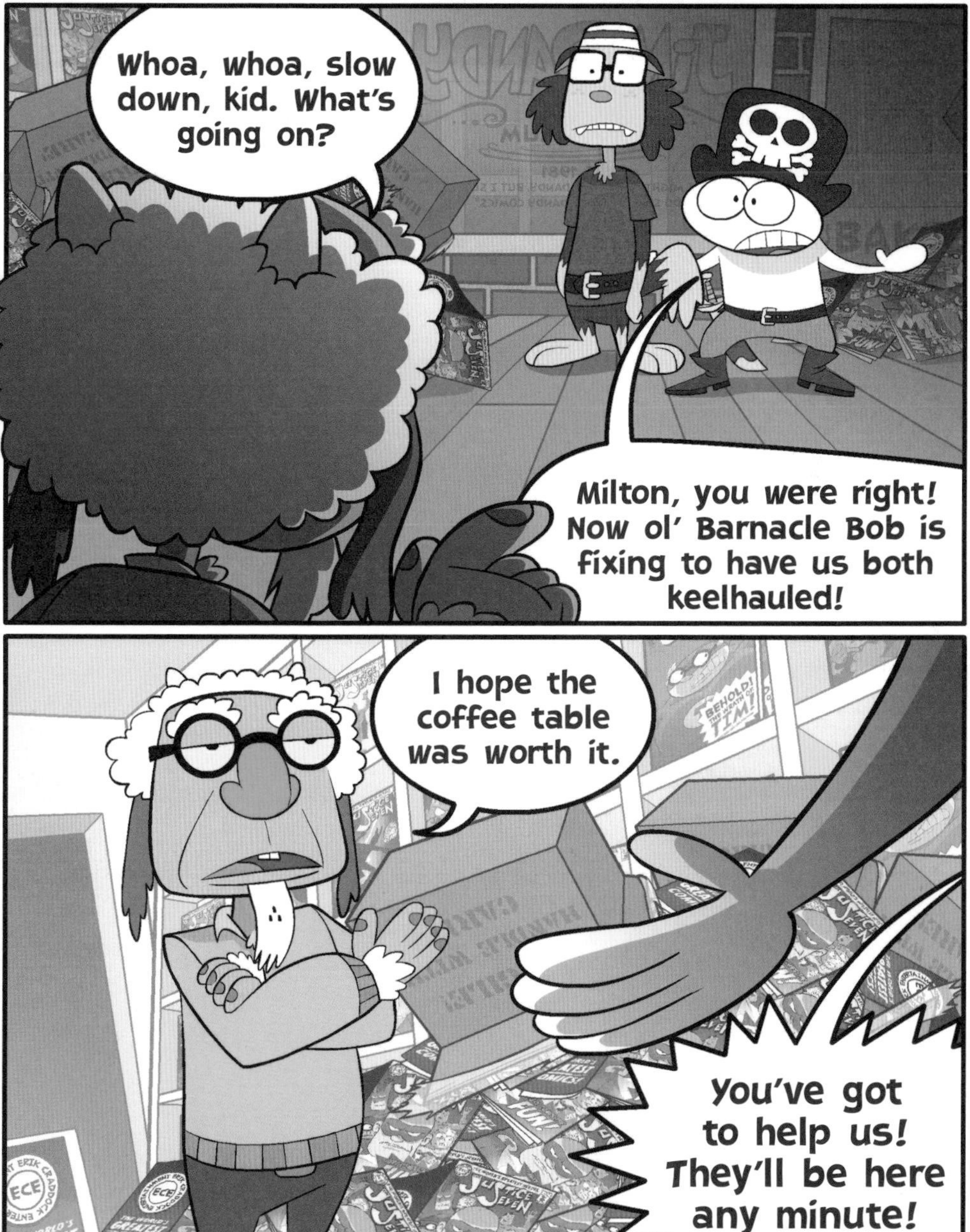
Whoa, whoa, slow down, kid. What's going on?
Milton, you were right! Now ol' Barnacle Bob is fixing to have us both keelhauled!
I hope the coffee table was worth it.
You've got to help us! They'll be here any minute!

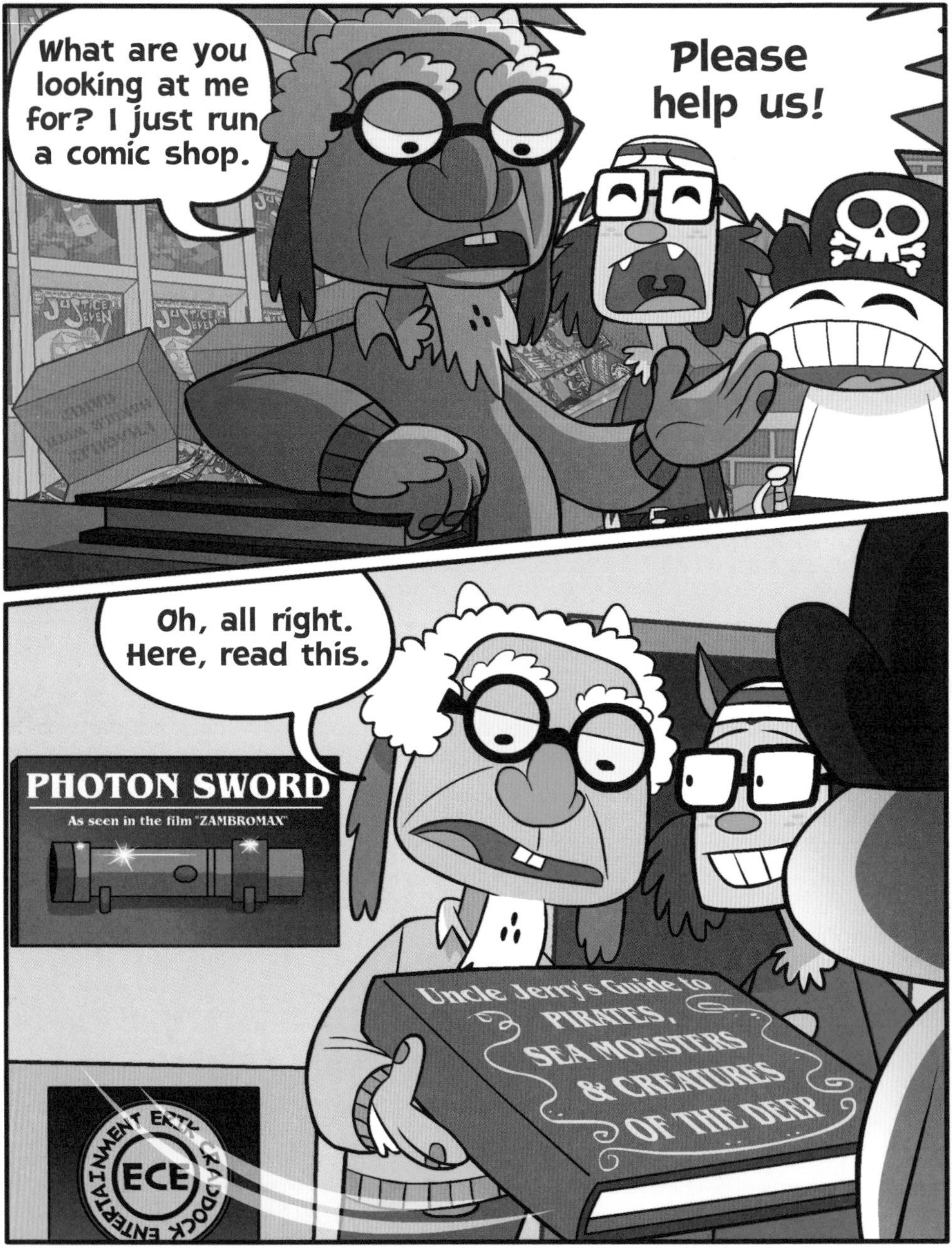
What are you looking at me for? I just run a comic shop.
Please help us!
Oh, all right. Here, read this.
PHOTON SWORD
As seen in the film "ZAMBROMAX"
Uncle Jerry's Guide to PIRATES, SEA MONSTERS & CREATURES OF THE DEEP
ERIK CRADDOCK ENTERTAINMENT
ECE

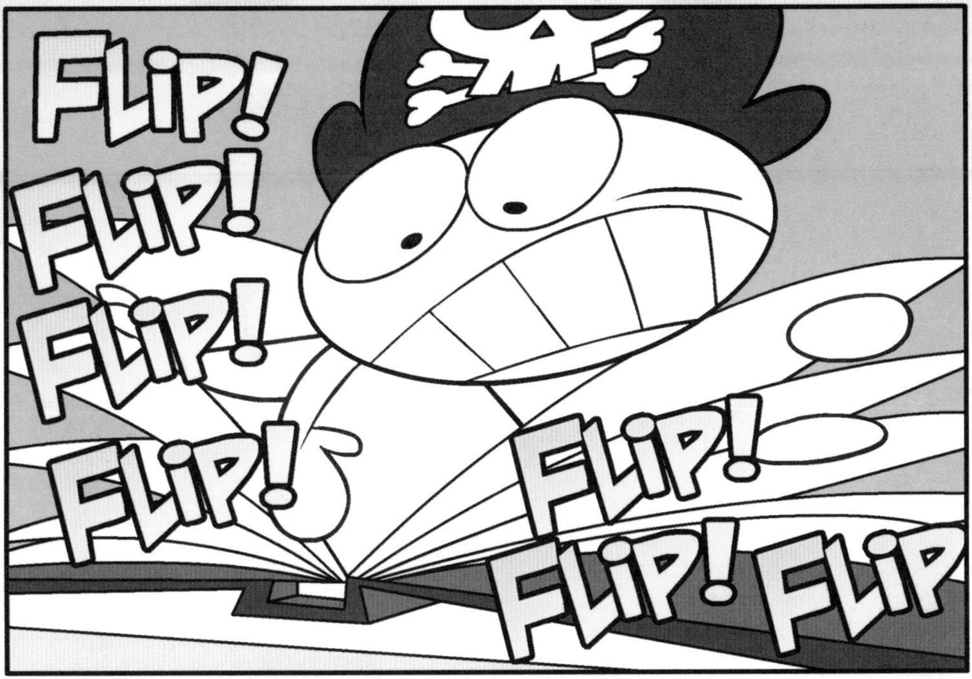
FLIP!
FLIP!
FLIP!
FLIP!
FLIP!
FLIP!
FLIP

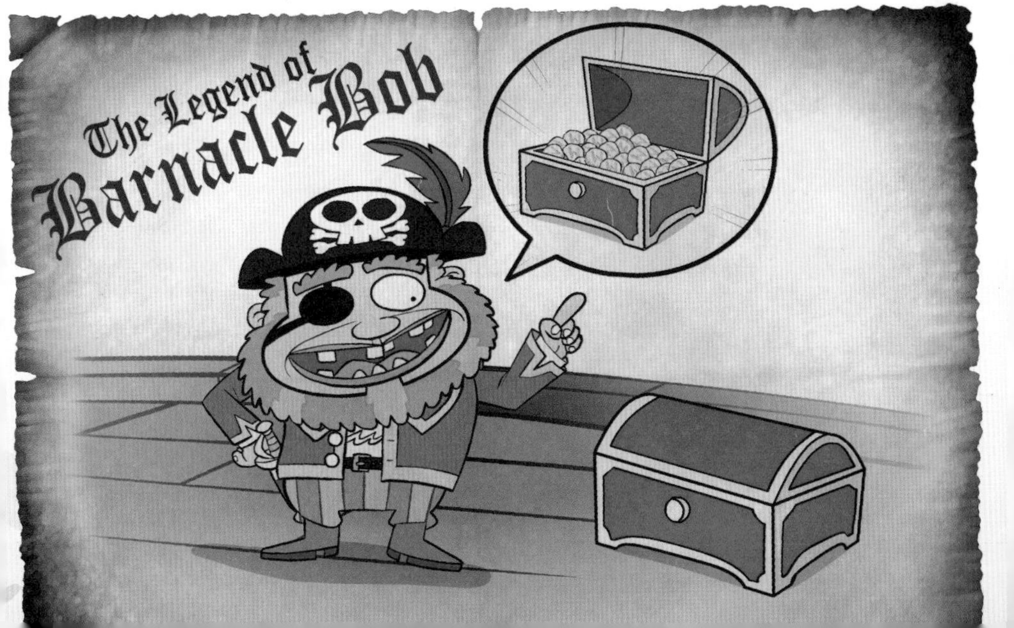
The Legend of Barnacle Bob

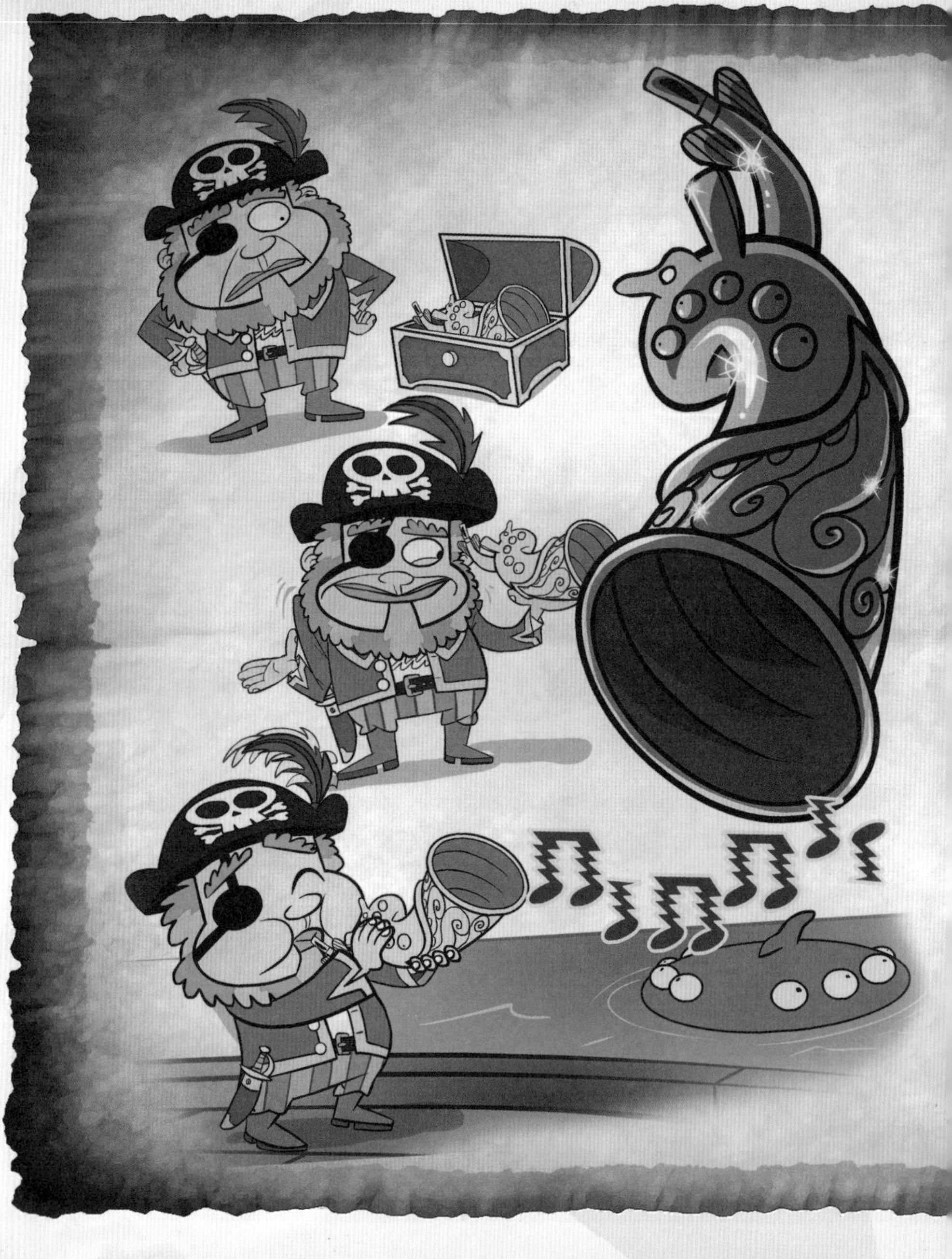

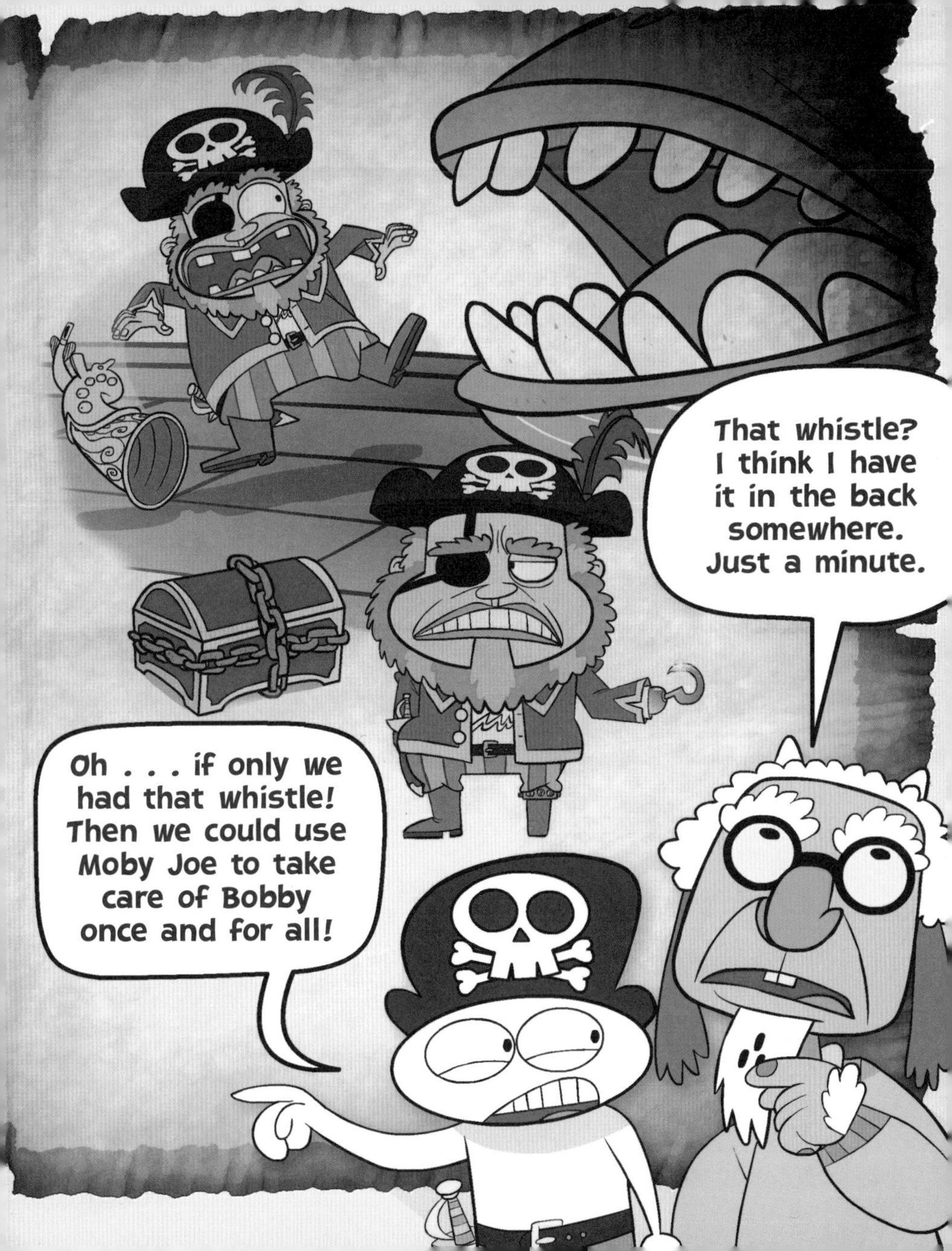
Oh . . . if only we had that whistle! Then we could use Moby Joe to take care of Bobby once and for all!
That whistle? I think I have it in the back somewhere. Just a minute.

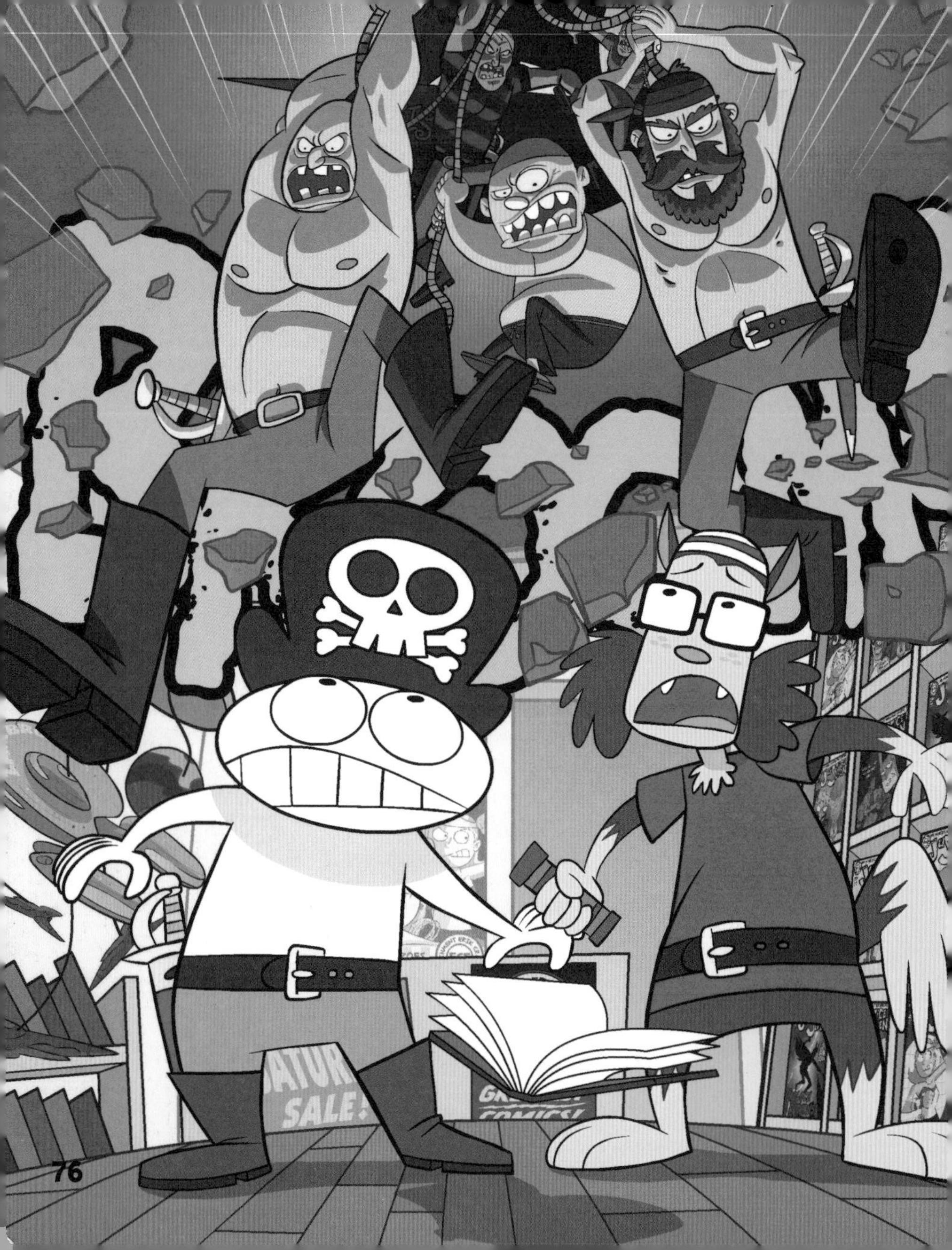
SALE!

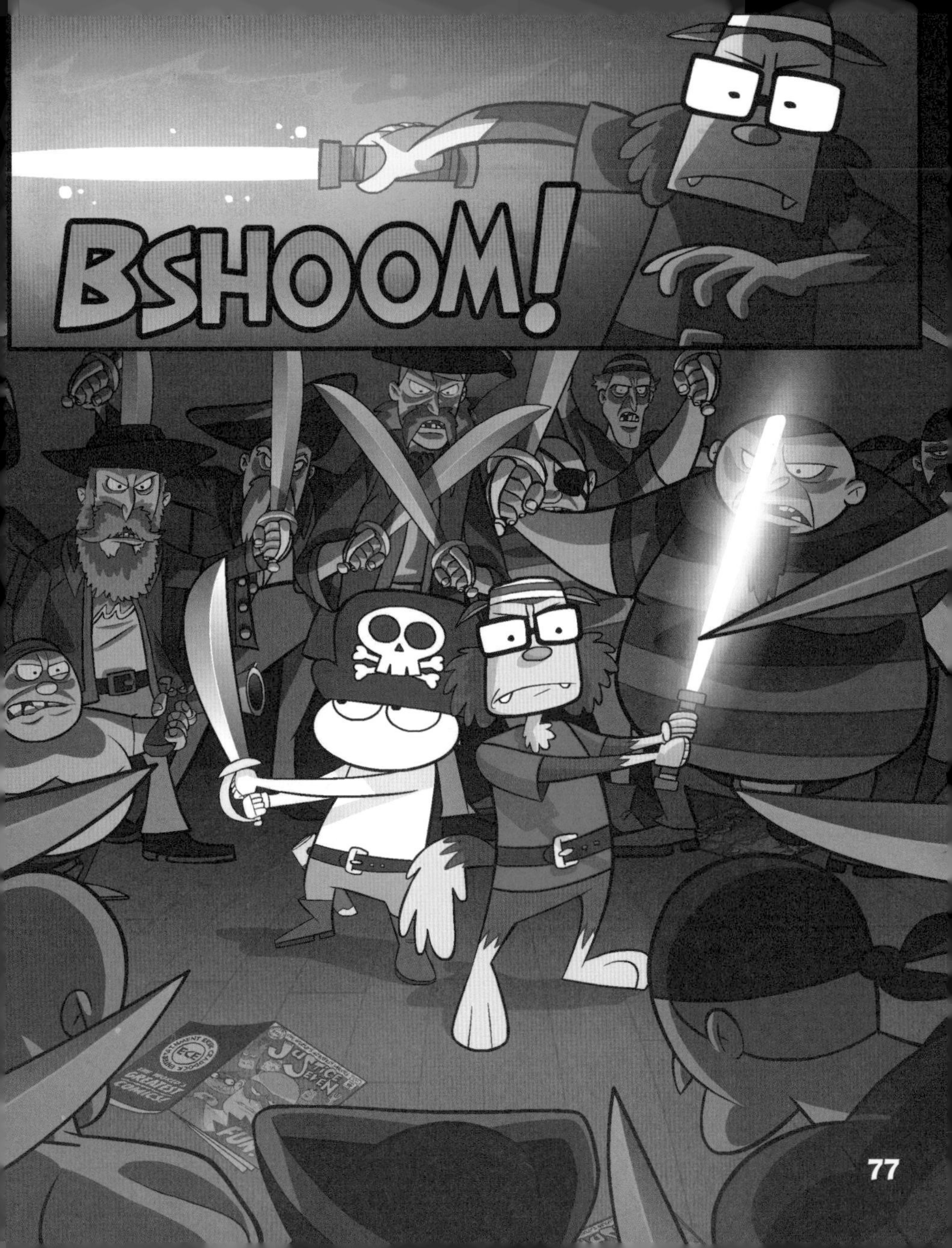
BSHOOM!
GREATEST
COMICS
JUSTICE SEVEN
FUN

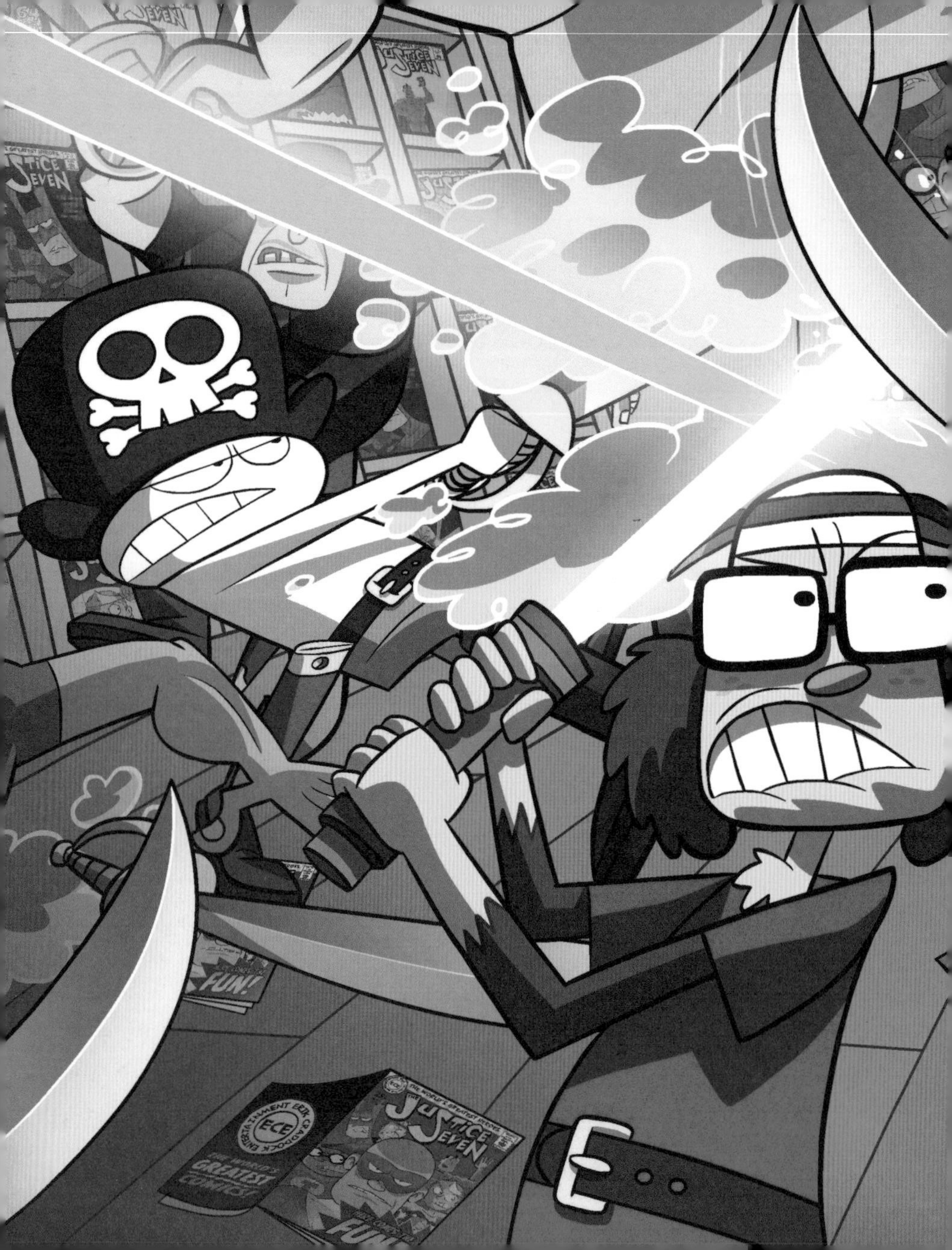
JUSTICE SEVEN
FUN!
ECE
THE WORLD'S GREATEST COMICS!
JUSTICE SEVEN

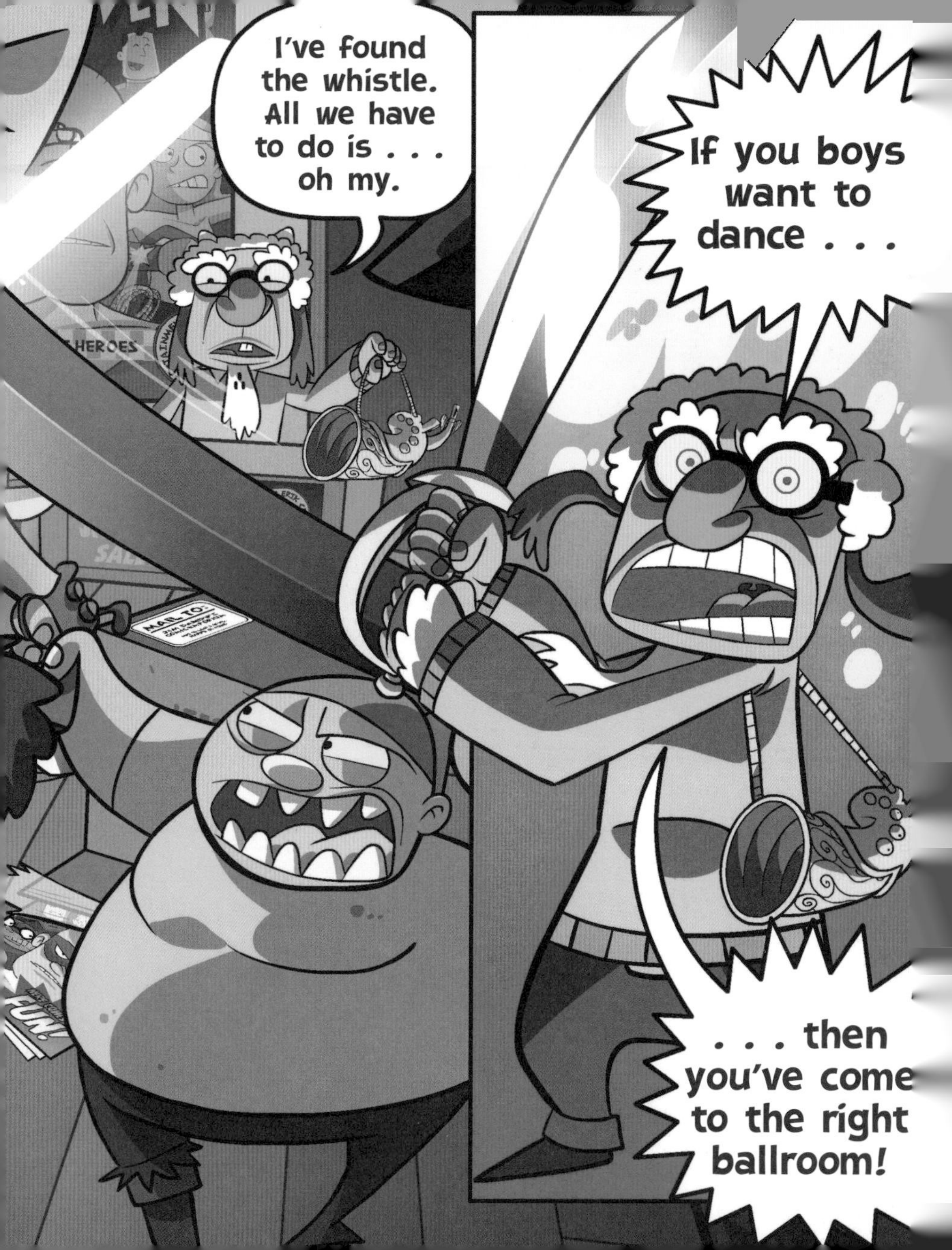
I've found the whistle. All we have to do is . . . oh my.
HEROES
MAIL-TO:
FUN!
If you boys want to dance . . .
. . . then you've come to the right ballroom!

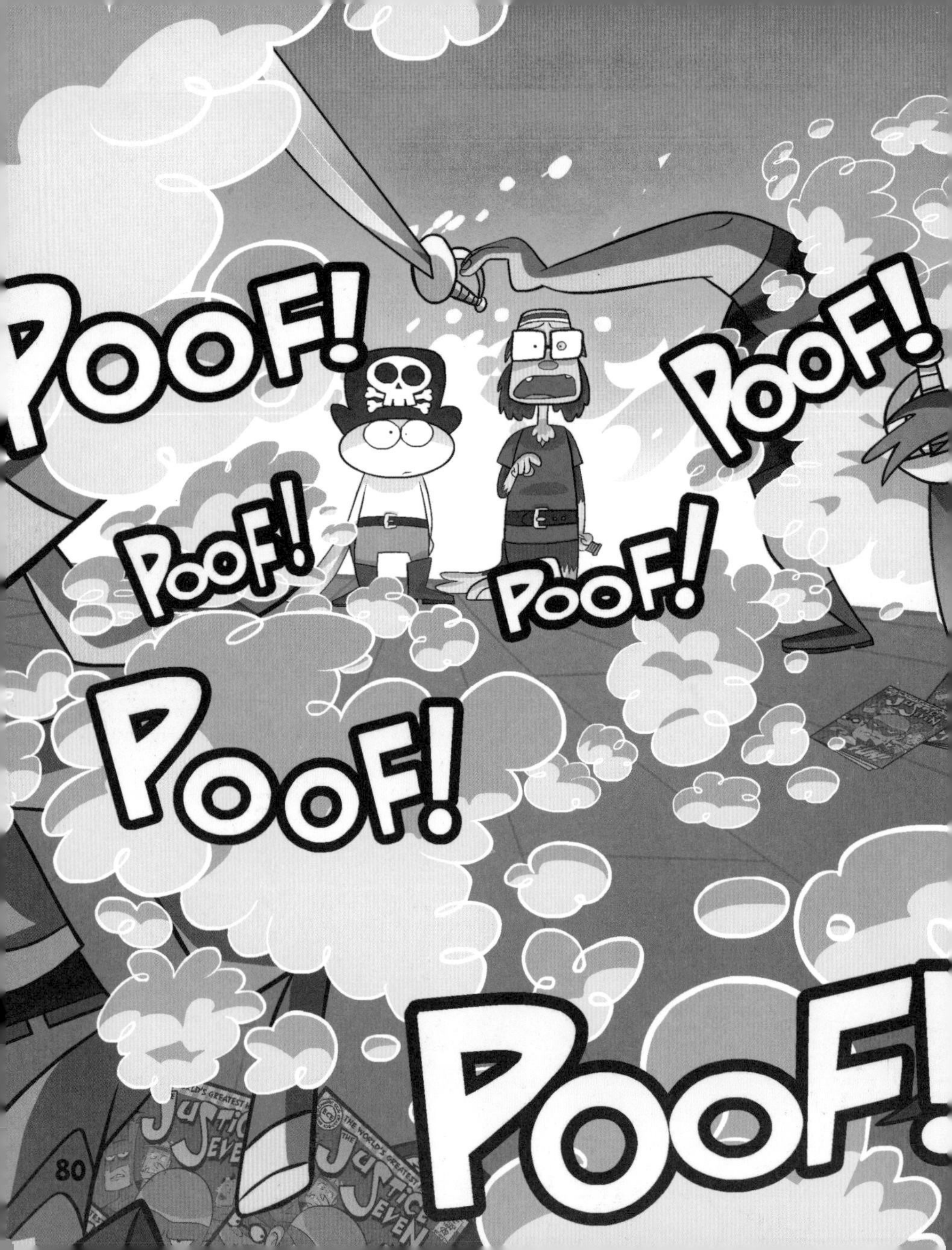
POOF!
POOF!
POOF!
POOF!
POOF!
POOF!

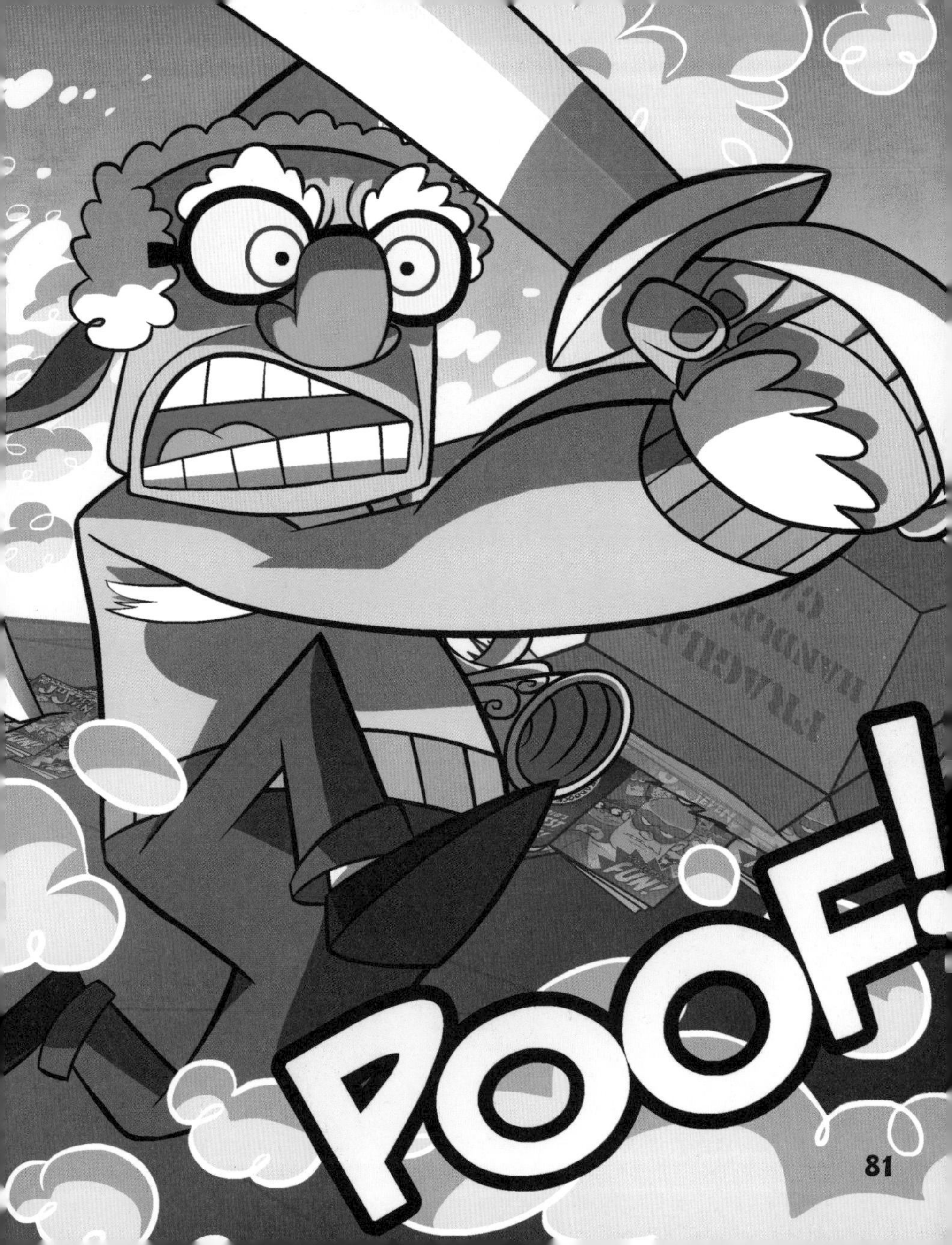
POOF!

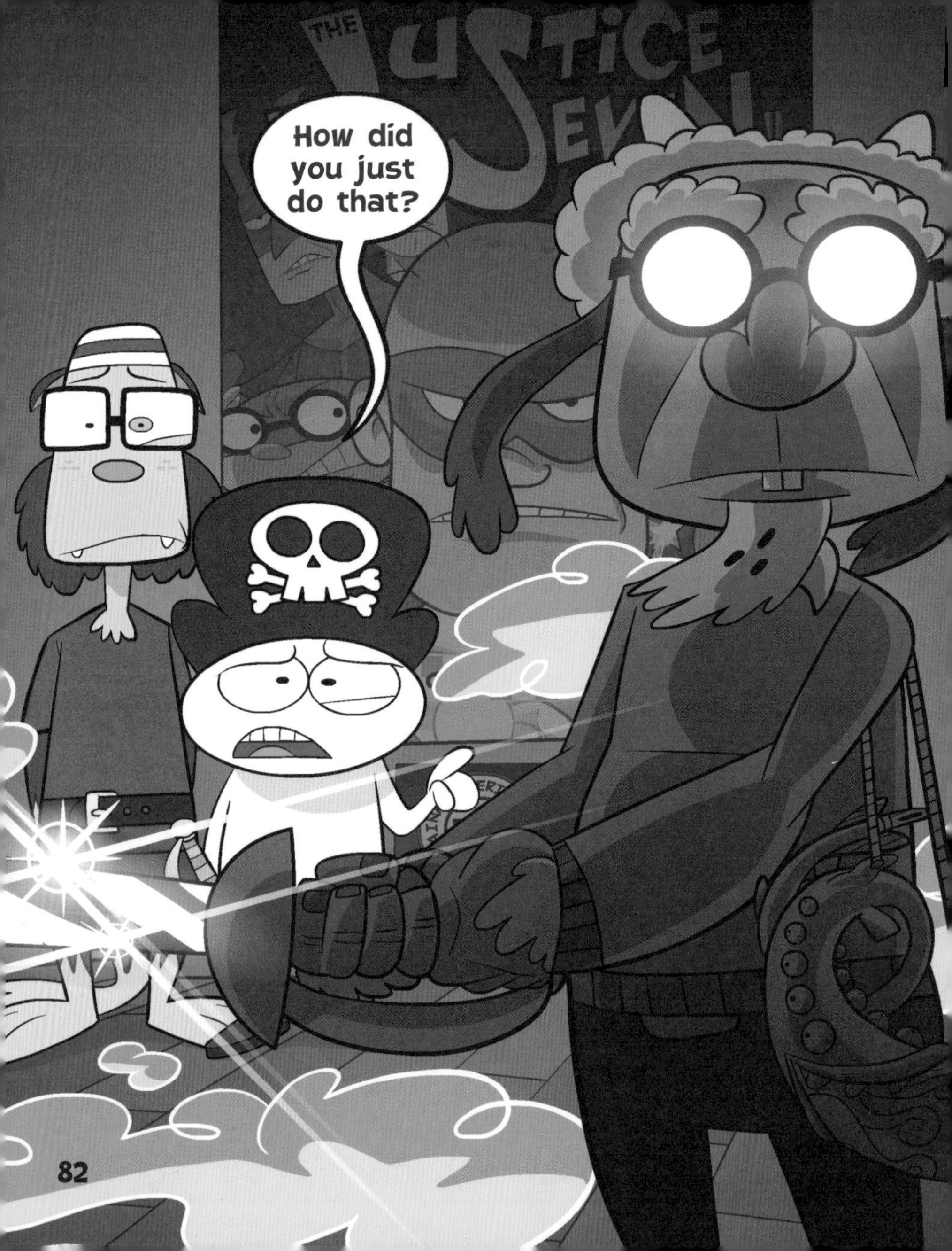
THE JUSTICE SEVEN
How did you just do that?

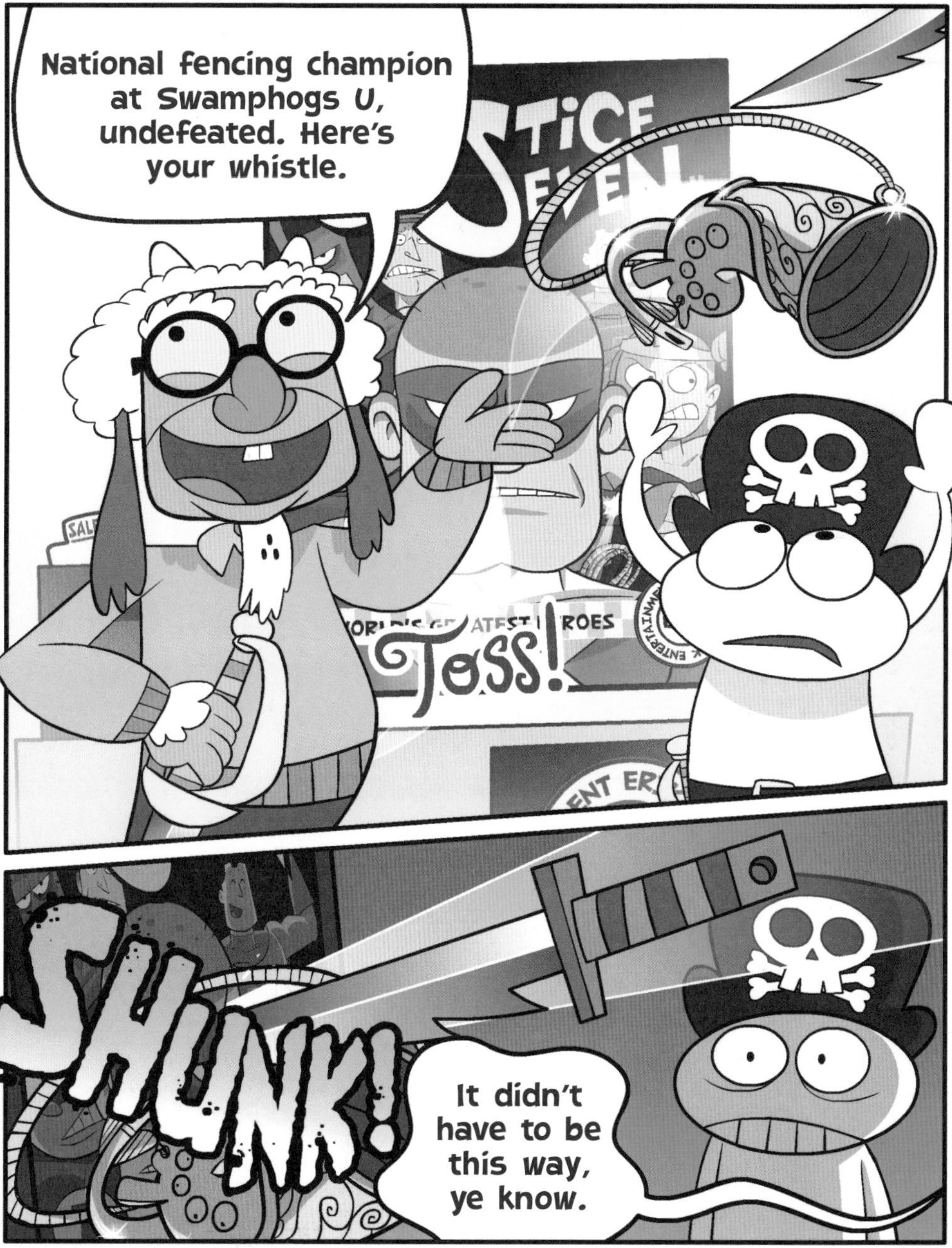

National fencing champion at Swamphogs U, undefeated. Here's your whistle.
TOSS!
SHUNK!
It didn't have to be this way, ye know.

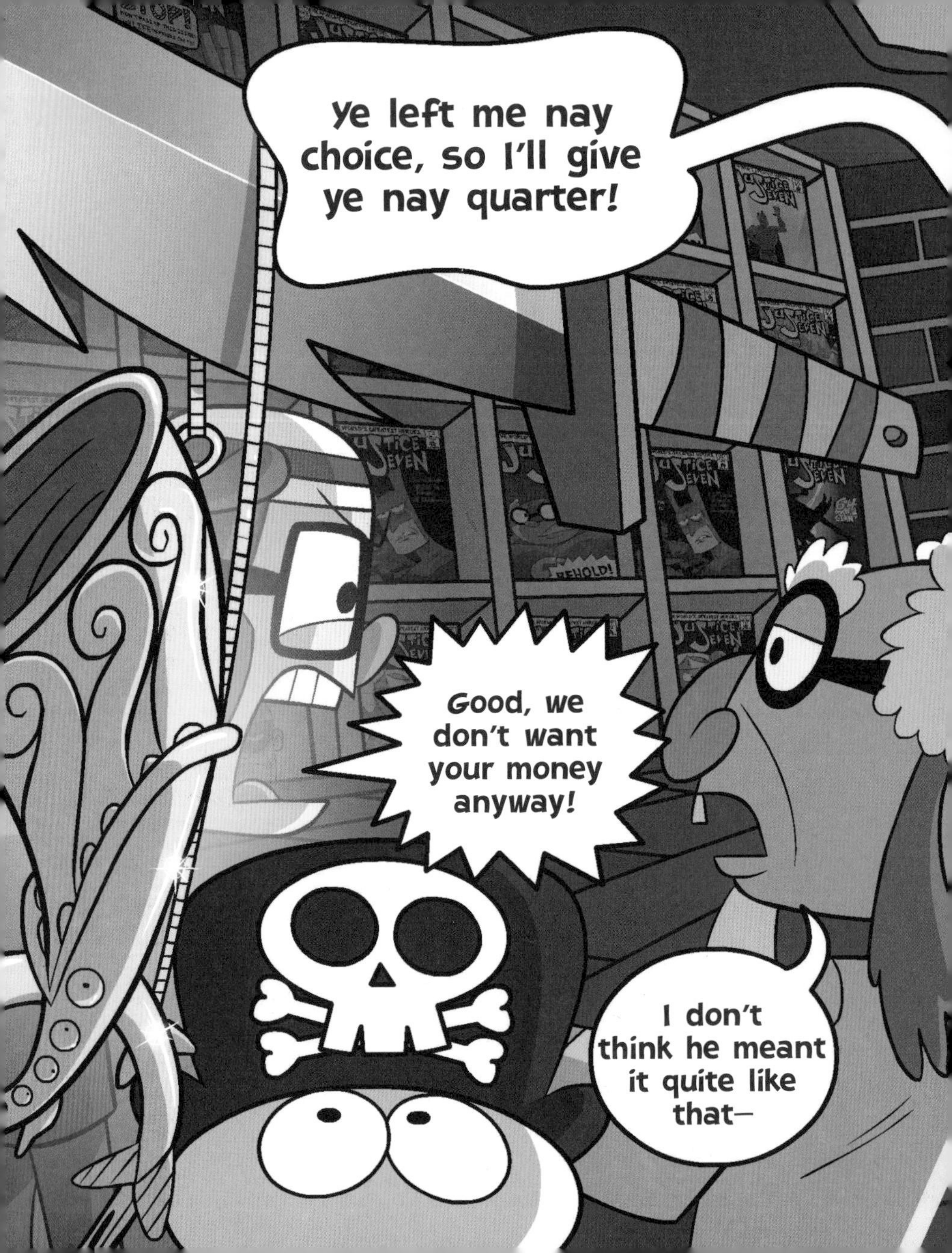
ye left me nay choice, so I'll give ye nay quarter!
Good, we don't want your money anyway!
I don't think he meant it quite like that—

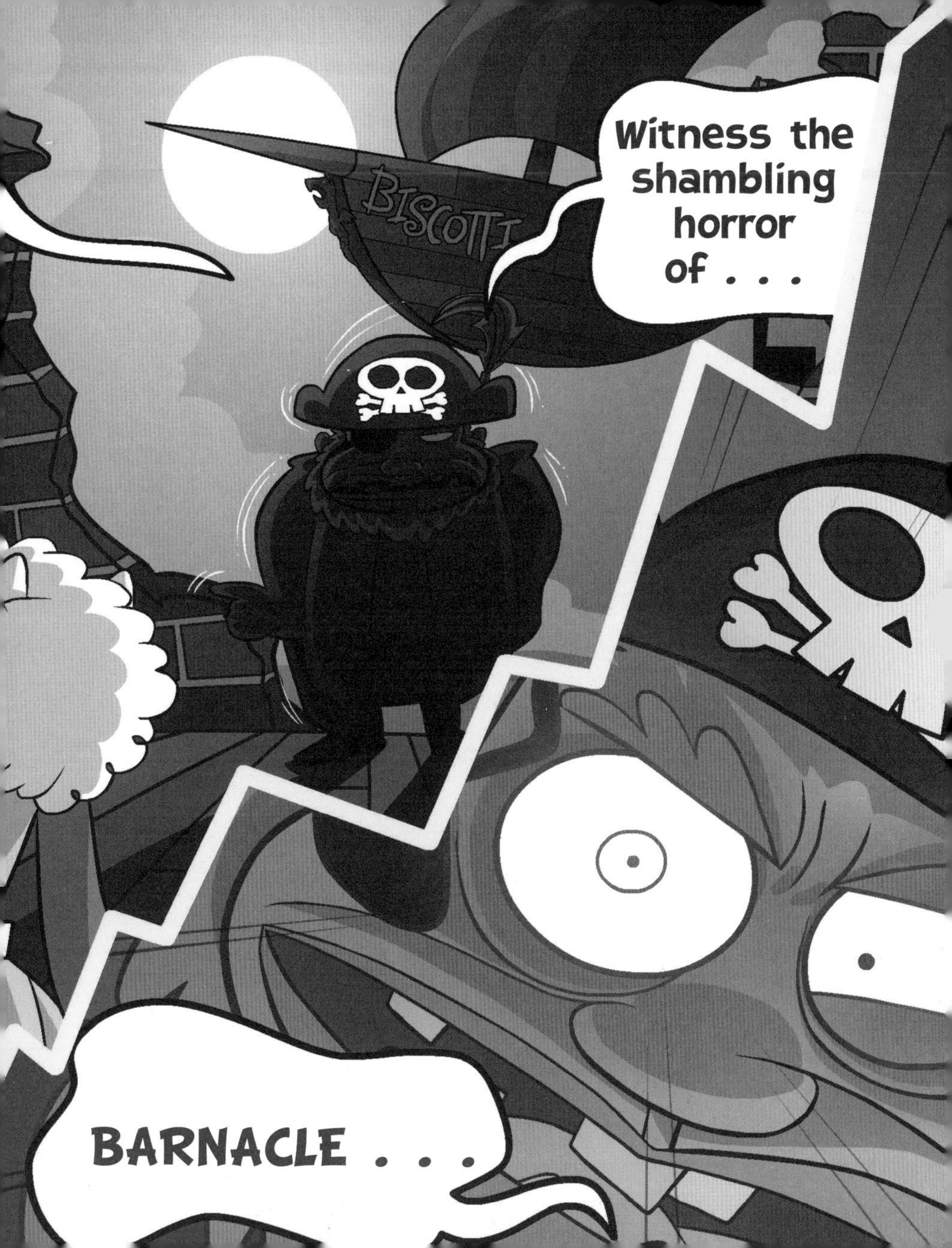
BISCOTTI
Witness the shambling horror of . . .
BARNACLE . . .

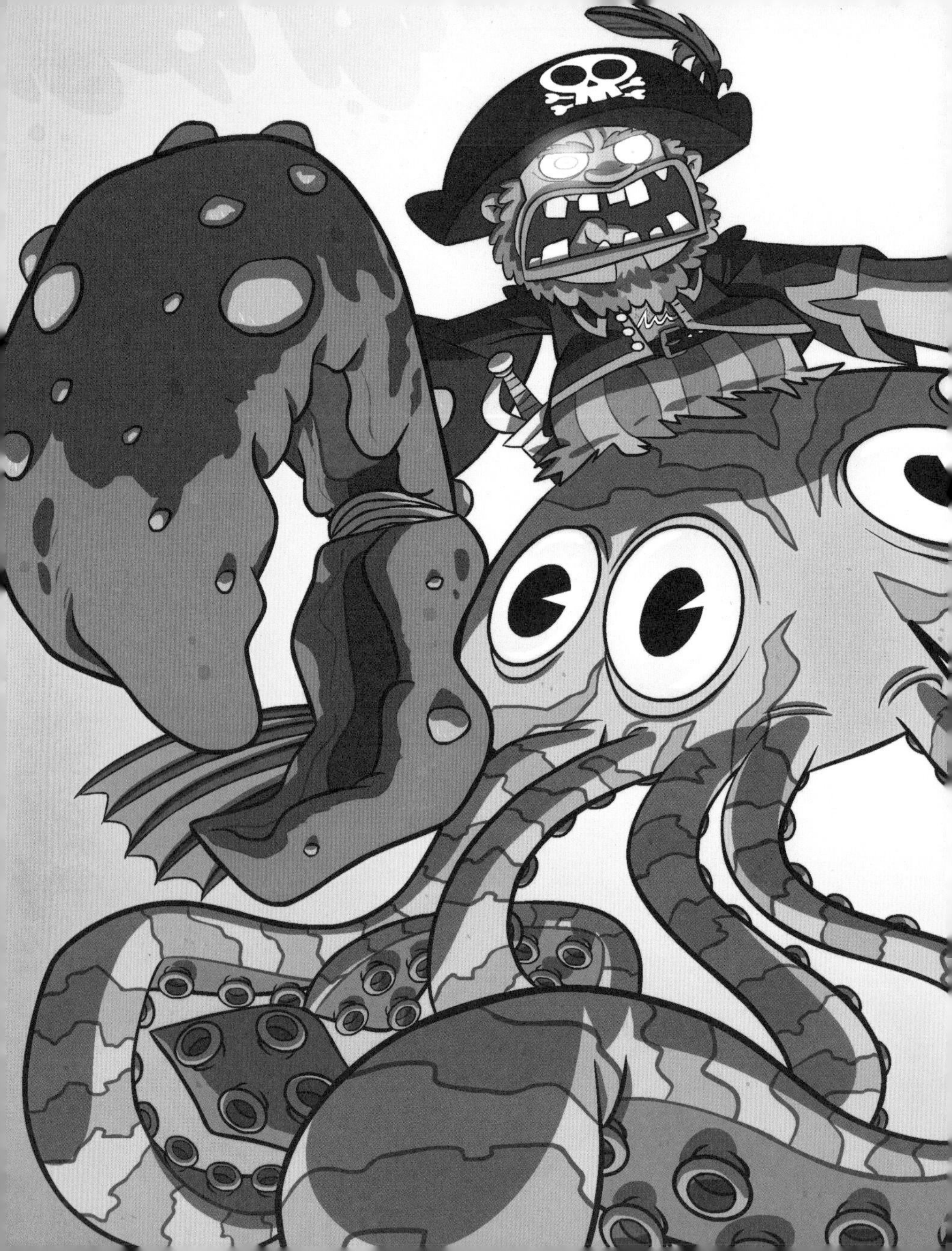

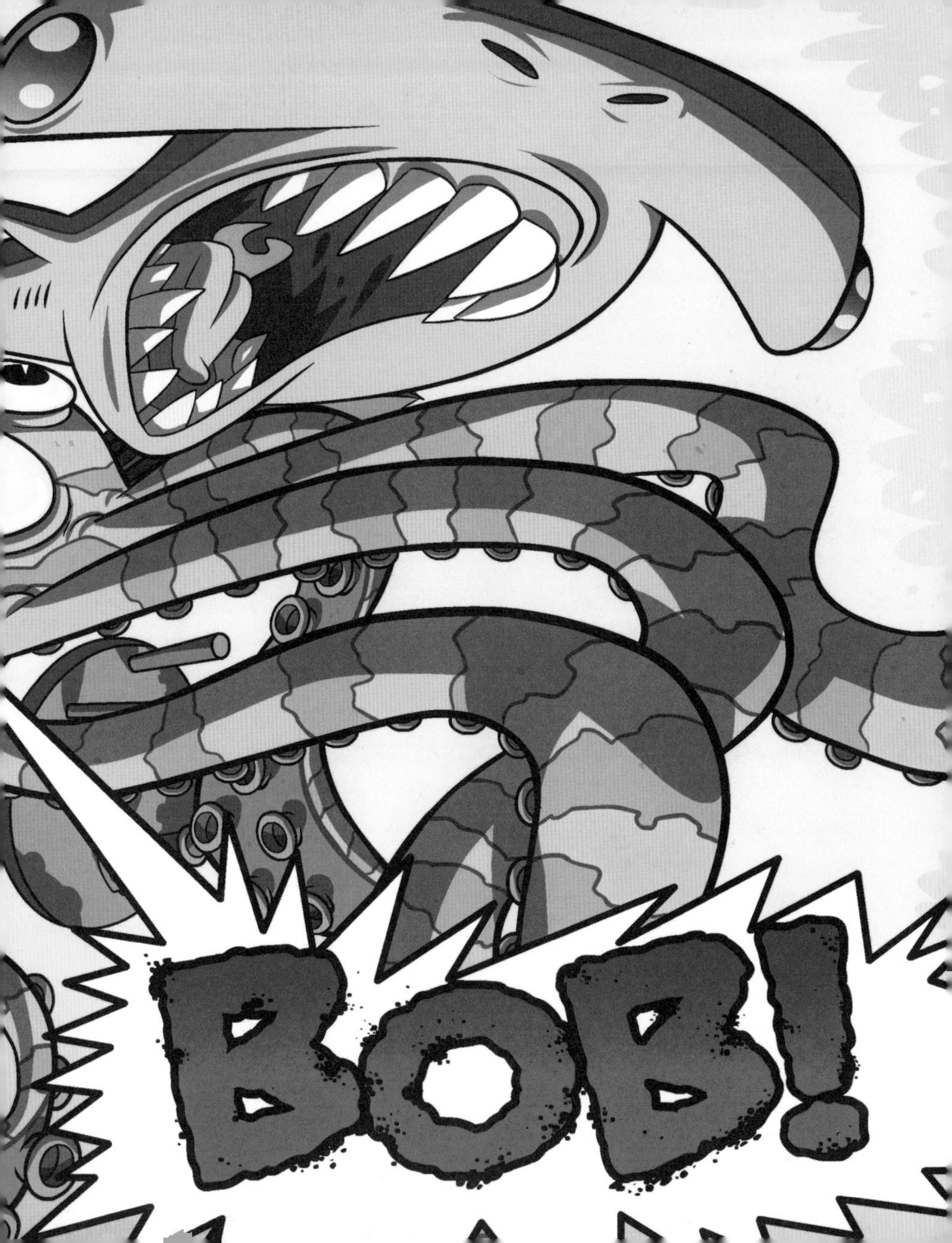
BOB!

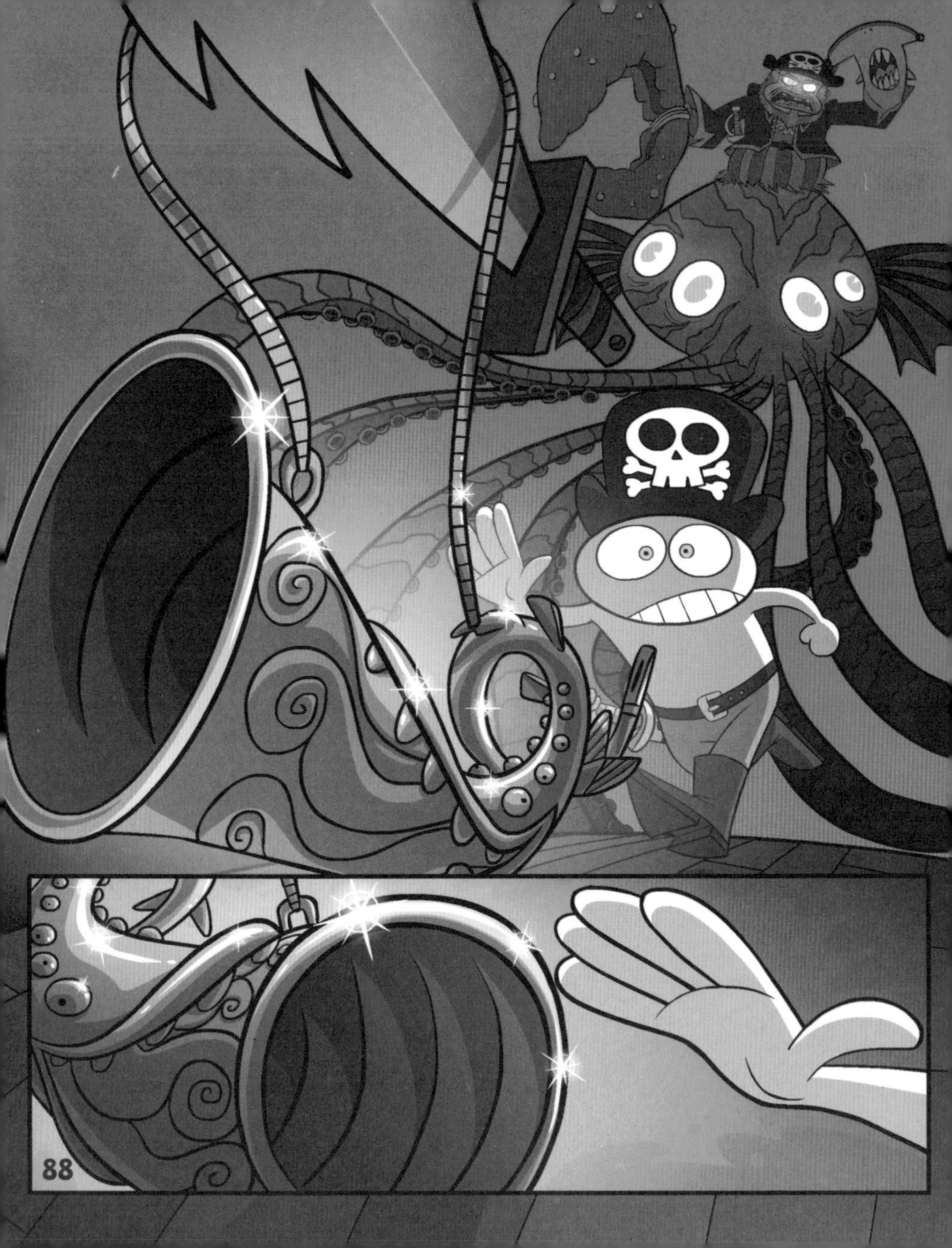

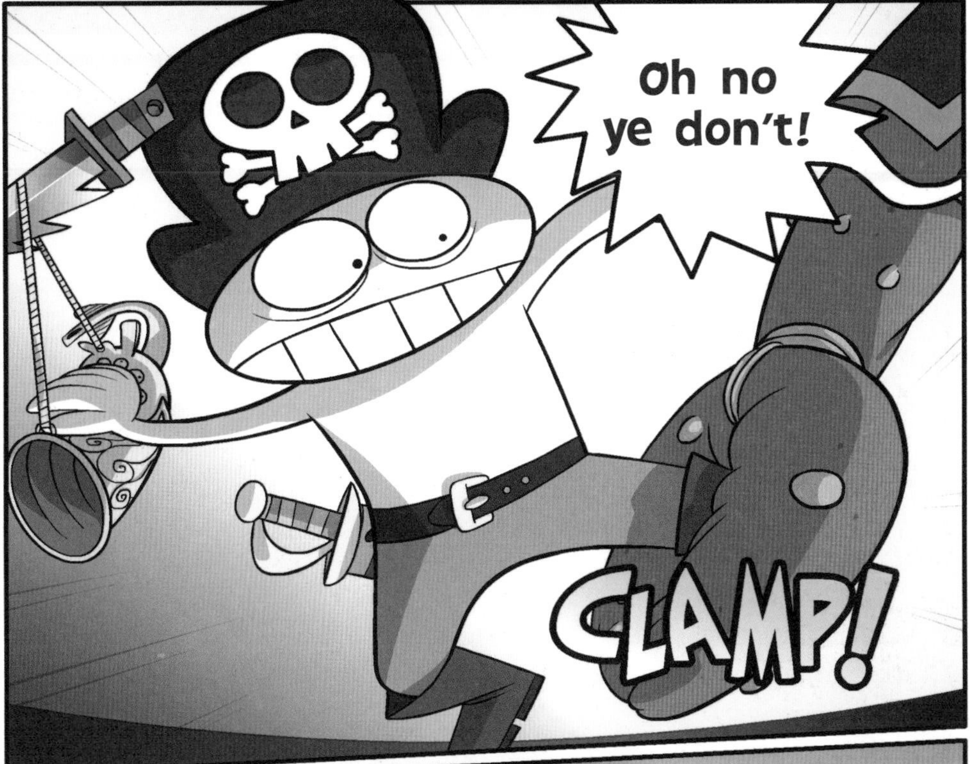
Oh no ye don't!
CLAMP!

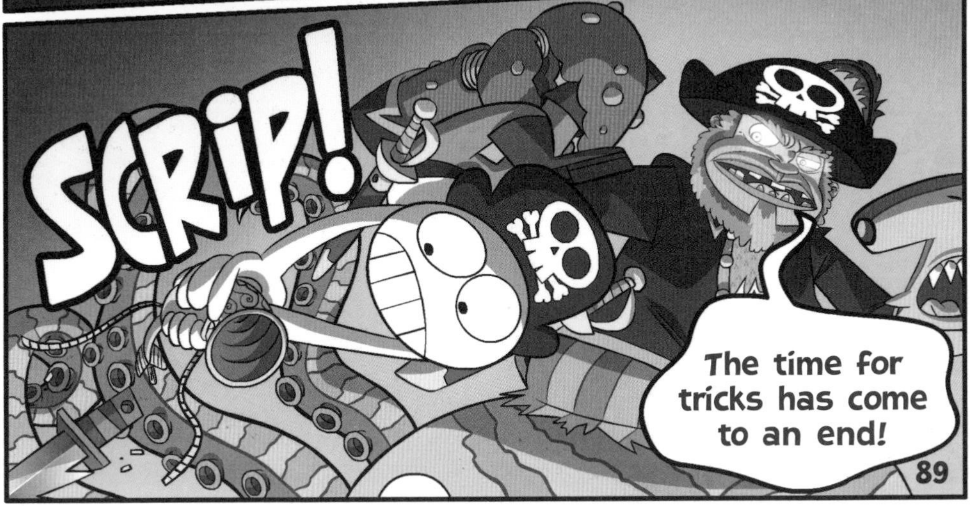
SCRIP!
The time for tricks has come to an end!

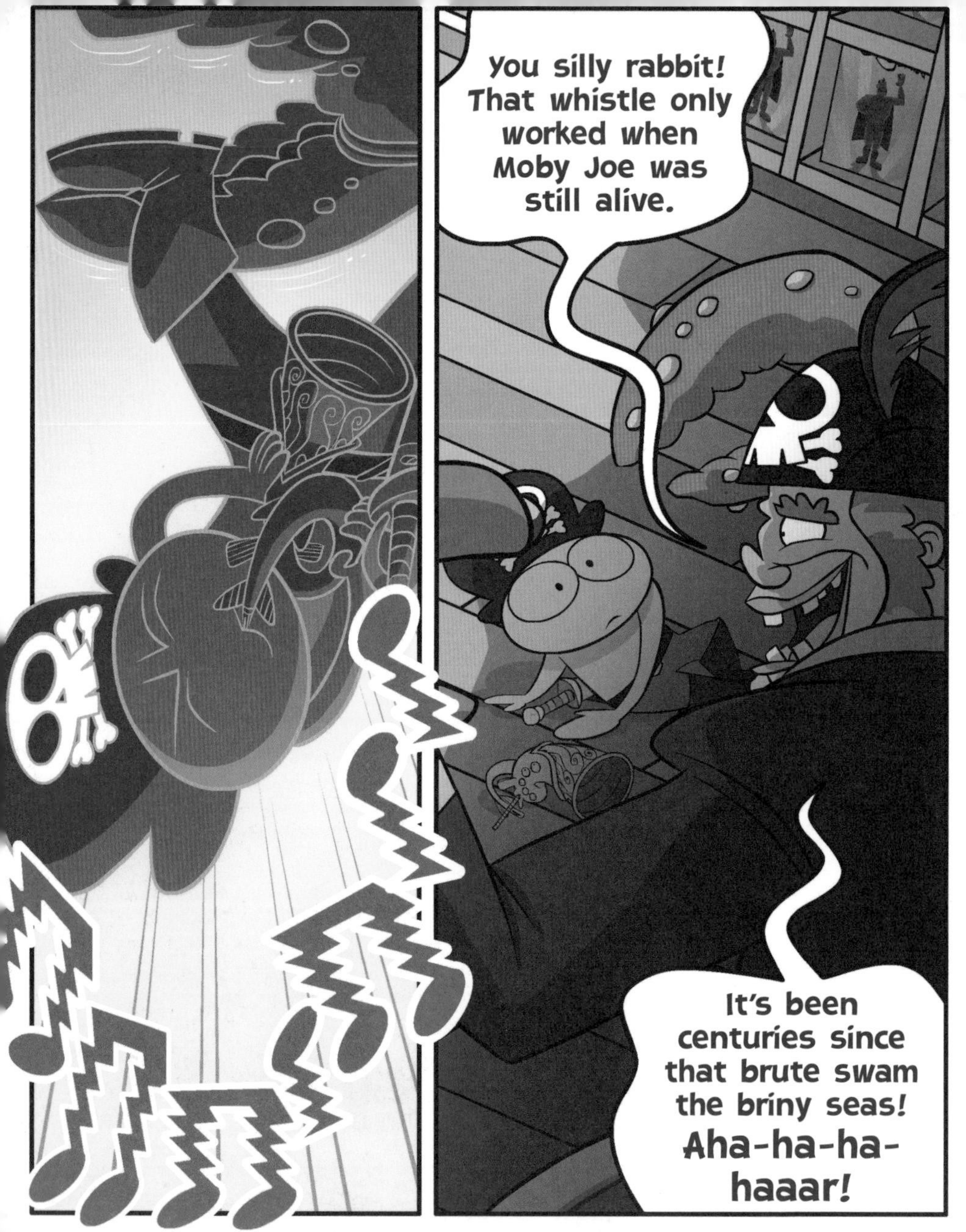
You silly rabbit! That whistle only worked when Moby Joe was still alive.
It's been centuries since that brute swam the briny seas! Aha-ha-ha-haaar!

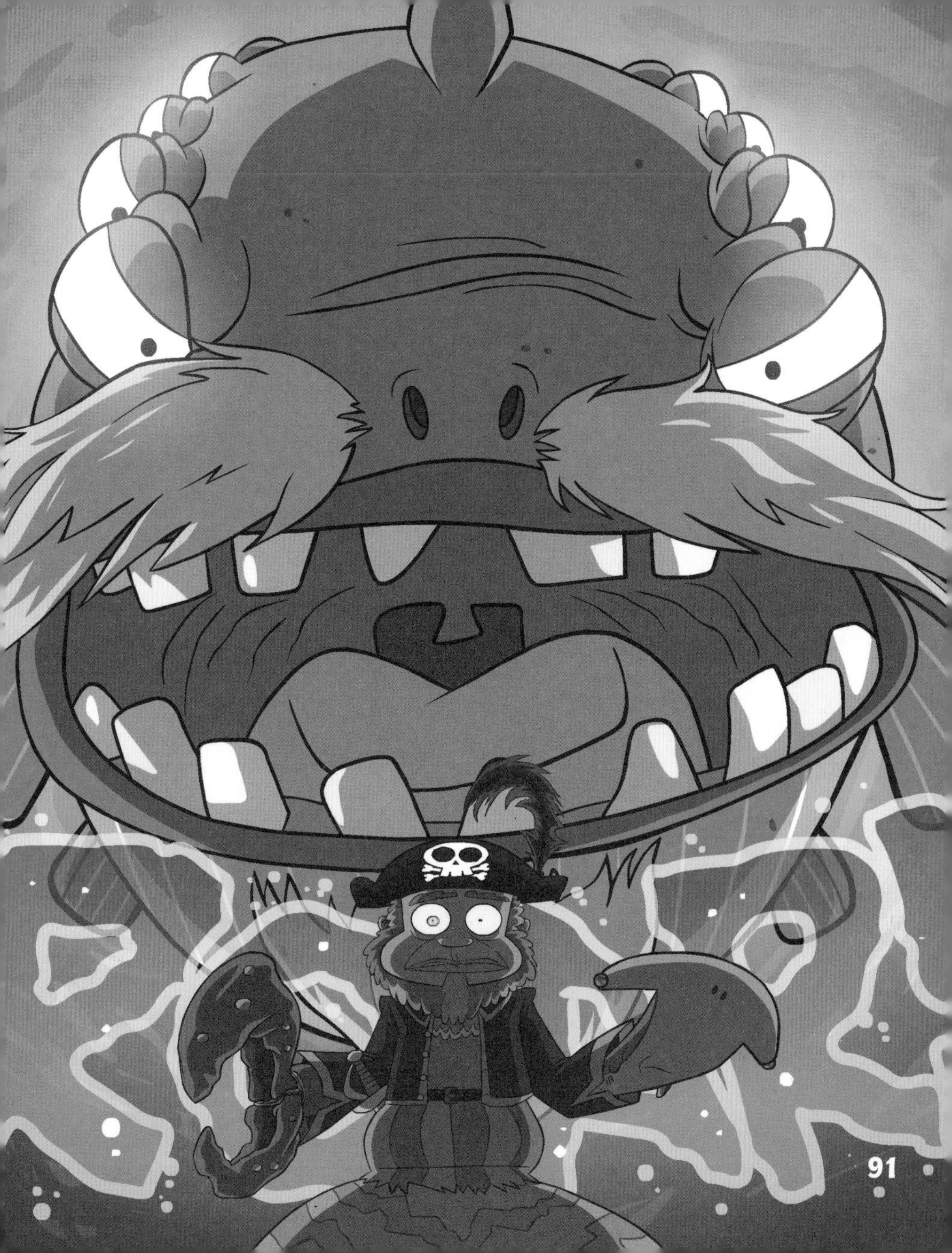

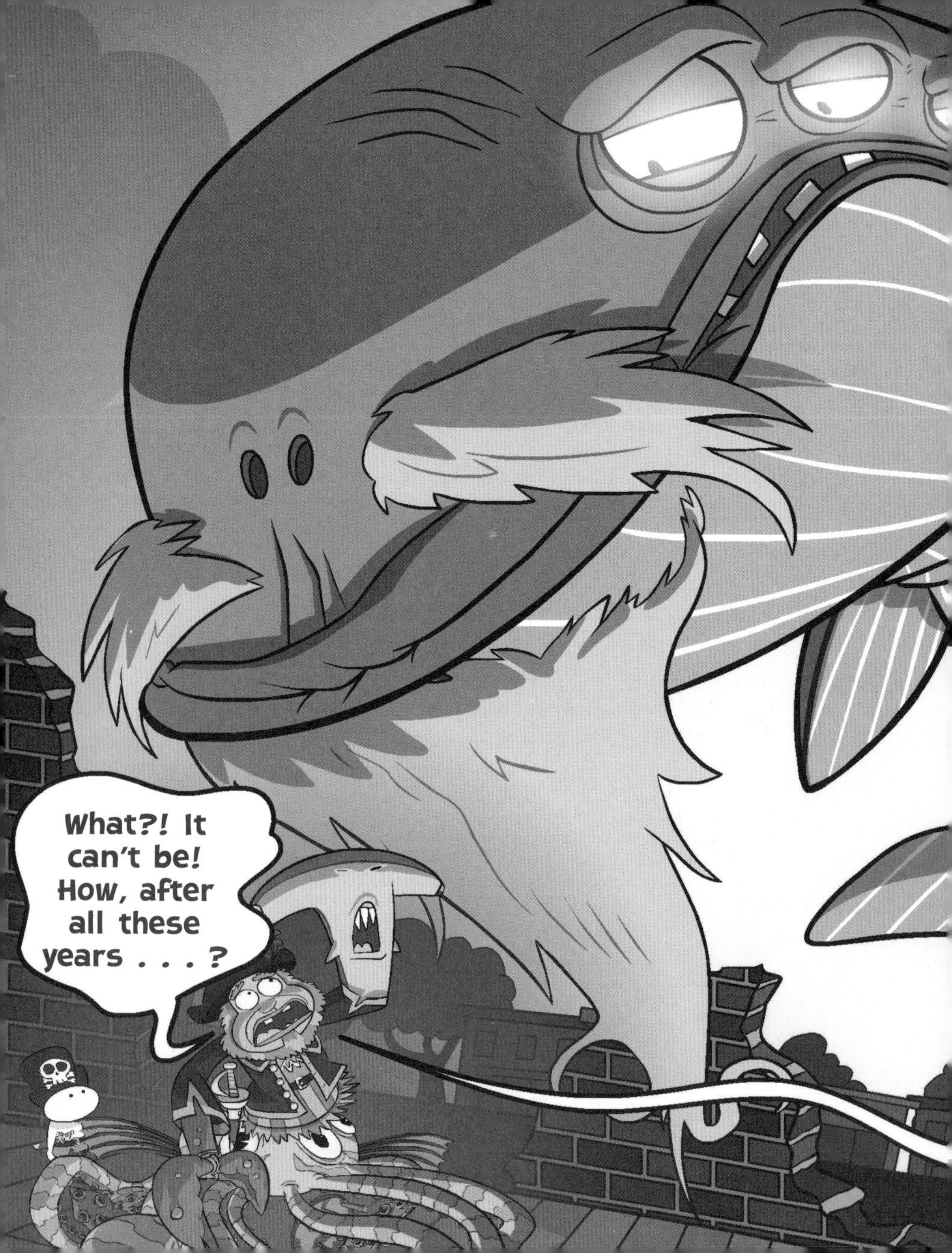
What?! It can't be! How, after all these years . . . ?

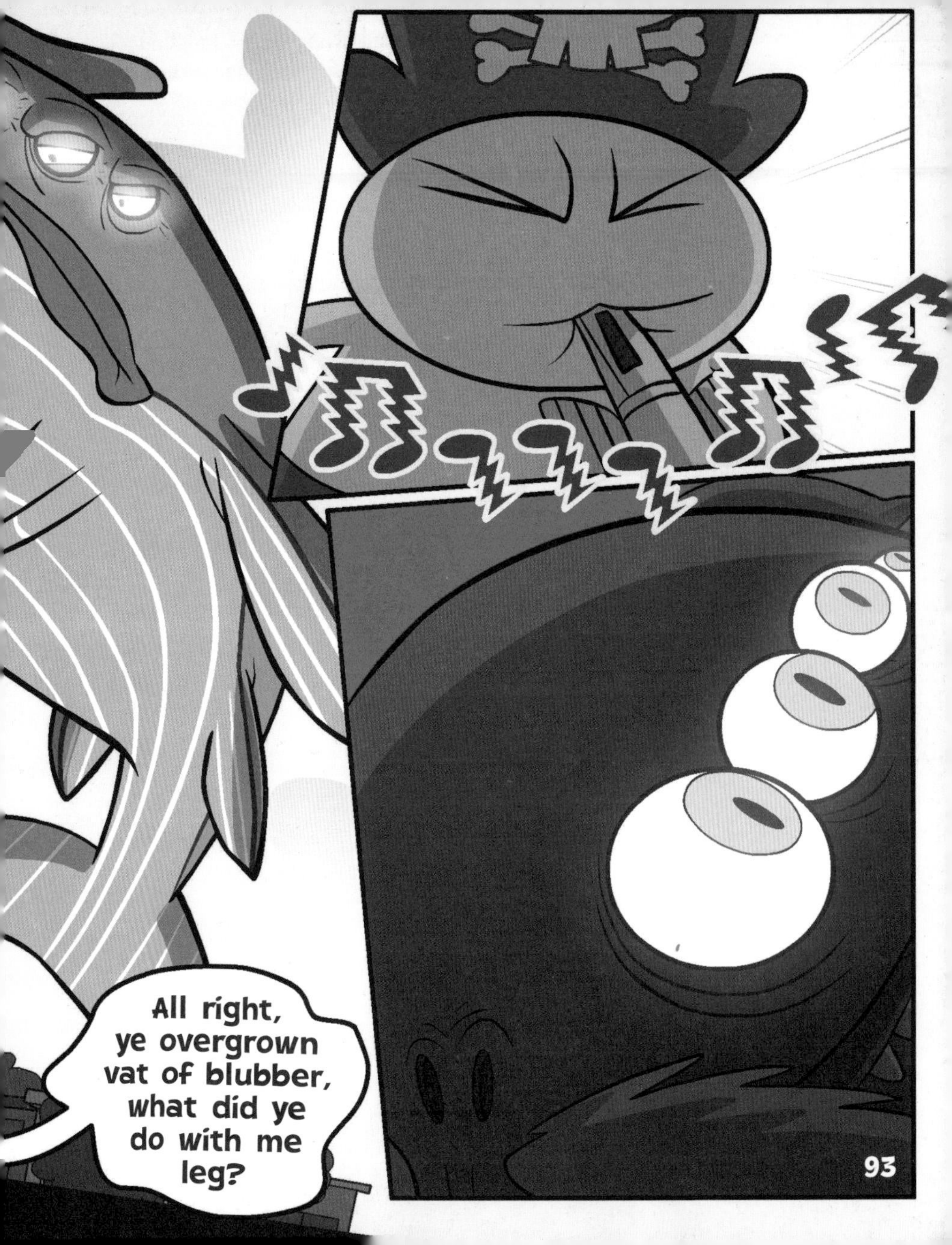
All right, ye overgrown vat of blubber, what did ye do with me leg?

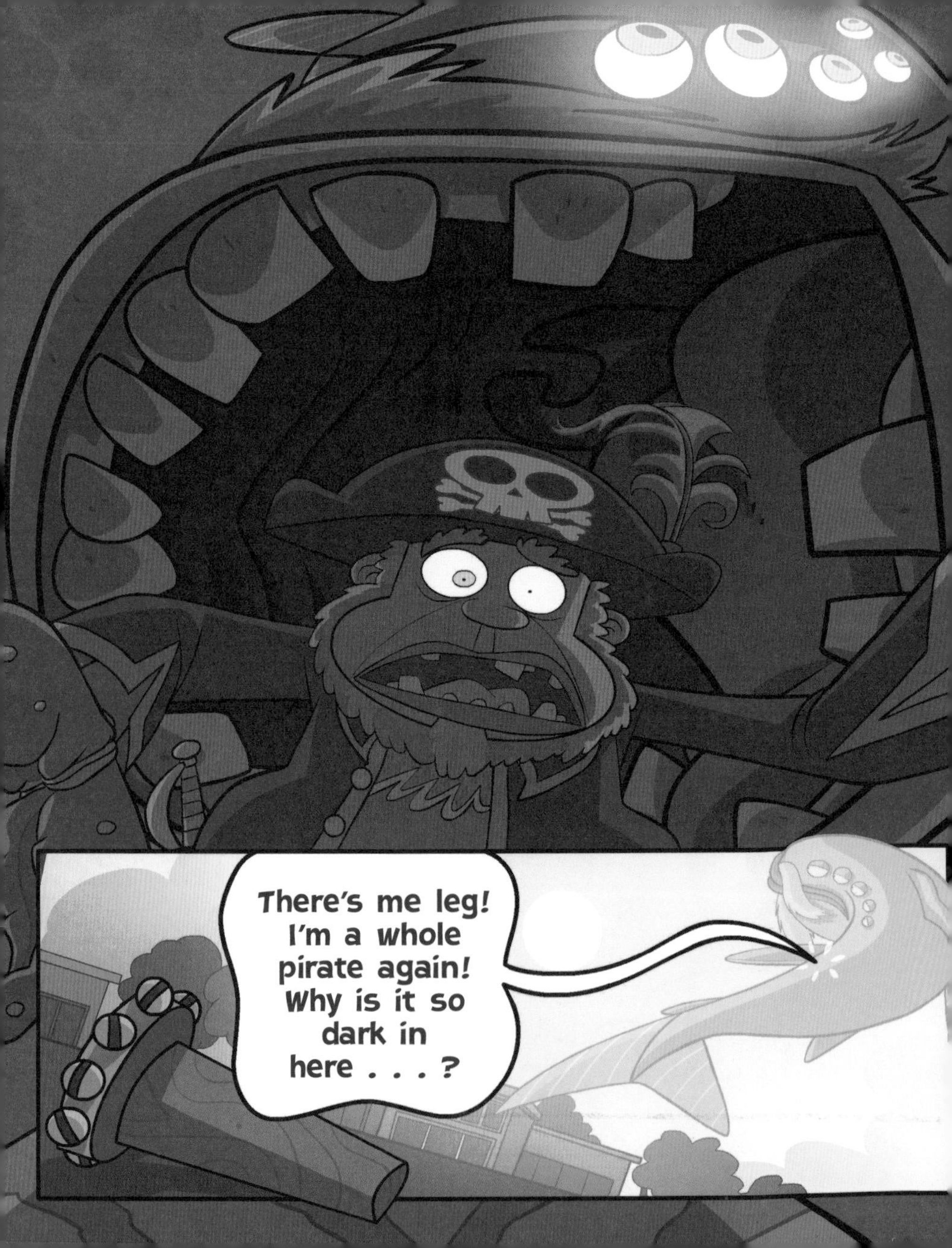
There's me leg! I'm a whole pirate again! Why is it so dark in here . . . ?

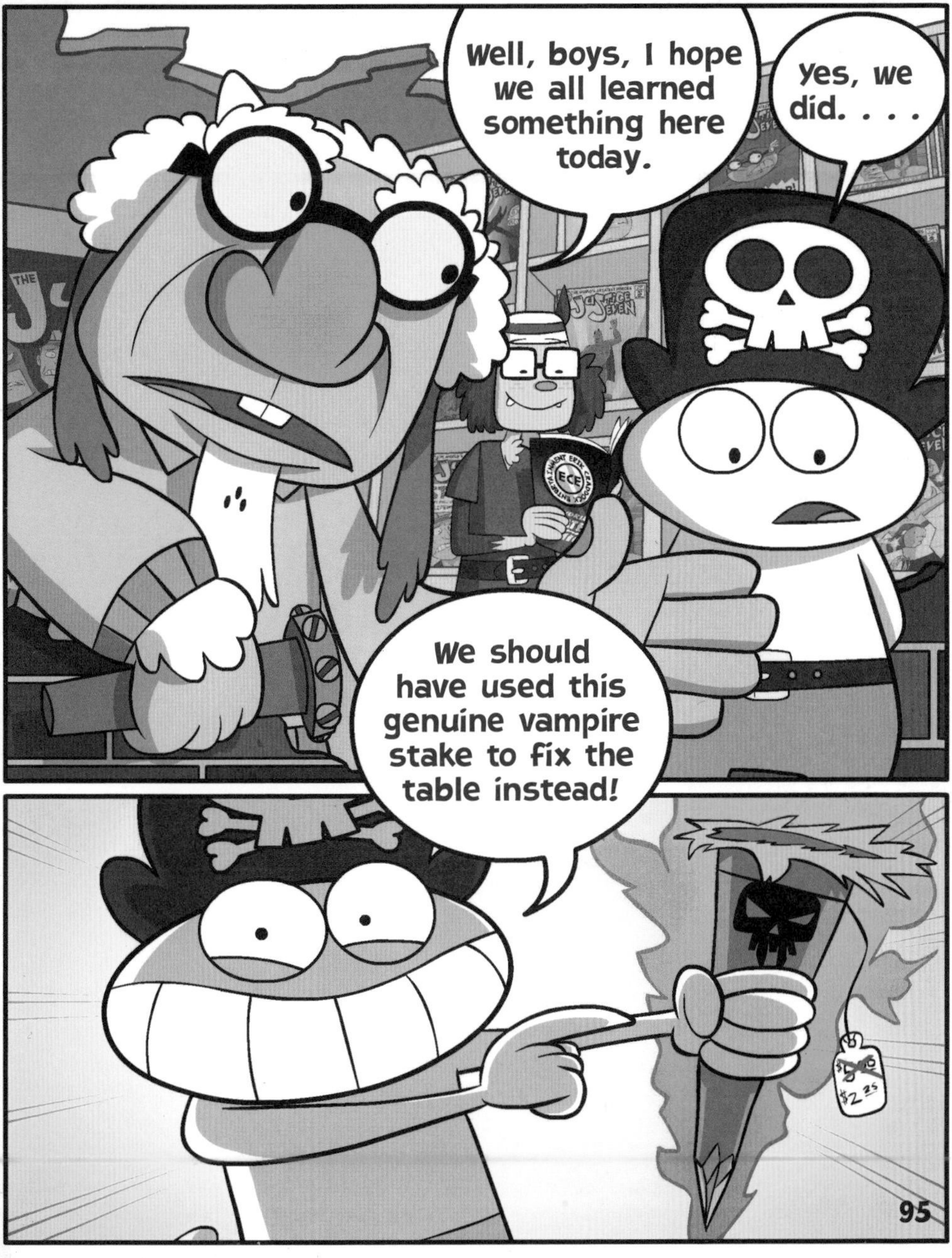
Well, boys, I hope we all learned something here today.
Yes, we did. . . .
We should have used this genuine vampire stake to fix the table instead!

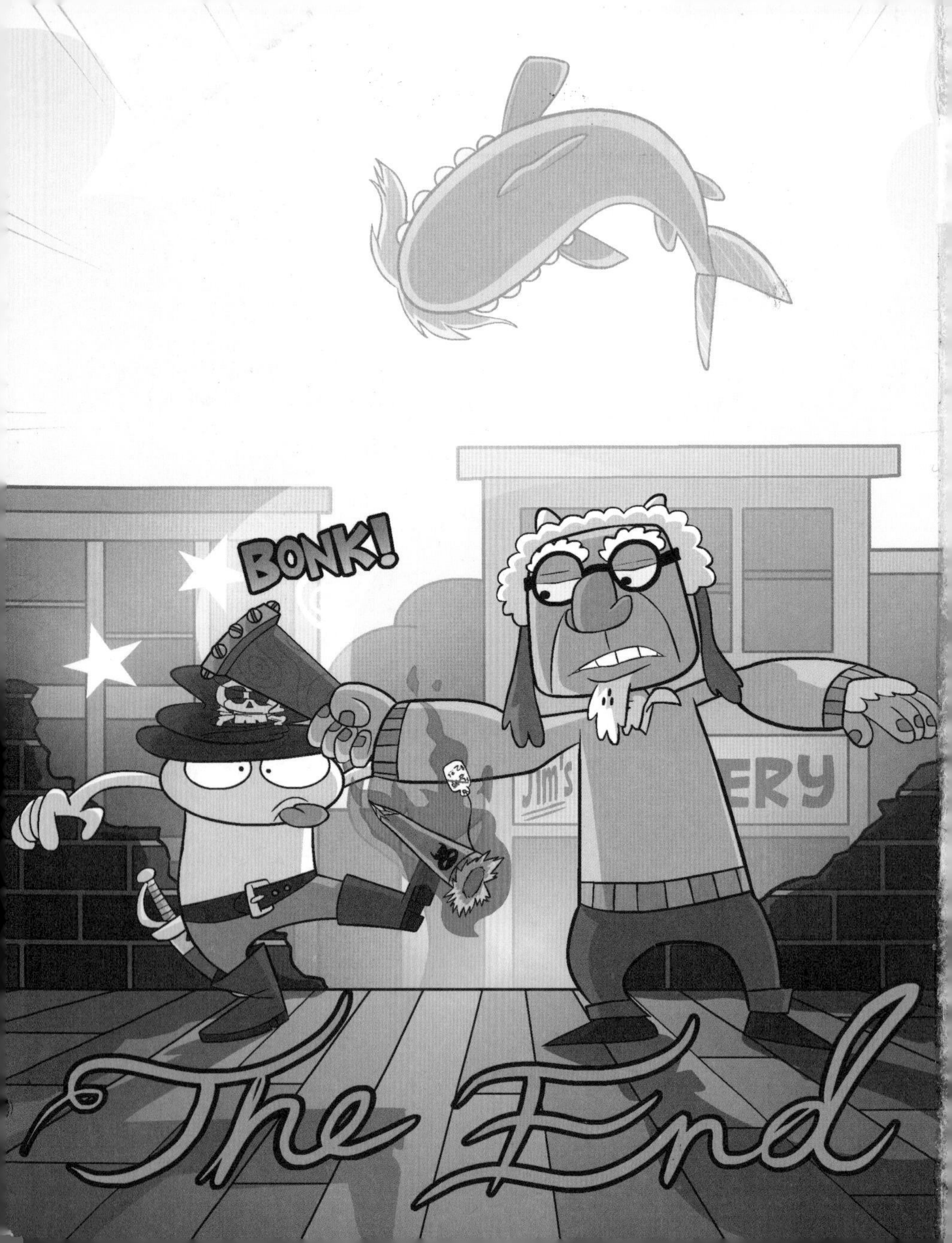
BONK!
JIM'S
ERY
The End